Nine Lives
and Alibis

Nine Lives and Alibis

CATE CONTE

St. Martin's Paperbacks

This is a work of fiction. All of the characters, organizations, and events portrayed in this novel are either products of the author's imagination or are used fictitiously.

First published in the United States by St. Martin's Paperbacks, an imprint of St. Martin's Publishing Group

NINE LIVES AND ALIBIS

For information, address St. Martin's Publishing Group, 120 Broadway, New York, NY 10271.

www.stmartins.com

ISBN: 978-1-250-88393-3

Our books may be purchased in bulk for promotional, educational, or business use. Please contact your local bookseller or the Macmillan Corporate and Premium Sales Department at 1-800-221-7945, ext. 5442, or by email at MacmillanSpecialMarkets@macmillan.com.

Printed in the United States of America

St. Martin's Paperbacks edition / September 2023

10 9 8 7 6 5 4 3 2

Acknowledgments

I've been obsessed with ghosts and funeral homes for many years, and I was thrilled to be able to combine the two in this book. Thank you to one of my best and oldest friends, Glenn Burlamachi, who runs multiple funeral homes and has given me so much good info I'll never be able to use it all. And for letting me sit in on all kinds of things that most people would think are way too morbid . . .

Thank you to my editor, Nettie Finn, for making the book even better; to my agent, John Talbot; and the team at St. Martin's for bringing this book to life. As always, the cover captures Daybreak Island perfectly—thanks to amazing designer Danielle Christopher and cover illustrator Scott Zelazny. And thank you to production editor Nathan Weaver for all your hard work on the logistics of getting the book out the door.

Thank you to my Wicked Author sisters—Sherry Harris, Jessica Ellicott, Maddie Day/Edith Maxwell, Julie Hennrikus/Julia Henry, and Barbara Ross for always being there for support. It never gets old to say I wouldn't want to be on this ride without all of you.

And as always, thank you to the readers—without you, this series wouldn't exist. Keep reading!

Chapter 1

From the Daybreak Island Chamber of Commerce website

Haunted Spots on Daybreak Island

While Daybreak Island has a ghostly history with its long parade of sailors and sea captains and the tragedies that naturally come with a life at sea, the Inn at Lighthouse Point in Daybreak Harbor is the only truly haunted residence on the island. It was built by Captain William Swain in 1850 for his bride. Sadly, Captain Swain died at sea shortly after his wedding, and his bride of ten days, Louisa, never recovered. She was said to have become a recluse in the house, leaving only at night to walk the cliffs, staring out to sea. Some said she was searching for her lost husband. Others said she was contemplating suicide on those nightly walks.

Until finally, she leapt from the cliffs on the one-year anniversary of her wedding.

The house sat empty for ten years, eventually

falling into disrepair, since Swain had no other family and no children. It was purchased by the Blair family in 1861, and they restored and renovated the home and turned it into an inn. It's been in the Blair family ever since.

Louisa Swain has kept the family company in her prior home from day one. She is said to walk the cliffs at night in her very best blue dress, the one she wore waiting for her husband to return from sea. Guests have reported seeing her roaming the property, watching for her husband, though they've only seen her from behind—she never turns to face anyone.

While Louisa is the first ghost to have graced the property, she's been joined by other spirits over the years. Guests have reported ghostly happenings, including furniture being moved around, the sounds of a child laughing, lights turning on and off, and music playing in the middle of the night. On the fifth floor in particular, guests have reported feeling violently cold air sweep through the room and have woken to find a woman standing at the foot of their beds.

If you're visiting the island and love ghost stories, this is the place to stay! The fifth floor is no longer open to guests, but there are plenty of haunted happenings on the other floors to experience. Make your reservations today.

Chapter 2

Monday

"What do you mean, the psychic can't stay at the haunted inn? That's kind of the whole point of bringing him here. To do readings at the haunted inn, in the haunted rooms. That's one of the reasons he agreed to come." Did I really need to explain this?

Planning for Halloween festivities was supposed to be fun. It was why I'd let myself get roped into being on this committee. Although to be honest, I didn't have much choice after my mother and sister agreed to spearhead this shindig. When one James got involved in something, all the Jameses got involved. But this—not fun right now. Not with so many egos and neuroses trying to fit at the table that there was barely any room to breathe.

My mother, sitting directly across from me, shot me a warning look. I was quite familiar with this look. It said, *Maddie, behave.* I'd been getting it from multiple family members since I was a little girl. Being Maddie James meant always being on my best behavior, because my parents were BIG DEALS on Daybreak Island. My dad, Brian, was the CEO of Daybreak Hospital, the only hospital on the island. My mom, Sophie,

was not only his sidekick but a force in her own right—
running multiple businesses over the years, managing
the hospital's social events, and participating in all kinds
of community events. In this case, she and my youn-
gest sister, Sam, had brought the idea of the Daybreak
Island Haunted Halloween Festival to the Chamber of
Commerce, whose leadership and membership had all
blessed the idea. As long as my mom took the lead.

Sure, she'd said. *Sam and I would be happy to.* Which
meant my sister Val and I had better be happy to also. I
wasn't really sure what my role actually was, though my
mother called me her right hand. Which meant she was
letting me handle all the day-to-day fun of planning this
thing. Val had been tapped to manage the events taking place during the festival, which was a coup for her.
She'd launched her own event planning business last
year and she'd already made a huge name for herself, especially after some celebrity attention we'd gotten over
the summer.

And Grandpa Leo was involved too. I'd made sure of
that. Our cat cafe, JJ's House of Purrs, was running the
pet costume parade, and I'd made Grandpa point man
on the project. It got him involved, but it meant he
didn't have to spend his time in meetings. Committees
weren't really his thing.

A shame, because I was totally contemplating handing my seat over to him. At least that way I wouldn't have
to sit in this funeral home any longer.

Oh yeah—we were having our committee meeting
in a conference room at the Tunnicliffe Funeral Home.
Someone's idea of a twisted joke, I had to assume. Picking this place for a meeting was weird, I don't care how
much of a Halloween junkie you are. The last time I'd
been here was when my grandma died a year and a half
ago, and I'd have been happy to never return. But no one

else seemed bothered, so here we all were. Right next to the room where Mrs. Phyllis Handy was getting embalmed. Well, maybe not right next door, but you get the picture. Creepy.

JJ, my orange rescue cat, didn't agree. In fact, he was in all his sniffing glory, nose pressed to the floor around us, intent on whatever smells were lingering inside this place.

I didn't really want to think about what those might be.

Jacob Blair, the owner of the haunted Inn at Lighthouse Point where the psychic was supposed to be staying and where a large part of the festivities were meant to occur, didn't seem to notice me teetering on the brink of self-destruction. He was too busy drumming his manicured fingers on the table as he stared into space, thinking very hard about this conundrum, taking all of it way too seriously.

"I would think this . . . psychic agreed to be here because he recognized that our town was quite up and coming on the Halloween front, not just because of the inn," he said finally, steepling his fingers under his chin and fixing his intense gaze on me. "Also, because his mother asked him."

That part was true. Balfour Dempsey, known in his circles as simply Balfour, the renowned psychic medium and tarot reader who usually spent his Octobers in the famed witchy town of Salem, had grown up on the island. He and his mother, Alice, had moved here when he was one or two years old. He'd left right after high school and never returned—something we'd had in common until I came back last year—but his mother still lived here. She actually worked part-time at the *Daybreak Island Gazette*, our local newspaper. So Sam had tapped into my best friend, *Gazette* editor Becky Walsh, to enlist Alice's help in getting him to commit.

"Maddie, forgive me for balking at such late notice, but I'm just not sure we want to . . . cheapen the inn's reputation by making it the setting for a, well, let's be honest—a show," Jacob said.

Sal Bonnadonna, owner of Bonnadonna Liquors—the giant liquor store that continued to be one of the most popular places on the island regardless of season—gave a thoughtful nod. "I agree. It's a little theatrical. But they're used to the way they do it in Salem, right? It's all a big freak show up there." His disapproval was obvious in the slight sneer of his upper lip as he tipped his chair back. I hoped the two back legs could hold out under his weight—Sal was a big, beefy guy, akin to a six-foot Danny DeVito. He had a lot of energy for a guy who had to be pushing seventy-five, and also a lot of weird-uncle vibes.

I felt myself gritting my teeth so hard I was sure I was going to chip one of them. I worked to turn my grimace into a smile. "Look," I said. "You know we set a goal to make Halloween a bigger deal this year. Get more people here, make it a week-long thing. Right?" I stared at them in turn until they all nodded. "And you know we have to really up our game to compete with Salem—"

Sal bristled. "We don't need to compete with Salem!"

My mother smiled. "Oh, Sal. Let's be honest with ourselves. Of course we do."

Everyone laughed.

I shot my mother a grateful look. "So, thanks to Sam, we signed on a high-profile guest who the entire island is talking about. Salem usually gets him, but this year, *we* have him."

Damian Shaw, my friend and the owner of the Lobstah Shack, applauded. "Yay, Sam."

Sam smiled modestly.

"Long story short," I said, "we're lucky we have

Balfour. He wants to stay at the haunted inn, we're having tours there, and it will add to the atmosphere, so I'm not sure what the problem is. What more could you want? You already agreed to this, and if you back out now you'll be turning people away. This is only a good thing for your business."

"And," Sam added, "he's definitely not a fake."

I sat back and watched all eyes turn to Jacob.

"Maddie's right," said Donald Tunnicliffe, the funeral director. Donald was short and round, with round glasses and a round, mostly bald head. "What's the harm? It will generate a lot of attention for you. I'd even offer to have him do the readings here, but I'm pretty much guaranteed customers anyway." He winked.

I resisted the urge to recoil. I supposed humor was a must in that line of business. But at least he was backing me up.

Jacob's face puckered, as if he'd been sucking on a lemon. My mother, sensing from across the table that I was about to lose my patience, jumped in.

"Is there something in particular you're worried about?" she asked, turning that charming, Sophie James smile on him. I'd seen that smile work on even the most disagreeable people, so I knew it would be no match for Jacob.

Within seconds, his face relaxed and he was smiling back at my mother. "I just want to be sure we're upholding the inn's reputation," he said. "I don't want it to become a kitschy tourist trap. People are already talking about some of the . . . history at the inn, which makes me wary of all the hype."

I assumed that in addition to the typical ghost stories the inn was famous for, he was referencing the unsolved murder that had taken place there forty years ago, not long before Halloween. Naturally, people were gossiping about the death like they did every year around the anniversary and, since Balfour had been known to work with police around the country on cold cases, there was a lot of speculation on his fan pages that he was here to solve the mystery.

My mother nodded sympathetically. "I completely understand, Jacob. And I can personally attest from the work I've been doing with the Chamber that your inn is one of the biggest draws to the island year-round. In the most serious way possible," she added, to ensure she'd made her point. "Haunted inns on islands seem to be treated with reverence because people feel like they can understand the stories that come from a hard life on the sea back in earlier times. And your inn, in particular, has such a fascinating history."

I had to hold back my laughter. My mother was a true master. I could feel the table holding its collective breath. Our whole event was built around this centerpiece, and to have it pulled now would do a lot of harm to the work we'd all been doing.

Jacob finally smiled and nodded. "Thank you for that, Sophie. As long as you promise me that the inn's reputation won't suffer, then I will allow it."

I let my breath out slowly, winking at Sam across the table. JJ jumped onto my lap, squeaking his signature squeak, a victory cry.

My mother beamed. "You won't be sorry. This is going to bring even more positive attention to the inn. People will be dying to stay there."

"Oh, Sophie, you're too kind. But that might be a stretch. After all, we haven't lost a guest in at least forty years," Jacob said.

I thought it was the first time I'd heard him crack a joke.

Chapter 3

With the crisis averted, my mother took back control of the meeting and ran down the official event timeline.

"Okay," she said briskly, tapping her iPad. "Balfour arrives tomorrow—Tuesday. Tours of the inn start on Thursday and continue through next week, up until Halloween night when we have our big bash. And Balfour will be doing readings beginning this Thursday night through next Friday night, with Monday and Tuesday off."

Sam piped up. "Don't forget he's touring the cat cafe."

"Right, but that's not public, is it?" My mother looked at me.

Sam answered first, which was good because I wasn't sure I'd remembered this part of the itinerary. "No. It's so he can get a feel for the place before he brings Balfour Jr. over to meet people for the cat costume parade."

My mother nodded. "Okay. Then the outdoor bazaar starts Friday and runs through this weekend and next weekend. It will remain open on Sunday, even though Halloween is Saturday. Gives people an extra chance to

shop. The cat costume parade is this Saturday—" She
glanced at me for a quick confirmation.

I nodded.

"—followed by the party for the cats at Damian's
where the costume winners will be announced. The chosen shelter cat will be master of ceremonies. Then the
pumpkin-carving contest is Sunday, then *Macbeth* is
Thursday night. Our horror author will be here Friday
night, then next Saturday will be trick or treat at the cat
cafe, followed by the big Halloween bash on Saturday
night at Jade Moon."

Jade Moon was a newer bar on the island. Jade Ben-
nett, the owner, was dating my ex-boyfriend, Craig Tomlin, who was a cop on the island. Jade and her bar were
cool. Too cool, almost. I could never tell what she really
thought of me.

My mother studied her screen for a second, then
looked up to see if anyone had any changes, corrections,
or objections. No one did. It was a packed two weeks, but
it would be worth it. If this went well, Daybreak Harbor's
Halloween reputation would be on the map. And that
meant tourism dollars for the island for at least an extra
month of the year, which was a good thing, especially for
all us business owners.

I was about to suggest we adjourn before someone
brought up something that would keep us here for another hour when the door burst open. All our heads
swiveled around to see Leopard Man standing there, his
face grave. Even his trademark leopard-print clothing
looked a little droopy today, and his tail was nowhere in
sight.

Leopard Man was our island's quirky character. He
did have a real name, which I'd found out much to my
chagrin. It was Carl. I never called him that. To me, he'd

always be the guy who wore head-to-toe leopard print, a matching tail on good days, spoke mainly in Shakespeare, and worshiped cats. People like that were not named *Carl*, for crying out loud.

He was on the committee, but he'd been absent today. Which was unusual for him. We'd been so busy dealing with the Jacob problem that I hadn't had much time to think about it. But now here he was, and he didn't look happy.

"What's wrong, darling?" His girlfriend Ellen stood up, a look of concern on her face. Ellen was one of the town librarians. They'd fallen in love over, you guessed it, Shakespeare. And they were co-leading the local production of *Macbeth* that was our Thursday-before-Halloween headliner. "Is everything okay?"

Leopard Man hesitated. "Though it be honest, it is never good to bring bad news: give to a gracious message a host of tongues; but let ill tidings tell themselves when they be felt," he said.

The man was brilliant—he could pull out a phrase from Shakespeare's most obscure work to fit any situation. Since I was just a tad competitive, I'd been refreshing my Shakespeare brain so I could identify the works. It was like my own daily trivia game. I didn't know this one, though.

But Ellen did, not surprisingly. "*Antony and Cleopatra*," she said promptly. "But does that mean you have bad news?"

"Unfortunately, yes. We may not have enough pumpkins for the pumpkin carving contest," Leopard Man said, his tone grim.

We all looked at one another. This was a new one. "Why not?" I finally asked, when no one else said anything.

"There's a pumpkin shortage," he said. "The weather has been so poor. Much too dry to grow quality pumpkins."

"Can we have them shipped in?" I asked. "Or is there, like, a nationwide shortage?"

"That's a very good question," Leopard Man said. "I have not gotten that far yet. I just got off the phone with Samuel the farmer, who sends his regrets that he won't be able to supply nearly as many pumpkins as we will need, and wanted to tell you all without delay."

"Okay, let's get what he's got and we'll figure the rest out." My head was starting to ache and I desperately needed a coffee. And to get away from the morgue. I swore I could smell the formaldehyde.

Leopard Man nodded promptly. "I did ask him to reserve all that he had for us. And he's looking into alternatives as well."

"Great. Anything else?" I looked around expectantly.

"One more thing," said Ellen. "How's the media plan coming?"

Shoot. This was actually *my* thing. The volunteer who did social media for the cat cafe had also volunteered to do all the festival's social, and she was already doing an amazing job on pre-promotion, but the rest of the media coverage hadn't been nailed down entirely yet. Which meant that Becky, who ran the only media outlet on the island worth noting, hadn't committed to how much space we were getting and what kind of coverage. I knew Becky would be all over it, but these guys wanted to see the confirmed plan in writing. Which wasn't normally how it worked, but here on the island, oftentimes traditional rules didn't apply.

"It's good. We're getting a lot of engagement on social, and we've gotten our pitches to the local paper and to the Boston outlets," I said. "I'm going to follow up with Becky today. Is the contract with Balfour officially signed so we can start doing press?" I turned to my sister expectantly.

Sam nodded. "Just got it back yesterday." She glanced around the table. "Sorry, should've mentioned that sooner. As you know, Balfour and his team arrive tomorrow afternoon. Maddie and I are going to pick them up."

I was hoping she'd forgotten that part, but apparently she hadn't. "That's great about the contract. I'm sure Becky's all over the coverage," I said. "I just asked her to wait until we had the executed contract in hand."

Everyone nodded. Thankfully, they had confidence in me. Either that or they knew Becky was a Halloween junkie and would be plastering this all over the paper with or without my ask.

"Anything else, or should we adjourn for the day?"

"I think we're good to go," my mother said. "Starting tomorrow, we'll be meeting daily for shorter time periods, to make sure all final details are handled. . . . At the Chamber office," she added, with a glance at me. "See you all at ten tomorrow."

"Did you not like the meeting space, Maddie?" Ellen asked sympathetically as she followed me out of the conference room.

I heard Sam snicker behind me and shot her a dirty look over my shoulder. "I just think it's a weird place to have a meeting," I said, pausing as JJ stopped for the millionth time to sniff something.

I almost jumped out of my skin when I spotted a man standing solemnly down a small dimly lit hallway. He was tall—almost freakishly so—and almost looked like a live Frankenstein lurking in the dark corner. Or maybe my imagination was just way overstimulated.

Frankenstein saw me looking and lifted a hand to wave.

Ellen waved back. "Hey there, Hobie! Hobie is the embalmer," she explained to me.

I shuddered a little. "Great."

"No need to be afraid of the dead," Leopard Man said, coming up behind us and grabbing Ellen's hand. "They mean you no harm."

"Which play is that from?" Sam asked with a frown.

Leopard Man grinned. "No play. Just my own words of wisdom."

Sam laughed.

"I'm not afraid of them, I just don't necessarily love to hang out with them," I said, tugging JJ to move faster. I didn't really want to hang out with the embalmer either. "So seriously? A pumpkin shortage? I don't think I've ever heard of such a thing."

Leopard Man shook his head sadly. "Just an unfortunate season. I hope I can track some down."

"Balfour needs pumpkins for his reading room too," Sam said. "Carved and lit. Different sizes."

"Can we get some fake ones at the Christmas Tree Shop or something?" I was kidding—sort of—but both Leopard Man and Sam stared at me like I'd just suggested we ask guests to bring their own pumpkins.

"We can't have fake pumpkins," Sam said, horrified. "That will never work."

I rolled my eyes. "Come on, Sam. First, I was kidding. Second, what if we can't get enough real ones? It's not like we're just refusing. I can't conjure them up out of thin air."

"Well, we really need to find some," Sam insisted. "He needs to have them. It's like, on his list. All celebrities have a list," she added, to ward off any commentary I might have about this.

"She's right," my mother said. She'd drifted over to us after spending a few minutes talking to Donald and Sal. "And the bigger the celebrity, the bigger the list. It's actually fun. Some people have such interesting needs."

I could tell she was about to launch into a story about some celeb or other she'd met—my mother has had an interesting life, despite living most of it on this island—and cut her off. "It's fine. Sam, can you just go to the grocery store and grab the ones for Balfour?"

She nodded. "Good idea."

My mother studied me. "Something wrong, Maddie?"

"Maddie's afraid of the funeral home," Sam teased.

"I am *not*." I bent down and scooped up JJ. "I have actual work I need to get back to."

"I will take care of the pumpkins," Leopard Man promised. "I'll move mountains if I have to."

Ellen gazed at him with adoration. "I have all the faith in you," she said.

I reached for my phone as it rang. It was Lucas, my boyfriend, so I excused myself and stepped away as more of the committee members came out and gathered again in a little circle around my mother. "Thank God," I said. "Tell me there's an emergency and you need me."

"What's wrong?" Lucas asked. "Are you okay?"

"Nothing's wrong. Just hanging out in funeral homes is not really my jam."

A pause. "I'm not even going to ask why you're hanging out at a funeral home."

"Not for fun, trust me. Our Halloween bash committee meeting was at Tunnicliffe's, of all places."

"Do they have snacks?"

I frowned. "Yeah. Why? Are you hungry?"

"No—I was going to tell you not to eat anything that touched the table."

I had to laugh. "We're not meeting in the morgue,

and hopefully the rest of it isn't covered in formaldehyde. Plus, Donald and his wife live here." Which was insane to me, but hey, it seemed to work for them. Their kids had even grown up here, in the apartment above the dead people. I was thankful my dad was only in the business of the sick. At least they were—usually—still breathing. "Anyway, where are you?"

"I'm outside on your porch. I just got here with a load of stuff, and someone is waiting with a certified letter. Want me to sign for it?"

"You mean *our* porch," I corrected him, smiling despite myself. Lucas was moving into my house. I still couldn't quite believe that I was in a functional, adult relationship that had progressed to this point. And even though our living situation was less than traditional—I lived in Grandpa Leo's house—which doubled as our cat cafe, JJ's House of Purrs—with him, my sister Val, her fiancé (and my business partner) Ethan Birdsong, all the cafe cats, and JJ—it was still really exciting. Lucas had basically been living with us for a while now anyway, but this was official. He had not renewed the lease on the beach cottage he'd been renting since he came to the island a couple of years ago, and he was moving his stuff today. Which meant Lola, his pit bull mix, and Walter, the dog my friend Katrina—also our town animal control officer and my official cat supplier—had conned Lucas into fostering, would officially be part of the family too. Katrina had totally played us with the Walter thing. She knew we'd end up keeping him. Plus, Val had also fallen completely in love with him, so he was kind of morphing into her dog. It was going to be a full house, but a fun one.

Grandpa's family had built the house generations ago, and our family had actually lived there for a while when I was a kid, back when it was just Val and me before

Sam came along. I'd loved it. I could've stayed there my entire childhood and been happy—nothing against my parents and the beautiful house we'd moved into after that, but being around my grandparents had always soothed my soul. Some of my favorite memories were long days on the beach with my grandmother, one of the original sun worshippers, and curling up in the book nook with Grandpa most nights to read stories. When I was little, he'd read to me. As I got older, we'd settled into our own books, but we'd still share that space.

So it was really special to be back here, living in that house again, with so much different but so many memories lingering in all the nooks and crannies. And cats. Cats were definitely now lingering in the nooks and crannies too. Grandpa had acclimated to the changes well, I had to say. Also he loved being involved in the cafe. He took his duties as a co-owner very seriously.

"You're right. Sorry. *Our* porch." I could tell he was smiling too.

I pushed the giddy Maddie aside and refocused. "A certified letter?"

"Yeah. It's addressed to you at the cat cafe."

Great. I could only imagine what that was about. I knew I'd paid my taxes, so not sure what else it could be. "Who's it from?"

"Your psychic. Or rather, his company. Balfour Dempsey, Inc."

"Maybe our contract," I mused. "Although I thought Sam received that already. Anyway, yes, if you wouldn't mind signing for it, that would be great. I have to stop at the paper and see Becky. And I probably need to get some coffee."

I could hear his grin over the phone. "I'll warn Ethan."

In the cat cafe, I was in charge of the cats, and Ethan was in charge of the cafe. He was the brains behind all

our food—and our coffee. He was a genius, and he kept
us fed—and me caffeinated, which was the most important thing for our business to run well.

"Thanks. That means I don't have to stop at the Bean.
See you soon."

"Love you," he said, before I could hang up.

I smiled. "Love you too."

Chapter 4

I hung up and hurried toward my car. I'd just settled JJ in the passenger seat when I heard my name.

"Maddie! Wait up."

Damian hurried toward me. I was happy he was also on the committee. It was nice to have someone my age, aside from my sisters, around. And he was a lot of fun. Damian had moved here a few years ago from the Midwest and bought the Lobstah Shack, which was down the street from our house and right next to the ferry, from a local family who'd owned it forever. He'd been systematically turning it into more of a restaurant ever since. Many islanders had snickered about this and placed bets that he wouldn't make it through one winter, but he was proving everyone wrong. Damian had thrown himself into island life with all kinds of enthusiasm. He was part of the Chamber of Commerce, which was how he'd ended up on this committee. He'd recruited a horror novelist to come do a talk on the night before Halloween, and he was also helping with the shopping bazaar, which spanned over the next two weekends.

"Hey," I said, slowing down to let him catch up.

"Jeez. You're in a rush."

"Yeah, well. I've got stuff to do."

He grinned at me. "Sure it wasn't our meeting space? You looked a little skeeved out."

I rolled my eyes. Was everyone going to give me crap about wanting to get out of the funeral home? "Why doesn't anyone else think that was an odd place for a business meeting?"

"*Odd* is relative," he reminded me, and I had to admit he was right.

"Okay, I gotta go." I grabbed my door handle, but Damian didn't move. "Everything okay?" I asked.

"Yeah. Fine. I just . . ." He trailed off, his face turning serious. "I need to talk to you."

Uh-oh. This didn't sound good. I braced myself for another problem I didn't need. "Don't tell me that there's a fish shortage or something." I hesitated. "Is fish on the menu for the Halloween night bash?"

He laughed. "No. It's nothing to do with the festival."

"Oh, thank God. So then what?" I demanded.

"Okay, okay." He sighed. "I have to ask you something. But you have to promise you won't laugh at me. Or judge."

"I swear," I said. "I don't usually judge my friends, by the way."

"Fair point. Okay. I wanted to ask you about Becky."

I waited. He waited.

"What about her?" I asked finally.

"Is she . . . like . . . seeing anyone?" His blue eyes were bright and serious behind those cute wire-rimmed glasses.

It took me a second to process what he was asking. "Whoa. Are you asking if you could . . ."

"I want to ask her out," he said.

I felt the smile spreading across my face. "You do? That's awesome. You totally should."

"I should?"

"Yes. The girl has not been on a date in—well, never mind. And don't tell her I said that," I added quickly. "What I mean is, I think it would be awesome if you two went out. She could use a little fun in her life. Her idea of fun is writing a front-page above-the-fold story. Anyway, the point is she works way too much."

Damian looked relieved. "You really think it's a good idea? I mean, I'm a Midwesterner. I know you New Englanders can be a little skeptical about us as a whole. Plus I can never tell if she thinks I'm an idiot."

"Nah. Just too nice." I winked at him. "Look. She'll definitely give you a run for your money. Becky's feisty, in case you hadn't noticed. And opinionated. And independent."

"Oh, I noticed." He grinned. "Those are all the reasons I like her. But she doesn't talk to me that much."

"That's because she's always running around working. She barely talks to me sometimes either. It's just how she is. She's got a one-track mind." I grinned. "I think you should totally ask her. Maybe you can help her chill out a bit."

He nodded. "I can try. Thing is . . ." He shifted from foot to foot, looking nervous. "Do you think you can find out if she's even interested? I don't really want to get shot down. It's a small island and I'll never be able to look at her again. Which would be super awkward since there are like, ten people here all winter long." He looked so earnest, with his too-long sandy hair flopping into his eyes.

I opened my mouth to decline—I hated playing matchmaker and had no desire to get in the middle of any kind of romance—but he was looking at me so earnestly that I couldn't say no. I almost pointed out to him that even if I did the asking, they would still both know the other's stance and it would be awkward anyway, but I took pity on him. "Fine, sure," I said. "I'm actually heading to the paper right now. I'll work it in."

Damian's whole face cleared and he reached over to hug me. "Thank you, Mads. You rock."

"Yeah, well. Don't blame me if things don't go the way you want," I warned.

He held up a hand solemnly. "I swear."

Chapter 5

Daybreak Island Gazette

October 5, 1983

Man Dies After Fall Down Elevator Shaft at Local Inn

An out-of-town investment banker is dead after a fall down a six-story elevator shaft at the Inn at Lighthouse Point.

Archibald "Archie" Lang, thirty-seven, was found deceased at approximately three a.m. Monday, after a number of guest complaints that the elevator in the historic inn was not working. When elevator technicians arrived on site, the body was discovered.

"It was pretty disturbing," said Eric Vasquez, the supervisor at Atlantic Elevator who handled the call. "I mean, you read about this kind of thing, but thankfully you don't see it a lot."

The suite in which Lang was staying had elevator access directly from the room. Andrew Blair, the owner of the inn, says the elevator was functional and there should have been no access to the shaft. Atlantic Elevator officials are investigating, but say it was likely a faulty door mechanism was triggered.

The coroner hasn't released a full report yet, but local officials said they are investigating the death as suspicious. Items were also missing from Lang's room—his wallet and a 24-carat-gold pocket watch that his associates say he was never without. Police are looking into robbery as a possible motive.

Lang is from Darien, Connecticut. He was in town with four colleagues from Green Farm Ventures, a venture capital firm based in New York City. The five went to dinner at Ventura's, then out for drinks at Strike 3. Lang and another colleague, Peter Jin, reportedly went back to the inn before the others. Jin said they each went to their respective rooms, and that was the last time he saw Lang.

"We are deeply saddened at the loss of our colleague, Archie," the firm's president, Nick Laskey, said in a statement issued early this morning. "We're offering any support we can to local authorities in this matter, and our deepest condolences to his family."

It's unclear if the Green Farm representatives were on the island on official business, and Laskey declined to discuss the matter in any detail. "Our team travels around the country for meetings and retreats," he said.

Lang leaves behind a wife and five-year-old son.

If anyone has information about Lang's death, they are encouraged to call the Daybreak Island Police Department's tip hotline at 1-800-555-1000.

Chapter 6

I rolled up to the *Daybreak Island Gazette* offices and was pleasantly surprised to find a parking spot right out front. The offices were smack in the middle of downtown, and since we had a lot of tourists here because of Halloween, it was busier than it usually was this time of year. I debated grabbing coffee at the Bean down the street first, then decided I would do that later. I picked up JJ and hurried to the door, pressing the newsroom buzzer at the entrance.

When Casey, the receptionist, answered I told her that her boyfriend was here to see her. Casey adored JJ and every time I brought him over, she spent the whole visit snuggling him.

She squealed and buzzed me in. I climbed the monster staircase up to the second-floor newsroom and deposited JJ on her counter. She immediately snatched him up and gave him a big hug. I could hear him squeaking—in protest, although I would never tell Casey—as I walked over to Becky's office in the back corner.

"Hey," I said, leaning against the open door.

"Hey." She didn't glance up. "Did I know you were coming?"

"No. I just left the event committee meeting and they put me on the spot about the PR plan."

Now she looked up, tucking a blond curl behind her ear, a grin playing over her lips. "Well then we should talk. Because I've got big plans for you, girl."

"I'm glad," I said, entering the office and dropping into a guest chair. "Aside from the cat costume parade, this is the big thing I'm responsible for."

"You won't be disappointed." She hit a few keys on her computer and pulled up a screen, then swiveled her monitor so I could look. "This is our story budget for the next week and a half. Front page *and* features abound." She grinned. "I've already got a front-page on Balfour coming, but you're making me wait on the contract." She eyed me. "Is it signed yet?"

"Sam just told me it was at the meeting, but just hang on until I see it. I don't want to go public if it's going to fall apart. Not that it will," I hastened to assure her. "I just like to be careful with these things."

"True. No need to have egg on the paper's face either," she said. "Since he's the big draw and all."

I tried not to let her words stress me out. Forget the paper—if Balfour backed out now, I'd probably feel like I'd have to leave the island. I remembered the certified letter Lucas had called me about. "I should have confirmation today."

"It will be a fabulous piece. I just know it. I can't wait till it runs."

I turned at the new voice behind me to find Alice Dempsey standing at the door of Becky's office. Balfour's mother had a proud grin on her face that deepened every time she smacked the wad of chewing gum that seemed to always be in her mouth. Alice was tiny— "five foot nothing," as Grandpa would say. She looked way younger than the sixty-something I assumed she was, given that Balfour was forty, at least according to his Wikipedia page. Her pinkish-red hair was short and stylish, and she had on her typical outfit of jeans, a blazer, and cowboy boots. Today's were silver with platform heels. She'd been working at the paper for the past few years on a part-time basis after retiring from her dental hygienist job. She wrote a "Householder Helper" column reminiscent of Heloise herself, as well as obituaries and other miscellaneous but necessary things that Becky threw at her. She was kind of the paper's Jane of all trades.

"I'm excited for it too," I said. "How are you, Alice?"

"I am *exceptional*," Alice said. "I can't wait until my boy comes home and wows this town."

Her excitement was contagious, and I couldn't help but smile. "We're all looking forward to this." I didn't tell her about Jacob's and Sal's earlier resistance to the whole thing. They were just being party poopers.

"I don't think a lot of people know about some of the high-profile stuff he's done. Like helping find that missing child in North Carolina. And of course, the body of that woman who had been missing for years." Alice clucked her tongue, shaking her head. "Terrible for the family, but better than not knowing what happened, in my opinion."

I glanced at Becky. "I didn't know that."

Becky nodded. "He was on that true-crime podcast for almost a whole season. The cops even went on record giving him credit for finding her."

"See?" Alice beamed. "My boy is the real deal. He was always so empathic, even as a very young child. I knew he was special before he could even speak."

I had to admit, that sounded impressive. I liked

psychics well enough, but I'd always thought of them as just something you went to see for fun. "I never thought of it as like, real. Sorry," I added with a glance at Alice.

"Oh, don't be. There are plenty of scammers out there. He's one of the few who really has a gift," Alice said. "Anyway, I didn't mean to interrupt. Becky, I wanted to let you know that the column for Thursday is filed. I did a Q&A this time. We had a lot of questions about getting tough stains out of white laundry, and I have a gem of a recipe that I use that I felt would be very generous to share."

"Awesome. Thanks," Becky said. "I'm sure it's great."

With a wave and a snap of her gum, Alice walked back to her desk.

Once she was out of earshot I turned back to Becky. "Wouldn't it have been better if he'd found that woman *before* she died?"

Becky snorted. "She died a long time ago. The family had been looking for her for like twenty years."

"Wow." I thought about that. "I didn't think the police went for stuff like that."

"A lot of them don't. But some are willing to be open about it."

I wondered what Lieutenant Mick Ellory would say if Becky told him Balfour had solved a forty-year-old cold case. Mick didn't seem like the type to be into psychics taking the credit for solving his crimes. "Have you ever met Balfour?" I asked Becky.

She shook her head. "He doesn't come here a lot, apparently. Alice said he's always too busy with his own stuff. I think it makes her kind of sad. But she was saying he may be around more after this. Anyway, she helped me get an interview with him. And he's going to go on the record with any insights he gets about the old cold cases."

"Remind me what the other cold case is?" I asked. "I know about the guy who fell down the elevator shaft." The story was big when I was a kid, even though it was almost a decade old by then. But it was never solved, and multiple theories abounded, including one about an evil ghost murdering the guy. The whole thing had shaken guests and staff alike and prompted Jacob's father, Andrew, who owned the inn at the time, to take that top floor suite out of use for guests. Which was part of the reason why, I assumed, it was such an attractive venue for Balfour's readings. Added to the mystique, and all that.

"The missing maid," she said.

"Oh yeah! Catwoman," I finally remembered. Barely a month after the elevator shaft incident, a young maid at the inn who'd left for a Halloween party dressed as Catwoman had gone missing. They'd found pieces of her costume—the ears, if I recalled correctly—on the road leading to the inn, but they'd never found any other trace of her. In some ways, it was almost scarier than the death; no wonder I'd put it out of my mind. Missing people tended to freak me out, especially ones who vanished under such seemingly sinister circumstances.

"Did you know your grandmother is quoted in the story? The first one after she disappeared?"

"My grandmother?"

Becky cocked her head at me. "Yeah. She worked at the inn at the time. You should check it out. I have a copy of it here somewhere."

We both glanced dubiously at the piles of loose papers, newspapers, books, and other miscellany stacked up on her desk.

"I'll find it," she said with a wave of her hand.

"That's wild. I guess I kind of forgot that she worked there." I had vague memories of my grandparents talking about her job when I was kid. She'd started before she and Grandpa got married and had kept working, which at the time wasn't usually done. But she'd been adamant that she wanted her own thing.

"I need you to go with me, by the way," Becky said.

"Where?"

"To the interview with Balfour. I want to pair it with a story about the overall festival, and it'll just be easier to get comments for both at once. Besides, he might be less uptight if you're there and we're talking about the festival instead of it just being all about asking him to solve something. Which I'm hoping he'll do anyway." She grinned.

"Well," I said. "That would be quite the scoop."

"Right? So you'll come?"

I sighed. "When?"

"Wednesday night."

"Okay," I agreed. What the heck, it might be interesting. Maybe I'd get a sense of whether he was for real or not. Alice was pretty adamant that he was, but after all, she was his mother.

"But back to the festival PR: I've got a lot of content planned. We'll do a Halloween front-page takeover featuring Balfour and anything he can give me about the old cases. Features about each of the main events including the cat costume parade and the *Macbeth* performance, a daily calendar, vendor profiles, and an interview with the mystery author. I've even got Leopard Man and Ellen coming on our podcast to talk about the play."

The newspaper had recently launched a new podcast—a spinoff on their features section. I knew Becky had plans to launch an investigative journalism series too—it was one of the things keeping her so busy lately.

"That sounds great," I said. "That's a ton of coverage."

"Can you imagine if Balfour could solve at least one of these things?" Becky was back on the track of an investigative journalism award. She looked starstruck just thinking about it. "It's such perfect timing—forty years ago this Halloween. Cue the spooky music. We mention both mysteries every year in the paper! It's fascinating. I mean, one day the maid was here and the next day, just gone. And of course, same kinds of theories abounded as with the elevator shaft guy. That one of the inn's not-so-nice ghosts got her. Wouldn't it be so amazing if Balfour could tell us what actually happened—to either of them? At least it's worth a try," she said, likely noticing my doubtful look. "Who knows, my next career could be true-crime podcasting."

"Maybe you and Balfour could pair up," I said. "Go around the country and solve the unsolved. The journalist and the psychic. It could be a whole schtick." I was kidding, but Becky immediately looked thoughtful.

"Don't laugh," she said. "I've learned to never rule anything out."

Chapter 7

I got up to go, then remembered what I'd promised Damian. I sat back down. "There's one more thing."

She'd already swiveled back to her computer. "I'll send you the story schedule for the committee," she said. "Actually, ask Casey on your way out. You know I don't usually share editorial plans with the public because things can always change depending on the news, but I'm pretty certain I'll make room for all of it no matter what happens. Just don't share it in writing."

"Thanks. I won't. But that's not it." I hesitated. Quite honestly, I wasn't sure what to expect from my best friend when I broached the subject of Damian. I'd known Becky my whole life. We'd grown up together here. She'd spent more nights at my house than I could count. My parents had treated her like their own kid, since her childhood hadn't been as idyllic as mine. Raised by a single mother who had to work two jobs, Becky had been alone a lot. As a result, she'd become part of my family. We'd started a business together (selling our mothers' makeup down at the ferry docks until we got caught), we'd gone on investigative journalism quests in our neighborhood (she'd been a newspaper woman long before she'd hit working age), and we'd spent many, many hours with my grandpa at the police station, which had further fueled her interest in bringing the stories of our island to the public. I knew her as well as, if not better than, my own sisters.

But right now, it made me feel really odd to realize that I had no idea what her dating life even looked like, or what kind of person she was interested in these days. Was Damian even her type? He was definitely a cutie. He loved animals, and he was generally a nice guy. She could also eat him alive. Don't get me wrong, she was an awesome person. And she looked like a living version of an American Girl doll with her shiny blond curls and innocent face. But she was ruthless. Newspaper people had to be, I guess. Damian was just as smart but much more laid back, super sweet, definitely a talk-about-his-feelings kind of guy. If she was willing to give him a chance, I actually thought he might be good for her.

I knew she'd dated on and off while I'd been away— she'd told me stories, but never super in depth. Part of it was her workaholism. She'd wanted this editor job at the paper since she could read, and she'd thrown herself into getting it from the day she returned from J-school. She had never been interested in going off to run the *New York Times*, or even the *Boston Globe*. She'd simply wanted to come home and bring her expertise to the place where she'd grown up.

The other part of it was the slim pickings here on the island. Sure, the summers brought an influx of people, but most of them left when the weather turned. It made it hard to find anything long-term. I still had no idea how Lucas had been so neatly delivered to my door. It almost seemed fairy tale–ish.

And I needed to get home to see him, so I had to get this show on the road.

"Damian wants to ask you out," I said without pre-amble.

Her hands stilled over her computer keys. She sat back, carefully. "What?" she asked finally, turning her full focus on me.

"Damian. You know, the Lobstah Shack guy?" Suddenly I wasn't even sure. Did she know him? Sometimes I had no idea if she was paying attention to anything other than the breaking news.

"I know who he is, Maddie," she said impatiently. "What was the rest of it?"

"He wants to ask you out," I repeated, slowly, to make sure she got the full effect. "He asked me to pave the way and get your reaction."

She folded her hands in her lap, swiveling her chair slowly from side to side, gaze locked on me.

I began to fidget. "Well?" I asked finally.

"Well," she said slowly. "That's quite a bomb."

"A bomb? That doesn't sound good." I sighed. "Beck. He's a great guy. Give him a chance! How long has it been since you've gone out and had some fun?"

"Give me a minute to process this," she said. "I wasn't really expecting it."

"It's a potential date, not an arranged marriage," I said, exasperated. "What's up? If you aren't interested, just tell me now so I can break the news to him and we can all move on. I should've listened to my mother about playing matchmaker," I muttered under my breath.

Once when I was in second grade I'd been tasked with telling my classmate, Henry Collins, that my friend Kaylee liked him. Henry was not interested. In fact, he and his friends spent the rest of that month making fun of Kaylee, doing all the obnoxious things seven-year-old boys did when they wanted to show off to their friends. Kaylee went home in tears every night for weeks and somehow I got blamed. I remembered my mother sitting me down with a cup of hot cider and telling me, very seriously, that matchmaking didn't work unless you were a professional matchmaker who had really excellent intuition about these kinds of things. I was sure most mothers wouldn't have included the last part, but that was Sophie James for you.

I'd had no idea what she was talking about back then, but the message had stuck. I'd always steered clear of setups. Until now, apparently.

Becky remained quiet. I waited for another minute that seemed like an hour, then stood again. "Well, think about it. I have to get home. Lucas moved in today."

"Oh, that's right!" she exclaimed, leaning forward in her chair again. "You think it's gonna be awkward? Since you all are like, living in a commune over there?"

I rolled my eyes. "No. If it works for Val and Ethan, I'm sure we can make it work." I didn't want to admit I'd been wondering the same thing. Lucas, however, didn't seem to share those concerns. He was so chill. It was one of the reasons I was drawn to him because, let's be honest, I could be a little high-strung.

"Well, I think it's great then," she said.

"Yeah, me too. Okay then. Let me know, I guess."

"Wait. I might be."

"You might be what?"

"Interested." She blew out a breath. "Can I think about it?"

Ugh. Damian was going to definitely ask, and *She needs to think about it* wasn't exactly the best message I could deliver. "I guess. Do you think you could think about it before tomorrow morning when I see him again? It's just a date. I'm betting you could use a night off of work."

"Hey, the news never sleeps. And I had a night off. Last week, when we went to dinner."

"Yeah, but that wasn't a date," I said pointedly. "When was the last date you went on? Unless you're hiding it from me, you haven't been out with anyone recently, right?"

"I'm not hiding anything from you. And no, I haven't been." She sighed, picked up a pen, tossed it down again. "It's kind of hard to meet people out here." There was a touch of defensiveness in her tone.

"I know it is." I sat back down. "Which is why you should totally give him a chance. Come on, what's the worst that can happen? He's a nice guy."

"That's the problem. I think he's too nice. He might not be able to keep up with me." She smiled a little. I couldn't tell if she was kidding.

"I'm sure he can hold his own. So do you still need to think about it, or can I tell him to call you?"

"Fine," she said. "Tell him to call me."

"Awesome." I stood and grabbed my bag. "I'm glad you're doing this. Let me know how it goes." I headed out.

"Tell him not to call me during work hours," she called to my retreating back.

I lifted my hand in a wave without turning around. Poor Damian had no idea what he was in for.

Chapter 8

Daybreak Island Gazette

November 2, 1983

The Case of the Missing Maid
Inn Employee Vanishes on Halloween

The police are searching for a local woman who hasn't been seen since she left for a Halloween party two nights ago.

Theresa St. Clair, eighteen, an employee at the Inn at Lighthouse Point, left the inn where she both lived and worked around seven thirty p.m. on Halloween, according to co-workers. She's five foot four with shoulder-length dark hair and brown eyes. She had a tattoo of Catwoman on her wrist and was reportedly wearing a Catwoman costume, of which police later found discarded pieces in the driveway of the inn.

St. Clair told a fellow employee she was attending a party, but did not give further details about where the party was, or the host.

The incident occurred less than a month after an unexplained death at the inn. Out-of-town investment banker Archibald Lang was found deceased at the bottom of the elevator shaft at the inn. Police suspect foul play, but have not made any arrests in the case.

"I'm terribly worried about her," said Lucille Mancini, front desk manager at the inn. "It's unlike her not to show up for work. She's very responsible."

Police Chief Jeremy Davies declined to comment on whether the two cases could be related. "We're looking into every possibility," he said in a statement.

St. Clair moved to Daybreak Island in October of last year, records show. She resides in one of the staff rooms at the inn and has been employed there as a maid since November of last year, according to Andrew Blair, the owner of the inn. Blair's family has owned the inn for three generations.

Blair said he hopes St. Clair is found quickly. "She's a great employee and a good kid," he said. "I hope nothing bad happened to her."

If anyone has information on St. Clair's whereabouts, they are encouraged to call the Daybreak Island Police Department's tip hotline at 1-800-555-1000.

Chapter 9

I stopped by the front desk to collect JJ and ask Casey to send me the story schedule for the Halloween event. She reluctantly gave JJ back, but was much more amenable to sending me the info. I gave her my email address and hurried out to my car, wondering if Lucas still had to make some trips back to his old place, or if we could make dinner plans tonight. There were a few things I needed to get done—like triple-check with Sam about Balfour's contract and call Katrina back about some cats she wanted to drop off at the cafe—but for the most part I was done for the day. Starting tomorrow, things were going to kick into overdrive and I was going to have approximately zero downtime, so I wanted to at least take one night to enjoy Lucas moving in with me.

Moving in with me. It still blew my mind. When I'd moved home last year I'd mostly sworn off men after a string of bad choices out in California. And coming back here, I'd resigned myself to the fact that since the population was so small and I'd known so many of the people since I was a kid, it wasn't likely I'd find my soulmate. I'd briefly considered picking up where I'd left off with my high school ex, Craig Tomlin, who was now a cop on the island—and admittedly super cute—but it felt too much like going backward. We'd dated all through high school and, like so many high school sweethearts, broke up when I left for college and declared I was never coming back. He, on the other hand, had made it clear he was never leaving the island, so we'd been at an impasse. And after moving back I'd simply banked on being alone for the foreseeable future.

Boy, was I wrong. I met Lucas nearly right away when I came back, and I'd been crushing on him since that first moment. He was a transplant to the island, and he'd opened up a grooming salon for both dogs and cats. We'd been thrown together a few times early on when he helped us with the strays who needed to get cleaned up before coming to the cafe for potential adoption. He was super hot. And a musician, which had always been my weakness. Unfortunately, those relationships had never worked out well—just a hazard of the occupation, I supposed—so I'd been skeptical. But he'd proven himself a million times over, even after a rough patch that I thought might derail us.

It hadn't. And now look where we were. So in retrospect, I'm glad Craig and I hadn't tried to date again. I had Lucas now, and Craig had found Jade.

I couldn't keep the goofy grin off my face as I drove home. I kind of wanted to stay in and have a cozy evening at home, but I didn't necessarily want to spend the entire evening with all our housemates. Although that was part of the unique package that was our life.

When I got back to the house, Lucas and Ethan were unloading boxes from Lucas's pickup. I felt a rush of gratitude for my business partner. Ethan Birdsong and I had been partners for the past seven years. We'd met in San Francisco when I'd moved out there, immediately clicked and became great friends. It wasn't long before we decided to go into business together. Ethan was an amazing chef, and I'd been wanting to open a business. We both had different skillsets, knew we'd never muck it up by dating each other, and were equally motivated by a desire to never again work for someone else. And we'd been right—our juice bar had been a huge success, and was actually still operating thanks to our awesome staff.

Still, I hadn't been so sure that Ethan would be open to upending his whole life and moving clear across the country to a tiny island for venture number two, but he had. And now he was not only living his literal dream of cooking and baking every day, but he was marrying my sister Val and we were considering how we could bring the juice bar either into the cafe or to a space elsewhere on the island.

Things just had a way of working out. I was beginning to believe that more and more.

I got out of the car and headed over to them. "How's it going?" I asked.

"This is the last of it," Lucas said, stepping over to give me a kiss. "Ethan has been a huge help."

Ethan waved him off. "My pleasure. Fresh coffee is on, Mads."

"You rock." I squeezed Lucas's hand. "Can you take a break to come have coffee with me?"

"I can." They each grabbed a box and followed me inside.

I took JJ's harness off and he scampered away to the French doors leading to the cat cafe, where he'd sit until Harry or Adele opened the door to let him in to play with his friends. Ethan and Lucas headed upstairs with the boxes and I went straight to the kitchen.

Val and Grandpa were at the kitchen table, drinking coffee and eating what smelled like freshly baked cookies. I saw a plate sitting between them heaped with the treats. They glanced up as I came in.

"Hi, Doll," Grandpa said. "Where've you been?"

"I had to stop by the newspaper to talk to Becky," I said. "Everyone's getting antsy about the media plan." I slid into a chair and grabbed a cookie.

"Oatmeal chocolate chip. A gluten-free and vegan version," Val said. "Ethan made them."

I glanced at the cookie dubiously. I wasn't sure how that sounded.

"They're delicious," Grandpa said, taking one as if to drive the point home. "So how was the meeting?"

I studied the cookie before answering. It looked normal enough. "Aside from dealing with Jacob's neuroses about the psychic, and finding out that apparently there's a pumpkin shortage, it went great."

"Well, " Val said with a wink. "And the funeral home?"

"The funeral home?" Grandpa repeated.

"We had the meeting at Tunnicliffe's," Val said with an eye roll. "It was a little weird, but Maddie felt way more strongly about it than everyone else."

"I'm not sure why that makes me weird," I said. "And why everyone has to individually give me grief about it!"

"Because it's fun?" Val suggested.

"You could have the meeting here next time," Grandpa offered.

"No," Val and I said at the same time, then looked at each other and laughed.

"We're going to be meeting every day pretty much until the event's over," I said. "I don't need *planning more meetings* on my list." I finally took a bite of my cookie. I shouldn't have doubted Ethan. It was delicious. The chocolate chips were still gooey too. "Yum."

Val and Grandpa high-fived.

"What?" I asked.

"We had to wait for a third yes vote before Ethan would put them on the menu," Val said.

"Oh. Well, good. How did he have time to do this while he was helping Lucas move?" I could barely manage pouring myself a cup of coffee someone else made before getting to work in the mornings.

"I helped," Val admitted.

"You took them out of the oven," Ethan corrected with a grin as he and Lucas came in. "But you didn't let them burn, so you can take extra credit."

"Gee, thanks," Val said dryly.

Lucas had an envelope in his hand, which he handed to me. The certified letter from Balfour. I'd almost forgotten. Hopefully it was just the executed contract and I could tell Becky we could move forward with the interview and the other stories. I stuffed the rest of the cookie in my mouth and reached for it. "Thanks," I said, sliding my finger under the flap to open it.

But when I scanned the letter, my smile faltered. "You have got to be kidding me."

"What's wrong?" Grandpa asked.

I was already reaching for the phone to call Sam. I scrolled to her number. While I waited, I said, "It's an addendum to Balfour's contract." Sam picked up before I could say more.

"I thought you had a signed contract for Balfour?" I asked her, foregoing all niceties.

"I do. I just told you that at the meeting. And hi to you too."

"I just got an addendum via certified letter," I said. "It wants us to dethrone the shelter cat who's supposed to be the master of ceremonies at the party following the cat costume parade so Balfour Jr.—also, who names their cat after themself?—can take his place. Did you know about this?"

Sam paused, clearly trying to keep up with my rant. "No, of course not. But it kind of fits with them being the guests of honor, right? In Salem, there was no doubt that he and his cat were like, the kings of the event. And he knows that we really want him. Besides, Tomas told me—"

"Who's Tomas?" I interrupted.

"Balfour Jr.'s handler," Sam said.

I snorted. "The cat has its own handler?" And everyone thought I spoiled JJ.

"Yeah, well, the human Balfour needs someone to look after him when he's busy. And Balfour Jr. is important to the production, so he also has stuff he needs. Tomas makes sure he has everything."

I refrained from commenting. "So Tomas told you . . ."

"Tomas told me that the Salem people offered Balfour a lot of money to come back when they heard he was going somewhere else. Like triple what he gets. He wanted to be here, though. He said he wanted to spend some time with his mother. Either way, he's taking less pay to come here so the asks are pretty minor, to my mind."

"I don't think Katrina will see it that way," I said. "It's kind of an important adoption event, you know?"

"I know," Sam said. "But maybe we can find a way to keep both of them happy. Let's talk about it tomorrow."

"Fine," I said. "But Becky needs to know the contract is all set before she can start running stories about him being the headliner of the festival." I could see Grandpa giving me that look out of the corner of my eye—the one that said I needed to watch my tone. I couldn't help myself—Sam wasn't used to managing stuff like this, and the potential for things to fall through the cracks was huge. Which meant more work for me, and I wanted to avoid that.

This was Sam's first real leadership role of any sort, and I couldn't help but worry that she couldn't handle it. She was nothing like Val or me. I was the typical oldest child—bossy, take charge, motivated. Val was a little more type A than me, but not much. Between the two of us, we got a lot of stuff done.

Sam, on the other hand, was the free spirit in our family. She'd kind of floated through life so far, trying a lot of different things and following a winding path of alternative healing. She had tried just about every career in the holistic fields—yoga, sound healing, Reiki, and some that I'd never even heard of. Her longest gig since she'd returned from college on the mainland had been as a yoga teacher, which she still did here and there, but now she was working as a barista at our cafe. And she was doing a decent job, I had to grudgingly admit. But it was Ethan who'd given her the job, against Val's and my warnings. I had to give him credit for that because I would've balked at hiring her—which was why my mother arranged Sam's interview with Ethan. But so far, it seemed to be working out well enough. It had been bumpy at first, though. And we didn't have a lot of time to course correct on the event like we did with her cafe employment.

"I'll call Becky," Sam said.

"It's fine. I'll let her know. Let's just figure out how to approach this addendum." I hung up, then looked around the table. Everyone was staring at me. Lucas was trying hard not to laugh. "What?"

"You're hard on your sister, Madalyn," Grandpa said. "She's trying. And this is supposed to be fun. It's really just a big Halloween party. The world won't end if something goes wrong."

"Exactly," I said, standing up to get more coffee. "It *is* supposed to be fun. That's why it's annoying that it's getting stressful." I refilled my cup, grabbed another cookie. Between Jacob's drama and now this, everyone was being so high-maintenance.

"Why is this such an issue?" Grandpa wanted to know.

"Because it's another way that Katrina gets to show off the shelter cats. And now, the cafe cats," I said. "We're showcasing the black cats for October. Doing a whole education campaign on why we don't adopt out black cats until after Halloween. We already picked Sylvester as the kitty." Sylvester was one of the cafe cats, a gorgeous long-haired black kitty with a perfect white spot on his chest. He'd been surrendered to us when his owner had to go into assisted living.

"There's room for two cats at the parade," Grandpa said. "Who's to say they can't share the stage? Maybe Balfour Jr. can be the main event, especially if people know him, and you can play up the whole rescue thing, a rags-to-riches story, and then tell Sylvester's story. Was Balfour Jr. a rescue?"

I stared at him, a smile spreading over my face. "You know, you're a genius, Grandpa. That could work. I have no idea if he was a rescue, but we could always tell Balfour we're not signing the addendum unless he goes along with the story and the new plan." I beamed. "You should just run marketing."

"Well," he said. "I could do with a promotion, now that you mention it."

Chapter 10

We all scattered—Lucas to unpack, Ethan and Val to the garage cafe, Grandpa to his basement office—when the doorbell rang. I'd been heading over to the cat cafe and I was closest, so I detoured over to the front door and pulled it open, surprised to find Lilah Gilmore standing stiffly on our porch. Lilah was Old Daybreak Money. She rarely left Turtle Point, where she and her husband, Henry, lived in a ginormous house, frequented the social club Tootsie's every weekend, and gossiped about everyone and everything. Lilah was the island busybody, no doubt about it, but she was too rich and powerful for people to take issue. She was Grandpa's age, but she was also good friends with my parents because she was very active in the community. She currently sat on the board of my dad's hospital.

All that to say she didn't usually stop by our house to say hello. I wondered briefly if I'd been supposed to show up for some fundraiser that I'd forgotten about, or maybe she was looking to hire Val for an event.

"Hi, Lilah. This is a surprise," I said.

"Hello, Maddie. I hope I'm not disturbing you."

"Not at all. It's nice to see you," I said. "Would you like to come in?"

"Thank you." She stepped inside. JJ, always on the alert for new people who might play with him, raced over and sniffed at her legs. She eyed him distrustfully. Lilah wasn't much of an animal person, though she had given the cafe a generous donation when we first opened. I think because of my parents, but really, who cared? The money was much needed for the kitties.

"Are you looking for Grandpa?" I asked.

"No, actually, I came to see you." Lilah took off her stunning coat, which looked like a very expensive cashmere even from where I stood, and adjusted her equally stunning pink silk scarf around her neck. "Can we speak in private?"

"Of course." I stepped forward to take her coat, then awkwardly hung it on a coat hook next to the door. She grimaced and took it back, folding it over her arm. Oops. I guess it wasn't the right kind of coat for a coat hook.

"Let's go talk in . . ." I hesitated, uncertain. Where did one entertain the Lilah Gilmores of the world? I had no sitting room or fancy parlor. My mother usually hosted her in the kitchen, but again, my mother could do whatever she wanted. Then I thought of my grandma's old sewing room. We'd half-heartedly cleaned it out and made it a den, but many of her things were still in there. No one really used it. I think it hurt Grandpa too much to imagine her in there working away, listening to Ella Fitzgerald. "Right this way," I said, leading her down the hall to the room.

I motioned her into a chair and closed the door behind us. She folded the coat in her lap. I sat across from her.

"So how can I help?" I asked. My mind was racing through possibilities, but I couldn't quite land on a good one for this visit.

"I have a request," Lilah said.

"Okay."

"I need a meeting with the psychic."

"You . . ." I didn't quite know what to say to that. Lilah wanted to meet with Balfour? Now that was something I wouldn't have expected in a million years. "Do you mean a reading?"

She waved at my words like she was swatting away a particularly annoying fly. "Reading, meeting, call it what you will. I need ninety minutes of his time."

"Ninety minutes," I repeated. "Well, Lilah, I'm not really—"

"Your mother told me you were running the event," she interrupted. "I need your help, Maddie, and I need for you to be discreet. There is no need for anyone to know I'm meeting with Mr. Dempsey."

"I'm not really in charge of his private readings," I tried again. "I'm happy to put the request in—"

"I would like it on Thursday night," she said. "That's the first night, yes?" At my nod, she went on. "Then that's what I want. At six p.m. I'll pay double his fee." She frowned. "Why aren't you writing this down?"

"Right. Sorry." I pulled my phone out of my pocket and typed in a note. "We'll have to work with Balfour's people," I said. "They're in charge of his schedule. We just facilitated his appearance."

"As long as no one from the island knows, that's fine. I need you to handle this, please. I'll also need a back entrance to the hotel. I don't wish to be part of the . . . mayhem." She paused, waiting for my confirmation.

I resisted an eye roll here. I also resisted telling Lilah that I was not her personal assistant, and whatever her "discreet" visit with Balfour was about—what was up with *that*?—it was not my problem to manage it. But it was Lilah Gilmore, and she'd no doubt find a way to throw me under the bus with my dad if I didn't play nice. So I smiled at Lilah and told her I'd certainly talk to Balfour's team. "I can't guarantee it of course, because I'm not in charge of . . . him, but I will tell them you should get priority," I said.

"Excellent. You can use the name Jane Cummings for the booking."

I was working really hard to control my facial expressions and had no idea if I was succeeding. Lilah Gilmore was going undercover with an actual alias for a reading with a psychic? I guess it was true that Halloween brought out all different sides of people.

"Got it," I said, noting that in my phone. "We're picking him up tomorrow, so I'll speak with them then."

"Thank you, Maddie. Please let me know right away when it's confirmed. And you're to speak to no one about it." She waited until I nodded, then stood. "I'll be going. Please tell Leo I said hello. If he asks why I was here, you can let him know that I wanted to personally give you a donation for the cats. You can buy them some . . . costumes or whatever it is you're doing for the holiday." She reached into her purse and handed me a check.

I took it, resisting a glance at the amount. "Thank you," I said. "That's very generous."

"You're welcome."

I followed her to the front door where she paused and slipped on her coat, then headed out. I watched her hurry to her car, slip in, and drive away.

I glanced down at the check and gasped. Ten thousand dollars.

Ten thousand dollars? To buy cat costumes? Or was this a way to guarantee a spot with Balfour? Or my discretion? I glanced back up to the street. Lilah's car was no longer in sight. But now I was dying of curiosity, and

I couldn't even talk to anyone about it because, well, I'd just been paid ten grand to keep my mouth shut.

What on earth did Lilah Gilmore want with a psychic medium that she'd fork over ten thousand in hush money?

Chapter 11

"Was someone at the door, Doll?" Grandpa asked, emerging from the basement as I closed the front door.

"Lilah Gilmore," I said.

He arched his eyebrows. "Really? What'd she want?"

"She gave us a donation. For the cat costumes." I didn't tell him how much. He might get suspicious.

"She did?"

"Yes. Very generous. I guess she's getting into the Halloween spirit." The whole encounter with Lilah had been weird. I was literally dying to ask my mother what the deal was, but I didn't want Lilah to find out and cancel the check or something. "How is the costume parade coming along?" I asked, hoping he'd let me change the subject. "Did we get a lot of local kitties signed up so far? I need to figure out if I have to do some paid social promotion for it. I want to make sure there's a good turnout."

"We have about sixty, last count."

"Sixty cats?" My eyes widened. "You're kidding. Is that including our cafe cats?"

"Nope." He grinned. "As soon as word spread about our famous judge, it was a no-brainer."

Ah yes. We'd gotten Balfour to agree to judge the contest, along with Leopard Man and Ellen. Grandpa had come up with the idea of the parade as a way to get some of the cafe cats attention during the shindig, as well as collect some donations by getting local people involved. Cat parents could include their kitty in the parade for a minimum ten-dollar donation. We'd asked for the street between our cafe and the ferry to be closed down to traffic, and we'd be starting here at the cafe and finishing with a reception at Damian's Lobstah Shack, where the judges would announce the winners.

We were also doing a photo shoot for the cafe cats once their costumes arrived, which we'd use on the website and social to push adoptions. We were hoping to get a bunch of interested adopters during the event. Also, it was great publicity for the cafe. Who didn't love cute cats in Halloween costumes? And with Becky's planned spreads in the paper combined with Balfour's celebrity, it would likely get picked up way beyond the island.

"Don't worry, Doll," Grandpa said, anticipating the million questions I'd have about the logistics. "I've got this."

"Thanks, Grandpa." I decided I wasn't going to worry about it. Grandpa Leo always had everything under control. "I'm going to go see if Lucas is done unpacking. I want to take him out to dinner to celebrate."

"You kids have fun," Grandpa said.

"Thanks." I hurried into the cafe to do a quick check on everyone and make sure the cats had enough food and water for the night, chatted with Adele for a few minutes, then headed upstairs.

When I stepped into my room, I couldn't believe how . . . neat it was. Like, neater than I'd remembered leaving it myself. The clothes I'd left haphazardly on the chair—and likely the floor—were now folded in a neat pile on my bed. My shoes, which were usually strewn around in a frenzy of me trying on and discarding, were lined up like little obedient soldiers in my walk-in closet. Which was where I saw the back of Lucas, as he hung clothes he was pulling out of a box. That one box was the only sign of his move, at least in here.

This guy was good. And fast.

When he heard me come in, he turned with a grin.

"What do you think?"

"I think . . . I have no idea. Where's all your stuff?"

"I put it away," he said, laughing. "Leo said to use one of the guest rooms, so a bunch of boxes are still in there, but most of the stuff I need is unpacked. I put kitchen stuff and other things like that in the basement. Your grandpa had some room down there."

"Wow. I'm impressed. And thanks for folding my laundry. I may get used to that." I went over and gave him a hug. "I'm glad you're here," I said into his chest.

He returned the squeeze. "Me too."

"But wait." I looked around, realizing something was missing. "Where are the dogs?" I knew it was way too quiet in here.

"Caroline kept them for me today. I didn't want them getting out in all the chaos of moving. I'm going to pick them up tonight." Caroline was his groomer.

"Smart. So you want to go grab some dinner? Then we can pick them up on the way back?"

"I'm starving. Give me ten minutes to take a shower and we'll go."

Forty-five minutes later we walked into Strike 3, one of our favorite restaurants for a casual—but still yummy—meal. Strike 3 was another family-owned business, here for the duration. It was a little famous because it was the last place Archie Lang, our dead guy from forty years ago, had been seen before returning to the inn and meeting his untimely death. It was also one of the only places on the island that was still open during the offseason, although this year with the promise of a busy fall, a few places had stayed open longer.

The island started to lose its appeal to outsiders right after beach season was over, although there were some who came to spend the holiday season here. But as of January, the place became a literal ghost town. In the height of the summer season we saw upward of twenty thousand people on our little island. In the winter, we had less than five thousand. Which was why it was so tough for some to make a living. The smart ones had figured out how to maximize their summer earnings and stretch them during the winter so they could stay here. It was why a lot of people had scoffed at "outsiders" like Damian, or Lucas, or Jade. But they'd all managed to figure it out and succeed.

And tonight there was a crowd at Strike 3—apparently some early Halloween guests had already starting migrating to the island. All the tables were taken, so we grabbed a couple of empty seats at the bar.

"So get this," I said once we'd put in our drink orders. "Damian is going to ask Becky out. Oh shoot—I forgot to call him." I smacked my palm into my forehead. I didn't know what was wrong with my brain right now. "Hang on one second." I pulled out my phone and fired off a text to Damian that simply said *Good to go!*

Then I put it on Do Not Disturb and turned back to Lucas. "Sorry."

"No worries." He grinned. "So you've added matchmaker to your list of jobs?"

"No! Ugh. I didn't want to. He put me on the spot. And you know Becky. Everyone's kind of afraid of her. Damian didn't want to be shot down."

"But she agreed?"

"In her very Becky way, yes. I'm worried, though. What if it doesn't work out?"

"Not your problem, babe. You can't control that. You did your part." The bartender placed our drinks down and took our dinner orders, then Lucas picked up his beer. "Cheers. To our new chapter."

"To our new chapter," I echoed, raising my margarita glass.

But I'd barely taken a sip when I heard my name being shouted from the other end of the bar. I turned to see Sal Bonnadonna—loudmouth that he was—waving at me. Vince Salvatore, the owner, stood next to him, wearing his typical white apron. Donald Tunnicliffe and Leopard Man sat on the stools next to him.

I gave a half-hearted wave back then turned away. "I really don't want to have an impromptu committee meeting right now," I muttered to Lucas.

"I don't think I've ever seen Leopard Man at a bar," he said. "Who's he with?"

"They're local business guys. And both on the Halloween committee. The guy in the middle? That's Donald Tunnicliffe. He owns the funeral home where we had our meeting today. And the big-mouthed guy who just yelled over here owns that big liquor store on the corner of Bicycle and Main." I hoped they weren't looking to chat.

But of course, they were. We'd just gotten our food—a burger and fries for Lucas and a grilled salmon salad for me—when I felt a tap on my shoulder.

"Sorry to interrupt your dinner," said Sal, not looking sorry at all. He turned a friendly smile on Lucas, offering his beefy hand. "Sal Bonnadonna. I'm sure you've been to my store before."

Lucas hadn't—we weren't big drinkers, normally just

a cocktail if we were out to dinner—but he politely nodded. "Lucas. Of course. Great to see you."

"We were just on our way out and wanted to stop by."
Sal leaned against the bar, getting comfortable. The guy
on the stool next to me shot a dirty look over his shoulder as Sal's beefy body invaded his space. "How you
holding up with all this craziness?"

"Craziness?" I repeated.

"This Halloween stuff."

"It's a lot of work, especially for you," Donald added
as he and Leopard Man came up behind Sal.

"Maddie can handle it," Leopard Man chimed in,
reaching over to lay a hand on my shoulder. "She and her
mother are doing a great job."

"No doubt, no doubt." Sal smoothed his chin stubble. "I
feel like we're going a little over the top, though," he said.

"How so?" I asked reluctantly, taking a bite of my
salmon. I hoped they'd get the point that I was trying to
eat dinner.

"This psychic guy. I mean, why we gotta act all
Salem-like?" Sal made a face. "We can just have *our*
stuff, can't we? No need to get outsiders involved and
have a whole carnival going on."

Donald laughed. "It's all in good fun, Sal. Besides,
psychics aren't real. We all know that." He winked at me.
"Right, Maddie? I get the sense you're too levelheaded
to believe in all that."

I resisted an eye roll. Honestly, I just wanted to eat my
dinner and talk to my boyfriend, not debate the validity
of psychics. "It's all in good fun," I said lightly, catching
Leopard Man's eye, a silent plea for help.

Thankfully, he was astute. "Okay, boys, let's get
going," he said. "Leave the lady to her evening."

Sal ignored him. "I just think, you know, we're gonna
get a reputation," he said. "We don't want to look like

we're tryin' too hard, or just copying Salem, you know? And this guy. Too good for this place, never comes back to see his mother and now he expects us to treat him like royalty?"

Jeez. It wasn't bad enough Jacob was whining about this, but now Sal was jumping on board too? "Well, I'm afraid it's too late to change it up this year," I said. "Contract is signed and our guest is coming tomorrow. We can discuss something different if we do another event next year. And really, it's none of our business how often he visits his mother." I took another bite of my food. "Besides," I said, once I swallowed. "Look at it this way. Lots of Halloween celebrating means lots of liquor sales, right?"

He considered this. "True. It's just—"

"Okay, let's go," Donald said, grabbing his friend's arm and pulling him away. "Have a good evening, Maddie!"

Sal let his friend lead him away. Leopard Man leaned over and gave me a kiss on the cheek. "Don't mind him. Our doubts are traitors and make us lose the good we oft might win, by fearing to attempt."

I frowned. "What's that from? I don't think I've ever heard it."

"*Measure for Measure*." Leopard Man winked. "A very good one, I should say. Good night Maddie, Lucas." He left, tail swinging behind him, as half the patrons in the bar—outsiders, of course—stared after him, likely wondering if they'd had too much to drink or if that guy really did, in fact, have a tail.

Lucas put his burger down and started to laugh. "And I wondered if I'd be bored on this island when I first moved here," he said. "I couldn't have been more wrong."

Chapter 12

Tuesday

I'd set my alarm for super early the next morning. It was going to be a busy day—we had an early committee meeting, then Sam and I had the honor of picking up Balfour and his team at the airport. I wasn't quite sure how I'd been chosen for the task, but once again, here I was.

Lucas and I managed to have coffee together before we went our separate ways for the day. He and the dogs were heading to the grooming salon, where Lola really enjoyed being the store mascot. She sat at the door and greeted people and other dogs as they came in, tail wagging all day long. Walter, on the other hand, basically ran around the store like a maniac until Lucas and Caroline had to put him to bed out back so they could actually get work done. Good thing he was cute.

Not to be outdone, JJ insisted on coming with me too, even though I tried to sneak out without him, since I couldn't bring him to pick up Balfour and his crew. I'd been informed that Balfour Jr. might not enjoy the company, since he'd be anxious from traveling. However, JJ could still come to the committee meeting with me, so I gave in and got him ready to go.

Although I'd braced myself for more drama about
Balfour, the committee meeting went surprisingly
smoothly, aside from a few sarcastic remarks by Sal and
some anxious questions from Jacob about our guests' arrival time. Damian was all smiles and told me on the
way out that he'd asked Becky out for Friday night, and
she'd agreed. Now he needed to figure out where they
were going to go.

I was happy for him and hoped it went well.

And as a bonus, there were no dead people in the room
next to us, since we were at the Chamber offices and not
the funeral home.

Since the meeting had been short, I had time to do
a few things in the cafe when I went home to drop JJ
off. Grandpa and Harry Timmins were there, ostensibly
cleaning but, since Adele was nowhere in sight, mostly
just talking and enjoying some kind of yummy-looking
pastry that I assumed was from our cafe.

Harry was one of our volunteers, and in his newest role, my shelter manager Adele's boyfriend. He had
somehow charmed his way into Adele's heart, which was
no easy task since she preferred the company of cats to
the company of humans any day of the week. But Harry
was a sweetie. Another retired cop who had plenty of stories to commiserate on with Grandpa, he spent most of
his time at our cafe so he could be with Adele. It was
adorable. He also worked security at the Inn at Lighthouse Point, which I hoped might be a positive thing for
us during the event, especially if Jacob made another
fuss.

When Grandpa saw me come in, he turned to me with
a big smile.

"There she is. You're picking up our guest today, yes?"
he asked.

I nodded. "Sam and I have to leave in an hour or so. Wish us luck."

Harry laughed. "It's not that bad, is it?"

"Easy for you to say. Jacob's being neurotic, Sal is being a jerk, and I have to deal with Balfour and the cat thing. I hope it's not a problem."

Grandpa waved that concern away. "Bring him here. I'll talk to him. And what do you mean about Jacob and Sal?"

"Jacob is worried that Balfour is going to put on a show that harms the inn's reputation. And I saw Sal out with Donald and Leopard Man last night. He made it a point to come over and pile on, telling me how silly he thought it was to have a psychic here, how it was going to mess up our reputation and make it look like we're following Salem or something. And how it's all not real, yada yada."

"You're kidding," Grandpa said.

"I wish I was. Sal's been kind of loud about it in the meetings too, glomming on to Jacob's negativity. It's so odd. What's up with these people? Why are they bothering to be on the committee if they're so against the whole thing?"

"I'm sure they wanted to be on the committee so they can say they're keeping an eye on things for the good of the town," Harry said with a shrug. "In Jacob's case, I'm sure he wants to feel like he's still in control since his inn just got offered up because of its status."

"Yeah, I guess we did kind of do that," I said. "Lots of peer pressure. I think a lot of it is that he's worried about them staying on the forbidden floor."

Harry made a face. "He's benefiting from it, don't you worry. And I'm getting some overtime, so thanks for that."

"No problem," I said dryly.

"Maddie, don't let a few sourpusses ruin it," Grandpa said. "It's going to be fun, and positive for us too. The cafe is booked out for the next few weeks. Not to mention there are tons of people excited for this. Me included. I can't wait for my reading. I got one for the first night." He looked proud of himself.

Harry punched him lightly in the shoulder. "You did? I'm on the wait list!"

"Well, you shoulda been on the ball," Grandpa said.

I stared at him. "*You're* getting a reading? From a psychic medium?"

He looked at me like I'd lost my mind. "Of course. Aren't you?"

"No, I wasn't planning to," I said. "I'm just going to hang around and make sure things are going well."

"I thought you loved Halloween?" Harry asked.

"I do. I just don't really believe in all the psychic stuff," I said, then cringed. "Now I sound like Sal. I don't mean it in a bad way. I think it's fun. I just . . . don't really have time for it. I'm running an event. Multiple events," I added defensively.

Grandpa and Harry exchanged a knowing look. Then Grandpa shrugged. "You'll be sorry you missed out. I'm looking forward to getting a message from your grandmother."

I stared at him, searching for a sign that he was kidding, but he didn't seem to be. "Really?" I asked finally.

"Well, he's a medium. That's what he does, Doll." He shook his head. "I thought old guys like me were supposed to be the crochety nonbelievers," he muttered, then handed me a litter scoop. "I hope he can prove you wrong. I think it would do all of us some good to hear from your grandmother right now."

I felt a little pang. There was nothing I'd love more than to hear from Grandma.

"And I'm really thrilled for Alice. She's so happy to have her son in town for this," Grandpa said. "She's a good egg, that lady."

"Hey, speaking of Grandma," I said, suddenly remembering the article from forty years ago. "Becky told me she's got an interview with Balfour. They're going to talk about the old cases from the inn that haven't been solved. I saw an old newspaper article about the missing maid. I guess Grandma knew her? She's quoted in it."

Grandpa nodded slowly. "She did at that. That was quite a case. Like something out of a novel at the time."

"You remember all that? Did you work it?" My grandpa's mind was sharp as a tack, but I still thought it was remarkable that he remembered so many of the cases he'd seen over the years.

"I was just a rookie, if you can imagine it." He grinned. "I know it's hard to believe, but your old gramp didn't know much about anything back then. Your grandmother was very upset. Insisted that something terrible had happened to her. But others speculated that she was the killer of the elevator shaft victim."

"Really? I don't remember hearing about that theory."

"It wasn't official. Meaning, there was no police theory. Just some people talking. I didn't believe it. First of all, it seemed very unlikely that a girl of her size could throw a man down an elevator shaft. And there were marks on his neck to suggest that's what happened. But you know how it is. It was too easy to look at her and assume she must be a gold digger who knew he had money, so she killed him and ran off with what she could. It seemed silly to me. There was also zero evidence to

support that theory, but it never stopped people from
talking. Your grandmother would get furious when she
heard it. I think she single-handedly shut the rumors
down, eventually."

"What do you think happened to her?" I asked.

He was quiet for a moment. "I assume she met with
foul play. It seems inevitable. And I always felt like I
let your grandmother down, not solving that case, even
though it wasn't mine to solve."

Later, as I drove over to my parents' house to pick up
Sam, I pondered what Grandpa had said. I'd had no
idea that my pragmatic, fiercely-grounded-in-reality,
law-abiding grandfather believed in psychics. Or was it
simply that he missed Grandma so much he was latch-
ing onto anything that might help him feel closer to her
again? She'd been gone only a year and a half, after all.
After more than fifty years together, that was still not a
long time to adjust. As I pulled into my parents' driveway, I decided to mention it to my mother. She would
know if Grandpa's appointment with the medium was
cause for concern.

When I got to the door, my mother opened it before I
had a chance to knock. "Great news," she said. "I got a
part in the play."

"*Macbeth*?" I asked.

"Of course *Macbeth*! It's the only play we're doing."
She rolled her eyes at me and held the door open so I
could enter.

"That's great, Mom. Which part?" I followed her
down the hall to the kitchen.

She glanced over her shoulder, eyes sparkling. "One
of the Weird Sisters."

I laughed. "Appropriate."

"Isn't it?" She beamed. "I'm thrilled."

"Kind of late notice though, no?" I asked. The play was a week from Thursday.

"Eh, it's fine." She brushed it off. "Fair is foul and foul is fair. Hover through the fog and filthy air," she recited. "See? Already know some lines."

Just what we needed. More people running around town reciting Shakespeare. Leopard Man would be in his glory.

"Anyway, Judy Milton was supposed to play the part but she backed out," my mother said. "Ellen called and asked if I could do it. She sounded a bit desperate. Of course I said yes."

"Yes, because you don't have enough to do, as chairwoman of the committee." I grinned at her and sat down at the table to wait for Sam. At least they hadn't asked me. Thank goodness for small favors.

My mother waved this off. "I love doing things for the town. You know that. And this is fun. I mean, who wouldn't want to be a Weird Sister?"

I laughed. My mother was weird, and I loved that about her. "I hear you, Mom. Hey, can I ask you something?"

"Of course," she said. "Tea?"

"Sure. Did you know Grandpa was doing a reading with Balfour?"

"Yes! He told me. I gave him the heads-up when the bookings were open."

I frowned. "You don't think it's weird that he thinks he's going to get a message from Grandma?"

My mother placed a mug with a tea bag in front of me. "The man is a medium. What did you think he was going to talk about?"

I sighed. Why was I starting to feel like the silly one? "You believe in that too, then."

"Well of course I do. Why would I bother getting a reading if I didn't? And yes, I was one of the first to sign up since I knew when the signups would open." She grinned. "These committees have their perks."

"So you don't think it's a problem that Grandpa's doing that?"

"A problem?" Now she laughed out loud. "I think it's great. He's very excited."

"What if Grandma . . . doesn't give him a message? He might get really depressed." I realized that was at the heart of what was worrying me.

My mother got up to take the kettle off the stove. She returned with it, poured the tea, then reached over and gave me a hug. "Sweetie. Grandpa will get his message, with or without Balfour. Don't you worry about that. Now. Drink your tea so you can go get our guest. You don't want to keep him waiting."

Chapter 13

My dad had left his giant Subaru Ascent for us so we would make a good impression on our guest, since I was still driving around in Grandma's old Buick. Also because it was big. We'd gotten notice that there were five people—plus the cat—in Balfour's party. Add Sam and me, and we'd never all fit in Sam's little Prius.

I knew Mom desperately wanted to come, and I would have even offered to let her do the honors in my place, but she now had a play rehearsal to get to. So Sam and I piled in and started the drive over to the small airport located on the other side of Daybreak Harbor. But of course, first we had to stop for coffee.

I pulled up at the curb in front of the Bean. Technically there wasn't parking, but Sam was staying in the car, so it was fine.

"What do you want?" I asked her.

"One of their witches' brew lattes with an extra shot, please." The witches' brew latte was an October creation that was a mix of caramel, mocha, and vanilla. It was delightful.

I hurried inside and ordered two. As I headed back

outside, I bumped into Lieutenant Mick Ellory coming in.

"Maddie," he said with a nod, holding the door for me, then looked pointedly back at my dad's car. "You're parked in a crosswalk."

I grinned. "I'm not technically parked. Someone's in the car."

He rolled his eyes. "How's the Halloween planning coming?"

"Heading to get our superstar guest as we speak. You guys excited?" I winked at him. I knew Grandpa had always loved when the town had big events, even if it meant extra work for the department. Some cops thought the same way. Others didn't—they just saw it all as one big headache. I wasn't totally sure where Mick fell on that spectrum.

"As long as things stay calm and quiet, sure." He finally cracked a smile. "Gotta run. Bringing Katrina a coffee before she heads out to save a possum." In a recent plot twist, Mick and Katrina had started dating—and it was going very well.

"Good luck. Make sure she doesn't try to sneak the possum into the cafe as my newest resident."

Now he laughed. "Hey, there are some things I can't guarantee."

I got back into the car where Sam was doing something on her phone and handed her the coffee.

"Thanks," she said, taking a sip. "I was just checking to see if there was any word from Balfour's team."

"And?"

"Nothing, which I'm hoping means everything's on schedule." She looked up at me. "I really, really hope this goes well."

She looked so earnest. I reached over and squeezed her hand. "It's gonna be great."

Mick exited the cafe, glanced at the SUV, then pointed at the crosswalk sign. I waved and pulled out into traffic.

The Daybreak Island Airport was the only airport serving the five-town island. Most of our "regular" folks, visitors and locals alike, traveled by ferry, while the airport was usually reserved for those with private planes. I didn't get over this way much, though it was only a few miles from our house. The airport was located on the east side of the island, technically in the town of Duck Cove, about three miles from downtown Daybreak Harbor. The drive took us only about twenty minutes. Another good thing about the offseason. Not a lot of traffic. I pulled into the parking area and glanced at my sister. "Do you know what time they're landing?"

The airport was small enough that we could see all the activity happening—which right now wasn't much. Everything was still, and on the other side of the building, the water glittered against the colors of the morning. I loved looking at the ocean. It would never get old.

"Yes, they're due in at noon. They'll text," Sam said. She checked her watch. It was quarter to noon.

I sipped my coffee, feeling happy about the caffeine rush. My mother's tea hadn't given me the jolt I needed—she usually tried to give me tea with no caffeine—and I knew it was going to be a long afternoon.

Sam picked up her phone as it dinged a text message. She groaned when she read it. "Jacob is being so high maintenance," she said. "What is up with him? He's usually a nice guy."

"What's his problem now?" I asked.

"He says he's getting a lot of questions about the tours and whether the top floor is included."

I rolled my eyes. "Can he just say no, that's where the psychic is staying?"

"You would think." She wrinkled her nose. "I hope Jacob doesn't mess this up."

"We won't let him," I said, then pointed to the small plane hurtling toward the runway. "I think they're here."

But it was an hour at least before any signs of life appeared from the plane. By that point, I'd long since finished my coffee and I had to pee.

Finally we saw a group of people walking across the tarmac. "Here they come," Sam said finally, nodding toward the activity, the relief clear in her voice. She knew I was getting antsy.

We got out of the SUV and went around to the front to wait for them. I focused on the five people heading toward us. One of them was also pulling some contraption, clearly not luggage, on wheels. The cat, I assumed. I couldn't hold back my grin. And I thought JJ was spoiled. "I wonder where they got that?" I said. "You think they had it custom made?"

"Shh." Sam stepped forward, transforming into a confident professional—someone I'd never seen before. "Welcome to Daybreak Island," she exclaimed. "We're so delighted to have you all."

A woman with long black hair cascading over her shoulders in perfect corkscrew curls strode over to shake Sam's hand. Her makeup was flawless, and she had nails that could easily be mistaken for Freddy Krueger's, although hers were perfectly oval and painted a deep purple with silver sparkles. "You must be Sam," she said warmly. "Maeve Sandler. So nice to finally meet you!" She appeared to be the group leader. Everyone else, including the man I presumed to be Balfour, stood behind her, seemingly waiting for their cue.

"Hi, Maeve! Likewise. Yes, I'm Sam, and this is my

sister Maddie. She owns the cat cafe, JJ's House of Purrs. You're visiting it this week. She's basically running the entire week of the festival."

"Well. That's quite a job." Maeve turned my way, sharp brown eyes sweeping curiously over me. "It's a pleasure to meet you, Maddie. I can't wait to see the cafe."

"Pleasure to meet you too," I said.

"And this is our guest of honor," Maeve said, standing aside and sweeping her hand in a dramatic gesture toward the man who waited behind her. I half expected a drum roll from somewhere in the distance. "Balfour."

I turned my attention to the esteemed psychic, who had really almost disappeared behind his commanding staff member. Balfour Dempsey was tall and skinny, with jet black hair that stood nearly straight up off his head, glistening with some kind of gel. In fact, he was so skinny I thought both of his legs might equal the size of one of mine. He wore psychedelic, purple-tinted glasses, black cargo pants, a black T-shirt under a black leather jacket, and combat boots. I couldn't see his eyes at all behind those glasses.

Sam and I both greeted him enthusiastically.

"Thanks so much for joining us this year. We're really excited to have you," I said.

"I'm excited too. But I'm not the real guest of honor. It's Balfour Junior," he said in a voice so soft I could barely hear him, motioning to the wheelie-cart thingie that another, silent man stood next to. "In any event, I'm pleased to meet you," he added. "Thank you for inviting me. I'm really looking forward to your event."

I swallowed my surprise. I'd honestly been expecting a loud, blustery guy who breezed in and started making demands, not this soft-spoken man.

"And that's Tomas," Maeve added, gesturing to the

silent man standing next to the cat carrier. "Tomas is Balfour Jr.'s handler."

Ah yes. The cat handler. I still found this quite funny, especially given how solemn and serious Tomas looked. As if he were Secret Service to the President or something. That made me almost giggle, and I had to cover it up by clearing my throat.

Tomas didn't seem to notice, he was so focused on his charge. Nothing else about him looked Secret Service–y, upon closer inspection. For one thing, he didn't look like he'd easily be able to pass a fitness test. He had a good-sized paunch around his middle, thinning hair and I could smell the aftermath of his most recent cigarette. He definitely dressed to impress, though, with designer jeans and a leather jacket that looked way too thin for this season. He didn't speak, just nodded solemnly and lifted a little shade on the wheelie contraption so we could see Balfour Junior. The sleek black cat was curled up on a purple pillow nestled on top of a bunch of blankets in his carrier, which sat atop this wagon-like thing. His yellow eyes glowed as he gazed out at us.

Sam and I oohed and aahed appropriately.

"And that's Sharlene and Manfred," Maeve added, pointing to the other two people standing behind all of them. I realized for the first time they were twins.

And perhaps just a little creepy. They had the same pale skin and tiger-colored eyes, same straight, straw-colored hair, although hers was a big longer—at least what was visible under the big floppy sun hat she wore—and the same expressionless faces.

I lifted my hand in a quick wave. They both gazed at me but said nothing.

Maeve didn't seem inclined to describe what Sharlene's and Manfred's jobs were. I assumed they were there to assist her in whatever she was doing to assist Balfour.

"Well, terrific," I said. "Shall we go?"

"Yes, please. Balfour is getting antsy," the senior Balfour said, glancing at the cat carrier.

This was going to get confusing. "Right this way," I said, leading them over to my dad's SUV and opening the back. Balfour's minions piled all the luggage in there. I watched as Tomas flipped a couple of locks on the cat contraption, extracting a smaller carrier from the larger one. He handed the now-empty one to Manfred and climbed into the back with his cargo. Manfred finished stashing luggage, then he and his sister piled in next to him. Sam asked Balfour if he'd like to sit up front. He declined, and he and Maeve climbed into the middle row of seats. Sam got into the front passenger seat.

"We can't wait to show you the inn," she said to no one in particular.

"We're super excited," Maeve confirmed. I could see from a glance in the rearview mirror she was already scrolling through her phone.

Oh yeah, this was gonna get interesting. "We'll be there in no time," I said cheerily, hitting the gas and zooming out of the parking lot.

Chapter 14

The ride was weird.

The strange twins said nothing the whole time. I kind of had the creeps thinking they were sitting back there staring at me. Maeve and Sam chatted, while Tomas talked to someone on his phone, contorting his body nearly in half trying to muffle his voice so no one could hear him. It was impossible, of course. And every few seconds, the cat would utter an ear-piercing scream that sounded like a baby shrieking. I drove with my hands clenched around the steering wheel, growing increasingly uncomfortable with the whole thing. Balfour didn't say a word the entire time.

After a few minutes, Maeve leaned forward and tapped me on the shoulder. "Once we're checked in, we should make sure all the schedules are confirmed. I know we have a tour set up for the cafe tomorrow, but we should check our list of the other places he'll be visiting to make sure we haven't missed anything."

"Oh, yes, of course," I said. "I have a couple of other scheduling things to confirm too." Like Lilah's secret appointment. It felt odd talking about Balfour like he wasn't even there, but he didn't chime in.

"Brilliant," she said, settling back into her seat again. "And how about a police detail?"

"A police detail?" I repeated, glancing at Sam. She gave a discreet shrug.

"We'd like to make sure he's not disturbed when he's trying to get around town," Maeve said.

"Okay," I said. "Was that part of the original list we got, or do I need to make arrangements now?"

"Hmmm. I don't think it was," Maeve said. "Apologies. But anything you can do would be helpful."

"Sure," I said. If the actual police didn't have time, Grandpa might want to do the job. I'd figure it out.

When I pulled up in front of the inn ten minutes later, I felt a quiet hush of anticipation come over the car. I drove into the circular driveway and stopped in front of the main entrance.

I hadn't been here in a long time, and now that I was seeing it again with fresh eyes I had to admit the Inn at Lighthouse Point was pretty breathtaking. It sat atop a cliff overlooking the sea at the southernmost point of Daybreak Harbor, set slightly apart from the businesses on the rest of the street. It was still walking distance to the bustling downtown but removed enough that it was quaint, quiet, and gorgeous. Jacob's family had done a lot of upgrades and refurbishments over the years, and had managed to achieve the perfect balance—in my opinion at least—between historical and modern. I knew that from the top of the property you could see almost the whole town. The water stretched out around us on every side, miles and miles of blue-green goodness that I never got tired of looking at. I'd loved San Francisco, but the Atlantic Ocean pulled me back every time. I even loved it in the cold weather. There was something about a deserted New England beach that still had my heart.

And to make it even better, the inn was completely done up for Halloween, but in a classy way. The purple and black lights outlining the building rivaled those of the most festive Christmas light show. There was a ghost hovering over the top right corner of the inn, looking for all the world like it really was floating up there. Orange candlelight glowed in every single window. I could see a makeshift graveyard on the front lawn and guessed that it had fake headstones for all the "ghosts" who were rumored to reside here. I loved what they had done with the place.

I could understand in that moment why Jacob was so protective of the inn. It was way more than a simple building or business. It was a family place, with history and memories and meaning. I felt the same way about Grandpa's house, which had been built by and passed down through our family. When someone had tried to take it from him, I'd nearly lost my mind. So if Jacob was feeling a bit insecure about his ghosts, I had to respect that. Halloween event aside, the place was booked out years in advance for most summers.

Of course, it was also the perfect setting for Halloween activities, as the décor clearly showed. Our guests would love it, especially paired with the ghostly legends they were likely coming to enjoy. I didn't personally love to scare myself, but to each his or her own, I guess.

"So here we are," I said, turning to look at Balfour, wondering why I felt the sudden urge to play tour guide. "I don't know if you know anything about the place, but it was built in—"

"I'm familiar, thank you," Balfour said softly, holding up a hand to stop my babbling. "I would like a moment to just take it all in."

I nodded. "Sure. I'll go get someone to get your bags . . ." I trailed off as I realized he wasn't listening.

Balfour opened the car door, got out, and walked slowly toward the inn, pausing on the lawn in front, almost like he was meditating. I risked a glance over my shoulder at his peeps. They were all checking their phones, unbothered. I guessed he did this often. I watched as Balfour walked slowly around the inn, disappearing from our view.

Maeve glanced at me, one side of her mouth lifting in a wry smile. "Don't worry. He has a process. He needs to get a feel for the places where's he's working and spending time."

I wasn't terribly worried about Balfour's process, but I really had to pee. "Great. I'm just going to go inside and make sure everything is ready for him," I said, sliding out of the car before anyone could object.

I hurried to the door of the inn and, before I could push it open, it swung toward me. Harry stood on the other side, grinning at me.

"Hey, Maddie."

"Harry. How did you get over here so fast?"

He shrugged. "We were done cleaning, and your grandfather and I thought an extra hand over here might be helpful to you."

"Oh, how sweet. Thank you."

"So where's our guest?" Harry peered past me at the SUV.

"Walking around. He's channeling or something right now and I need the bathroom."

"Right over there." Harry pointed to a corner of the lobby. "Want me to call the bellhop?"

"Please. They're an interesting crew," I called over my shoulder as I raced to the ladies' room. "Get ready!"

I rounded the corner and almost slammed into Jacob Blair, who was coming out of the men's room in the same little alcove.

"Maddie! I'm so sorry," he exclaimed, reaching out an arm to steady me.

"No problem," I said, trying to get past him. But he seemed like he was in the mood to chat.

"Has our guest arrived?"

"He has. He'll be in in a second," I said.

"Ah, wonderful." Jacob clasped his hands together and studied me, looking like it was anything but wonderful. "Anything I need to know?"

"I don't think so," I said. "I think we're well prepared for them at this point." I edged closer to the door, but he kept talking.

"Excellent. Well, I have the top suite ready. It took a bit, since we don't put guests up there anymore. That floor has been used as mostly office space for many years."

I tried to ignore the passive-aggressive statement. "Great. I'm just going to—"

"Did you know they've requested a special room for the cat?" Jacob continued. "So he has a space to retire to if the readings become too much?"

"I didn't. But we appreciate you accommodating him," I said, reaching for the door handle.

He nodded. "Luckily there are multiple rooms. I was able to give them the connecting rooms. Of course, I had to move all my files out. I was using one of the rooms as an office," he added, just to make sure I got the point. "So there's no bed in the cat's room, just a couch, but I trust it has its own bed?"

"The cat is a he. His name is also Balfour." I ignored Jacob's smirk. "And I'm sure he does have a bed. Thank you," I repeated. "I'm sure it will be great." I turned to the bathroom door again, just as a young guy wearing a bellhop uniform skidded around the corner.

"Mr. Blair? There's a man trying to climb down the cliff."

"*What?*" Jacob looked suddenly apoplectic. "Get Harry."

The bellhop nodded and took off.

"Climb down the cliff?" I repeated, a sinking feeling in my stomach. It couldn't be Balfour . . . could it?

Jacob looked at me and shook his head. "These people. Always tempting fate. We couldn't make it clearer that they are not allowed to go anywhere near the cliff. Excuse me." He hurried away.

"Thank God," I muttered, heading into the bathroom. Even if it was Balfour, it would have to wait.

When I returned to the lobby a few minutes later, there was a lot of commotion. Which I assumed meant my gut had been right.

"It's part of his process," I heard Maeve's unmistakable voice ring out. "He needs to assess the surrounding area for any psychic activity." I rounded the corner to find her towering over Jacob, her stilettos adding a few inches to her already impressive height. She stood toe-to-toe with him, and though her voice was pleasant enough, I could tell she was daring him to dissent. The rest of Balfour's entourage gathered around. The cat was silent in his wheelie, most likely asleep. I envied him.

I spotted Sam standing just outside the fray and beelined over to her. She was watching the whole thing nervously. "What's going on? Please tell me Balfour didn't try to scale the cliffs like Spider-Man."

"He was just trying to see the property. He tried to go in the back, you know, where the path leads to the cliff? I figured he wanted to check out the ocean but they got upset and made him come back up." She spoke in a stage whisper, but everyone's head whipped around to us.

"It's dangerous," Jacob snapped, his temper thinning for the first time. "No guests are allowed down there. There's a civilized path to the beach, but it entails a bit of a walk. I'm happy to show Mr. Dempsey—"

"It's fine." Balfour's quiet voice floated over the room, pausing all activity. I turned to where he'd entered, Harry by his side. Harry looked faintly amused by the whole drama, but tried his best to keep a straight face because Jacob clearly was not amused. "I apologize for worrying you. I just needed to get a sense of any activity around the building before I came inside. With seaside inns with cliffs, especially historic ones like this, there are likely a lot of potential spirits who are more attached to the outside of the property. I need to know that before coming in."

"Yes, well. We'd prefer not to obtain new ghosts on our watch," Jacob said dryly. "Those rocks are dangerous, and the path leading down to them are off-limits to all guests, even psychic ones. That's why there are signs posted and a fence out there, to deter people. I'm only concerned for your safety, Mr. Dempsey."

Balfour merely looked at him—at least I thought he was looking at him. I still couldn't see his eyes behind those glasses—and didn't even respond. Instead he turned to Maeve. "I'd like to be shown my room now."

"Of course. I'll finish checking us in." With one last, faintly threatening glance at Jacob, Maeve clacked over to the check-in desk.

"Did they get your luggage out of the car?" I asked Tomas brightly, mostly because he was standing closest to me.

Tomas nodded. "I believe we have everything. Thank you."

"Great." I turned to Sam, waiting for her cue to tell me what we were supposed to do next.

"We should check the room," she said in a low voice. "Make sure Jacob gave them everything they asked for."

I resisted the urge to tell her she should've done this yesterday.

"He didn't finish until this morning," she said, reading my mind.

"Fine," I said. She was probably right, given Jacob's resistance to Balfour. We'd need to make sure he had all his demands met, otherwise I'd probably get a call at midnight looking for some crazy thing that he needed to channel someone. And since I was kind of curious about upstairs, I didn't protest too much.

We went over to Jacob, who was watching the whole procession with some disdain.

"Can we just go take a quick look before they go up?" I asked.

He looked offended. "Of course. Though I have been doing this professionally for many years, Maddie."

"Look"—I lowered my voice—"this is a big deal for the town. You know this. Let's just all play nice and make it an event to remember. We're all going to make a lot of money this week, don't forget. And we need to make sure we checked all our boxes."

He sighed, still put out, but my words had registered on some level. "Fine. Follow me."

Chapter 15

Sam and I followed Jacob to the elevator. He pressed the button for the fifth floor. "We need to take the stairs from the fifth floor. There's no elevator access to the top floor," he explained.

"Why?"

"Because we took that floor out of commission after the unfortunate event a number of years ago," he said. "Now. Do you need to see all the rooms, or just his? His is the only one on the top floor. Well, and of course the cat's. I put the rest of them on the fifth floor."

"Just his," Sam said. "I can't wait to see the cat's room."

I couldn't hide my giggle. I was a total cat fanatic and I did more for cats than I probably did for the humans in my life. But for some reason, the separate, connected room for the cat seemed super funny to me. If I was being honest, I had to say I admired the way the guy treated his cat. It said a lot about him as a person.

The doors whooshed open on the fifth level. Jacob led us down the hall and around a corner to a stairwell. He unlocked the door, pushed it open, and motioned us through. I followed Sam. Jacob closed and locked the door behind us, then led us up the two flights to the top

floor. He unlocked the door at the top, once again holding it open for us. I stepped through into a hallway that
looked nothing like the rest of the inn, or at least what
I'd seen of it. I'd been to the inn a few times for events
before I'd moved away, but I hadn't been here since I'd
been back. And I'd never been up here—it had been out
of circulation since before I was born.

The floor was huge. Jacob could be renting this out as
a honeymoon suite, or even to a whole wedding party. I
wondered if the murder was the only reason why it had
been out of commission, or if all the haunting rumors
had played a part too. I made a note to ask Grandpa. He
would know the deal. Especially since it was related to an
unsolved murder. Maybe Grandma had told him all the
dish from back then. I wished she was around to ask now.

I walked down the hall slowly, taking it all in. This
floor looked older than the rest of the inn, as if they'd
made every effort to retain some of the original feel
even when they'd done upgrades; the décor was historical but expensive looking. The hallway rug was probably Persian—I didn't really know my rugs, but I could
guess—and the paintings of people along the wall were
in heavy, brass, antique frames. On the opposite side of
the hall were framed photographs that appeared to span
decades. I paused to look at them and realized with a
start that my grandmother—a much younger version of
her—was in a few of these. Which made sense, since
many looked like staff photos. In one, she was in the
middle of a group standing in front of an older version
of the front desk. She wore a uniform, and I could see a
name tag pinned to her chest. Her dark hair was cut into
a bob that I'd never seen on her before, but her smile
was unmistakable. In another, she stood with a group of
women all dressed in maid's uniforms. The one next to
her had an arm slung around Grandma's shoulders and

an impish smile on her face. I could see a tattoo on the woman's inner forearm. My grandmother wasn't looking at the camera, but turned slightly toward her, laughing.

"Sam," I said, motioning her over. "Look, it's Grandma."

Sam joined me in front of the photo, her mouth widening as I tapped Grandma's face. "Wow. She was so pretty," she said softly.

"Ah, yes. Our staff and many guests from over the years," Jacob said when he saw what we were looking at.

"Who's that?" I asked, pointing at the woman—girl, really—whose arm was around Grandma.

Jacob gazed at the photo. "Theresa St. Clair," he said finally. "The woman who went missing."

"Oh, wow," I said, stepping in closer for a better look. Theresa looked like she could be the life of the party. Her eyes flashed with spunk and her pose, even in her uniform, was slightly provocative.

"So much of the inn's rich history is on these walls," Jacob said, motioning to some of the other photos. He moved down the hall and pointed. "This is Captain Swain, who built the inn for his bride. He died at sea, as so many of these sea captains did back then. And this was his wife, Louisa." He pointed to the picture hanging next to the sea captain. The woman in the painting was exquisite with curly brown hair cascading around her shoulders and eyes the color of the ocean at night. She didn't smile so much as smirk, and I felt like she was trying to tell me a secret.

I realized suddenly that it was cold up here. Like, at least ten degrees colder than downstairs. I instinctively rubbed my arms, trying to get rid of the goose bumps. "Is the heat not working?" I asked.

Jacob frowned. "It was working this morning."

I looked at Sam. She didn't look freezing, but I could feel my teeth starting to chatter. "Seriously, it's cold up here," I said. "Is it just the hallway? Hopefully the rooms are okay. Did they specify a temperature for Balfour?" I was being a little snarky, but it really did feel cold.

But both Sam and Jacob were looking at me oddly. Jacob marched over to the thermostat on the wall and peered at it, then turned back to me. "It's seventy-two degrees up here," Jacob said. "And heat rises, so I expect it will get warmer as the day goes on. It's not terribly cold out today. But we can ask Mr. Dempsey what his preference is. And he can control the air in his suite."

Weird. It didn't feel seventy-two. I shrugged it off and turned away from the line of paintings. "Okay, let's do this. They're going to be up here any second."

Jacob led us to one of the doors and waved a card in front of the little black sensor. It flashed green and he pushed it open. Sam and I both peered inside, my mouth dropping open slightly.

First, he wasn't kidding. The suite spanned almost the length of the whole floor, or at least that was the perception. The living area was bigger than the entirety of my old apartment in San Francisco, and the kitchen rivaled the one in Grandpa's house. The door to the bedroom was open, and I caught a teasing glimpse of the view out the slider door—the sea, churning below, crashing on the rocks. It gave the illusion that the balcony hovered over the edge of the cliff.

But my gaze was drawn back to the living room. I could see where the old elevator shaft must have been— the wall was completely different in texture and color, a probably hasty job that no one had bothered to upgrade since they'd closed the area off to guests anyway.

The room had clearly been decorated to Balfour's specifications. It was low-lit with purplish lights, casting a witchy glow into every corner. And it was entirely draped in scarves. Black, silver, purple scarves, some sheer, some glittery. An amethyst stone as tall as my knee stood in front of the full-length window, which also had a breathtaking view of the ocean. A circular table with purple chairs was placed off to the side—ostensibly the psychic reading table. Sam had gotten the requested pumpkins, and someone had even carved them.

"Wow," I managed finally. "This looks great. Very impressive."

Jacob nodded, clearly proud. "It is."

"The amethyst is so gorgeous, isn't it?" Sam went over to admire the stone. "I got it on loan from this really cool woman I met at a fair. She's coming to be a vendor this weekend, actually. But she agreed to ship this over early so we could get the room ready."

We didn't have a good crystal shop on the island. I didn't know this because I personally bought crystals (I didn't), but because Sam had lamented this fact many times. "Who is she?" I asked.

"Her name is Violet Mooney. She owns a crystal shop in Connecticut," Sam said. "The Full Moon. She's super cool. I met her at the Spring Equinox Fair last year. She reads auras too. You'll love her, Maddie."

I had no idea what *reading auras* meant, or what the Spring Equinox Fair was. And Violet sounded more like Sam's type of friend than mine, but I nodded anyway as if this all made perfect sense. "Awesome. Well, glad it worked out." It was cold in here too. I looked around for the thermostat and spotted it right near the door. But when I went over to look at it, it swore it was also 72 degrees in here.

I hoped I wasn't coming down with something. I certainly had no time to be sick. I turned to Sam. "We good to go?"

Sam was scrolling through the list of demands on her phone, mentally checking them off. When she was done, she nodded. "Let's check Balfour Junior's room before we go."

"Right this way," Jacob said, ushering us back into the hallway. "You can get to it through the bedroom, but it's locked right now from the other room."

We traipsed back out into the hall and to the next door. When Jacob unlocked it, I was amused to see there were scarves and crystals in here too. The room had no bed, as Jacob had mentioned, but there were multiple couches set up in the living area. "The cat needed some crystal healing support for travel," Jacob said dryly when he noticed me looking at the stones. "They sent them ahead of time."

Sam stepped in and looked around, nodding approvingly. "The only thing we'll need is a purple blanket for the couch. He likes purple. It's calming."

Jacob pulled out his phone and made a note. "I'll get one sent up right away. Although I'm sure I'll have to buy one. I don't believe purple is in our color palette."

"And just make sure the connecting door is unlocked before he comes up," she added, sounding more and more confident with each ask. Maybe this role was good for her.

Jacob marched over to the door and unlocked it. "All set." He was being polite, but I could tell he was kind of holding his nose at this whole thing.

Oh well. Came with the territory of being the haunted inn owner. And really, I wanted to get off this freezing cold floor and into my warm car. "We ready?" I asked Sam again.

"Yep. Let's go," she said.

I opened the door to the suite and stepped out into the hallway, then paused when I saw a woman halfway through the door of Balfour's suite.

Chapter 16

"Can we help you?" I asked. I assumed the woman worked here. How else would she be letting herself into Balfour's suite? Although her outfit was not the typical black pants and white shirt I'd seen the other staff members wearing. The geranium-pink dress she wore did not flatter her white skin and dishwater-blond hair. It was accented by a screaming yellow scarf with orange tigers on it around her neck that reminded me of the ones flight attendants wore. She was wearing way too much blush the same color as her dress. I didn't see a name tag or badge.

Maybe she worked in the office and was just helping out. With Balfour coming, all hands were probably on deck.

The woman froze, half in and half out of the door, then stepped out into the hall. Her face was like a deer in headlights.

"No, I . . ." she began, but Jacob came out into the hallway and stopped short.

"Who are you?" he asked the woman, looking at me as if to get some clarity. I shrugged. I certainly didn't know her, but it was kind of disturbing that he didn't seem to either.

"I'm sorry. I . . . think I took a wrong turn." She began edging away, looking for all the world like she was about to make a run for it.

"I should say so," Jacob said. "What exactly were you looking for? And how did you get in there? Or even onto this floor?"

"I was looking for a restroom," she said.

"Up here?" Jacob's tone was incredulous.

I echoed his disbelief. What hotel had the public restrooms on the top floor?

"May I ask how you got up here?" he asked. "This is a private area."

The woman shrugged, her jaw settling into a defensive line. "Through the stairwell. I saw a doorway and it was open. Like I said, I thought it was a restroom."

"Are you a guest?"

"Uh. No. Not yet. I was hoping to be," she added. "I just came in from out of town and was . . . checking the place out."

"Well, the booking agents are in the lobby. Along with the restroom. Let me take you." His tone left no room for argument. He glanced back at us. "Are you ladies all set with the accommodations?"

"Yes, it's great. Thanks, Jacob," I said, still dying of curiosity about this woman.

"Don't forget the blanket," Sam added.

"I will see to it right away." He checked to make sure both suite doors were locked, then ushered us all toward the stairs. Before he followed us down, he checked the door to the stairwell to make sure it was locked, then repeated the procedure at the bottom level.

When we got to the lobby, he pointed to the desk. "They can help you."

"I'll use the restroom first," she said.

"To the left of the desk, down that hallway."

The woman scurried off. We all watched her duck into the bathroom, then I turned to Jacob.

"That was weird," I said. "Do you really not know her?"

"I do not," Jacob said, tightlipped.

"That's not good," Sam said.

"It certainly isn't," he agreed.

"Do the suite doors lock on their own?" I asked.

"Of course. We had the locks changed when we upgraded all the rooms, even though we don't put guests up there."

"So how did she get in?" I asked. "She had the door open and was halfway inside."

Jacob's lips pursed. "I probably didn't shut the door all the way. As for how she got upstairs, she must've gotten through the stairwell door somehow."

We both fell silent. I knew we were thinking the same thing—I'd seen him lock it, and he probably remembered himself locking it.

"I thought I locked it behind us. And no one should be able to access that floor without a specific key card. There are only two of them." He sounded troubled, although I could tell he was trying to make light of it. "Tourists. We do get some ghost-crazed ones who try nutty things. But don't worry. There are only two keys to that floor and I have one." He took it out of his pocket and waved it at me.

"Well, who has the other one?" I asked.

"My night manager. I'll make sure it's still in her possession. I promise you, this won't happen again," he added, as Sam opened her mouth, ostensibly to tell him that Balfour wouldn't like surprise guests.

He didn't wait for the commentary and hurried away, muttering something about the purple blanket. I looked at Sam. "Strange, right? I guess it was just some star-struck person who heard that's where his room would be. Although I swear he locked the door."

Sam sighed. "It's bound to happen. People are obsessed with him. I just hope it doesn't happen again when Balfour is there. He wouldn't like it."

"I don't think anyone would like it," I said. "I'm sure Jacob has it under control. I'll mention it to Harry on the way out. So do we need to meet with Maeve now, or do they want to settle in first?"

"Let me find out." She hurried over to where Maeve and Balfour stood near the front desk, heads huddled together as they talked in low voices. I wondered if he was telling her about the spirits he'd already bumped into.

I scanned the lobby for any other interesting activity. As I did, a flash of pink caught my eye—the woman from upstairs, exiting the bathroom. As I watched, she slipped right past the front desk without stopping and hurried out the door.

Guess she hadn't really wanted a room after all. Curious now, I slipped out the door and caught a glimpse of her getting into a white SUV. She looked right at me as she took off out of the parking lot, driving a lot faster than was probably prudent for a smallish parking lot.

Her gaze was not friendly.

I watched the car speed past, noting that it was a Kia. I glanced at the license plate and caught two letters—BD. Just for the heck of it, I noted them in my phone, then went back inside.

Sam waved me over. "They just took Balfour up to his rooms. We're going to talk to Maeve now."

"We should tell her about the woman," I said.

Sam looked doubtful. "That might upset them. Shouldn't we just let Harry know?"

"We need to tell Harry too. But they should be on the lookout themselves." We headed over to where Maeve waited in the lounge for us, her iPad in front of her.

"Great," she said. "This shouldn't take long."

I pulled out my phone and checked my notes for the alias Lilah had given me. "Before I forget. We still have some overflow readings open, right?"

"Yes, of course. I left enough space for two per night."

"Great. I need one for Thursday."

"You're getting one?" Sam squealed, excited.

I shot her a look. "No. It's for . . . a client who asked me about it. She wasn't sure how to book. Hey, can you go let Harry know about that thing?"

"That thing?" Sam looked confused.

I sighed. "The thing upstairs." I didn't want to say more yet.

It took her a second, but thankfully the light dawned. "Oh. Yes. Got it. I'll be back." She hurried off.

I turned to Maeve, who watched us with interest. "Sorry. Anyway, this lady. Her name is Jane Cummings. She'd like Thursday night."

Maeve used an Apple Pencil to tap her screen. "The only slot I have left on Thursday is an abbreviated one," she said.

"Can we move something to make him available at six? This person—er, Ms. Cummings said she'd pay extra."

Maeve paused, glanced at me. "I'll have to see if I can swap the current person. How much extra?"

I suppressed an eye roll. "Double his fee."

"The person I have in here now at six on Thursday is Becky Walsh. Do you happen to know her?"

Relieved, I nodded. "Yes. We can totally move her. Don't worry about it."

"Will Ms. Cummings still pay double for the efforts?" Maeve smiled sweetly.

"I'm sure she will," I said.

"Excellent. I'll have to move"—she peered at the spreadsheet—"Leo Mancini too."

"You know what, keep him at the same time. Becky can go later, or the next night?"

She nodded. "I'll make the switch. Will you tell Ms. Walsh I'll be in touch with a new time before I send the new confirmation?"

"Telling her now." I fired a text off to Becky, then turned back to Maeve.

"So what happened upstairs?" Maeve asked. "If it's anything to do with Balfour, I'd appreciate knowing. I need to be one step ahead of him at all times." She smiled, but her eyes were sharp and evaluating as she watched me.

"Yes, of course. I was going to tell you when we were done with your agenda." I hesitated. "There was a woman trying to get into Balfour's suite upstairs. She somehow got into the stairwell, which is always off-limits to the public. Jacob assured me there are limited keys, and I'm going to talk to security, so you should be fine. But I wanted to let you know."

"A woman? What did she look like?"

I described the woman. Maeve stared at me while I talked, her unwavering gaze a little unnerving. When I was done, she frowned and muttered something that sounded like "Not again."

"Sorry?" I asked.

"Nothing." She pulled out her phone and typed

furiously for a moment. "Is she still here?" she asked, not glancing up.

"No. I saw her drive away."

"Thank you for the heads-up. Why don't we spend a few minutes tomorrow when we come for the tour at your place talking about the other tours? There's something I need to take care of." She stood, not waiting for my response. "Oh. And please do let me know about the police detail."

I stood too. "Do you know that woman?" I asked.

She fixed those intense eyes on me again. "What makes you say that?"

"You didn't seem surprised when I mentioned it."

"I'm not," she said, her face relaxing into a smile. "Balfour has many types of fans. It's just part of the reality of his life. Just make sure we get that police detail sorted out, please. He's going to want to visit his mother today." With a tight smile, she hurried away, leaving me staring after her.

"Today?" I said to the empty spot she'd left. "Is she freaking kidding me?" I looked at Sam, who had just walked up behind me. "Why didn't they ask for this detail in their contract?"

"I don't know," Sam said. "I swear I didn't forget, because they wouldn't have signed it."

"Unless there's a separate addendum," I muttered.

"What?"

"Nothing," I said. "But I got the sense she was familiar with this woman."

"You did?" Sam said. "Wonder what that's about."

"No idea. But I wonder if it's why they're worried about police escorts." I checked my watch. "Let's go. I'll call Mick and ask him." I knew that police details weren't just simple affairs that you called up and requested. There was a process that occurred, usually far in advance.

We hopped back into Dad's SUV and I told Siri to call Mick's cell. When he answered, he sounded like he was outside somewhere. "Hey, Maddie. What's up?"

"The psychic and his people just got here."

"Great," he said, in a tone that told me he wasn't sure why I felt the need to fill him in on this.

"They asked for a police detail for Balfour. When he needs to get around. Like, starting today."

He laughed. "You want a police detail. Today."

"Well, I don't want it. They're kind of demanding it."

"Maddie. That's impossible."

"I figured you'd say that." I sighed.

"Ask your grandfather."

"He was my backup plan," I said. "But Mick? There was something weird that happened today." I told him about the woman trying to get into Balfour's suite. "When I told his handler about it, she didn't seem surprised. And she got very squirrelly."

"He's a psychic. I'm sure he's got all kinds of weirdos following him around," Mick said. "And it's just my luck they're all descending on our island. Because Halloween isn't kooky enough around here." He disconnected.

"Bummer," Sam said. I'd had him on speaker so she'd been able to hear the whole thing.

"I figured. It's not that simple to just set one of these up. Unless . . ." I asked Siri to call Craig.

He picked up on the second ring. "Hey."

"Are you working tonight?"

"No, I just got done with my shift a few—"

"You wanna make some extra cash?" I interrupted.

He was silent. "Doing what? Is it illegal?"

Sam giggled.

"Who is that?" Craig asked.

"It's Sam," she said.

"Oh, hey Sam. So, you didn't answer me, Maddie."

"It's not illegal. I need a police escort, basically. For the psychic."

"For the . . . jeez, Maddie. What's he doing that he needs an escort?"

"I think he's just going to visit his mother. Alice Dempsey."

"And he needs an escort because . . ."

I repeated what I'd just told Mick. "I don't know if that would be the reason they'd give you, but I'm thinking it's something to do with it. We'll pay you a hundred bucks an hour." I glanced at Sam to convey she needed to work it into the festival budget.

"Okay," Craig said.

"Okay?" I was surprised.

"Why not? Jade's working and I had no plans. What time and where?"

"We'll work out the details and call you back," I said. "Thanks, Craig. I owe you."

"Yeah, you do. But what else is new?"

Chapter 17

The next morning, Lucas and I got up early, poured some coffee that Ethan had kindly left for us into to-go cups, and got the dogs ready for a walk.

We were definitely not the earliest risers in the house. Ethan would already be out at the cafe getting today's menu prepped and goodies into the oven. There was evidence Grandpa had been downstairs too—his coffee mug still sitting on the table in the kitchen next to the newspaper, which was unsurprisingly open to the police log page. I glanced at it to see if there was anything interesting, but nothing jumped out at me.

I wondered if Grandpa was out with Harry doing security for Balfour. Craig had told me he could only help out yesterday, since they weren't approved to provide that service for Balfour. So I'd talked to Grandpa, and he said he and Harry would take care of it.

It was the best I could do with the last-minute notice. Honestly, I was annoyed; Harry and Grandpa both had other things going on right now and this could potentially take up a lot of their time. But, we had to do what we had to do.

"Ready?" Lucas asked, handing me my travel mug. He

held Lola's leash in his other hand. She sat at his feet, tail thumping excitedly. The dogs loved their walks.

"Ready." I sipped the coffee, then zipped up my hoodie and took Walter's leash. We slipped out the back door and down the path leading to the beach. There really was nothing better than where we lived, I had to admit, even though I did miss San Francisco sometimes. But the Atlantic Ocean had always held a piece of my heart. The longer I was back, the more space it seemed to fill in there too.

"What's on tap for today?" Lucas asked when we paused to let Lola sniff and do her business. Walter, ever the puppy, was running in circles around my legs, kicking up sand and having a grand old time. I tried not to let him trip me.

"Balfour's coming to tour the cafe," I said.

"He is? Shoot. I wish I didn't have appointments." Lucas looked disappointed. "I'd love to meet him."

"Aw. I'm sorry, babe. You'll have plenty of chances," I said, squeezing his hand. "He'll be here for two weeks."

"I know. I have a reading with him. It's just so cool. I mean, he solves cold cases and stuff. It's pretty awesome."

I had to laugh. "You have a reading too? You're as starstruck as everyone else, then."

"Of course! Aren't you?" He looked genuinely surprised.

"I mean, I just want the event to go smoothly. As long as everyone's happy, I'm good." I looked down in dismay as Walter happily peed on my shoe. "And I guess I'm changing shoes before he arrives."

"That's a good sign," Lucas reminded me. "It's how we met, remember?"

It was true. I'd met Lucas in a pet shop with one of

his grooming charges, who had promptly peed on my leg. It made for a good story.

And this particular incident was, I hoped, a good omen for our festival.

When we got back, I took off my shoes and left them on the back porch to deal with later, then headed to the cafe to see how it was coming along for our guests. I had to go do some work for the cafe that I'd been putting off—intake forms for new cats we were getting this week, vet checks on some potential adopters, and some updates to the website. We were selling Halloween merchandise right now. Cat costumes, mugs and totes with a picture of JJ in his costume, which was the cutest ever—he was Sherlock Holmes—and some other really fun items. I'd even sourced some super funky, unique Halloween jewelry made by a local artist. We had some stuff in stock here, but things were selling like wildfire online. Our social media volunteer was, as usual, killing it.

As was Adele. She was already here working her miracles. The place looked like a million bucks despite us having way more than the ten cats I'd originally said we'd keep in here. I wasn't sure when Katrina had started ignoring me and bringing over as many cats as she wanted, but I'd lost count at this point. With all the kittens we currently had, we were probably up to at least thirty.

In any event, someone had gotten the Halloween decorations up, the floors gleamed, the litter pans were clean, and not a thing was out of place. I sometimes wondered if Adele slept here. The cats were mostly taking their morning naps. Except for some of the kittens, who thought it was playtime all over again. I watched them pounce on one another, little wrestlers with boundless energy. They made me smile.

Adele had a couple of our steady volunteers helping

her. Harry had been commissioned to do the security detail this morning to get Balfour and team over here.

"Hi Maddie," Mish Warner called. "Big day! Adele told us all about it."

"I didn't say it was a big day, for the record," Adele informed me. "I just said we needed to spruce the place up because the bigwigs are coming."

I had to laugh. "Bigwigs?"

Adele shrugged. "Out-of-towners."

Adele thought everyone who wasn't local was either fancy, rich, or both. Of course Balfour with his celebrity status would most definitely fall into that camp. "I think they're more interested in the atmosphere. He's got this thing where he has to feel out any place he's supposed to go to for any kind of psychic activity." I figured it was for show, but didn't say that.

"That's so cool," breathed Clarissa, our college student and social media expert. "Is he willing to be on our social?"

"We'll have to ask him," I said.

"I have guests scheduled for right after them, so hopefully this won't take more than an hour," Adele reminded me. She was nothing if not structured.

"I know." We'd had to close the cafe for the tour, which wasn't ideal since we had a lot of people trying to get on the schedule who were in from out of town. "I'll do my best."

"You think he's gonna get hit with a psychic whammy here?" She looked around with anticipation, as if expecting a ghost to pop out and yell *Boo!*

"I doubt it. So do you need me for anything? They're due in a few minutes."

"Nope. Told you I had it under control," Adele said.

Just as she said that, we all heard the universally recognized sound of a cat getting ready to throw up. The hacking, gagging sound of a particularly large fur ball. All our heads turned toward the sound, and we watched in horror as Monty, our big orange guy, threw up right on one of the oversized floor pillows we had scattered around for guests to sit on.

"Oh, man," Clarissa said.

"Yeah," I agreed.

Adele sighed. "That's gonna leave a stain. And I'm out of Furry Freshness."

"Why don't you use the stuff in the closet?" Grandpa asked from the doorway.

"What stuff? You're holding out on me?" Adele demanded.

Grandpa laughed. "No. It's been here the whole time. It's pretty good too. Locally made, nontoxic. I actually forgot we had a stash of it." He went over to the little closet near the office area and returned with a gallon of cleaner. "Your grandmother swore by this stuff," he told me. "It was apparently a Blair family recipe passed down for generations and used at the inn. They sell it now."

"You're kidding. Jacob sells cleaner?" It didn't seem to fit his image.

"Yeah, although I'm guessing he had very little to do with it," Grandpa said with a laugh.

"Amazing," Adele declared. "It better work, Leo."

"I take full responsibility if it doesn't," Grandpa said solemnly.

Adele marched off to clean up.

Grandpa and I headed to the kitchen to get coffee. "All set for today, Doll?" he asked.

"I think so," I said. "I need to go check on Ethan though."

"He's fine. I just saw him. Val is helping out too."

"Oh, perfect."

Grandpa poured two mugs and handed one to me. "So what's Balfour like?"

We hadn't gotten to catch up last night. Grandpa had been out at a card game with some friends when I finally got back. "He's . . . fine," I said. "Quiet. I was expecting someone, I don't know, louder."

"So you're going to talk to him about the contract addendum, then?"

"I am. You're coming for the tour, right?"

"Of course I am. I told you I can't wait to meet him." Grandpa grinned.

Right on time, a van with the Inn at Lighthouse Point's name on the door pulled into our driveway. I could also see people lining up along the street. Word must've gotten out that Balfour was coming here, and his followers were going to try to get a glimpse. I didn't know psychics had such rabid fans.

Harry emerged from the driver's seat. He opened the back driver's-side door and Balfour and Maeve slid out. The twins got out of the other side. I stepped out of the side door, which was the cafe entrance, and waited for them to reach me.

Harry led the group up the driveway. Balfour trailed behind the lot of them, craning his neck to look at the house, his eyes still covered by those purple-tinted sunglasses. I wondered if he was getting any "psychic hits," as Adele would say, from it, or if he was going to need to visit our attic or something weird. Balfour Jr. and Tomas were not in attendance.

Harry turned to say something, pointing toward the cafe. The twins turned in unison and made a beeline for it. As they passed, their pale eyes swept over me without reaction. Man, were they weird. I sent good thoughts to Ethan.

"Welcome to JJ's House of Purrs," I said, putting on my best hostess smile for Balfour. "So glad you could come!"

"Thank you for having us," Balfour said in that quiet voice. "It's a lovely home."

"Thank you." I held the door for them. JJ waited just inside, his tail swishing expectantly. He loved company.

Balfour reached down to pet him, smiling as JJ pushed his head into his hand. "Lovely cat," he said. "Isn't he, Maeve?"

"The cutest," she agreed. "Is he up for adoption?"

"No. He's my cat," I said. "The rest of them are up for adoption. Come right in, the cats are this way." I led them inside. Harry remained outside, still on security detail I presumed.

Grandpa had joined Mish and Clarissa. They were all standing at attention. Adele was still there too, but she was at the desk working on something. One of Ethan's avocado and egg sandwiches sat on a plate on the desk next to her, barely a bite missing. She, unlike the rest of the island, didn't seem that enthralled with all the psychic hype, but I'd warned her to at least have some manners when they came, so she did stand up and greet them.

I introduced all the volunteers. "And this is my grandfather, Leo," I said, pulling Grandpa over. "He helps run the cafe. This is his house."

"*Our* house," Grandpa corrected. "It's a family affair." He smiled at Balfour. "A pleasure to meet you, son."

Balfour shook Grandpa's hand. "How old is your home? It's gorgeous."

I turned to Maeve as Grandpa launched into the history of the house. "They might be a while," I said. "Would you like to meet the cats?"

"I can't wait," Maeve said. "I *love* cats. Balfour Jr.

doesn't give me the time of day, and it always makes me sad. I might have to adopt one of my own."

I wasn't sure how I felt about any of this crew leaving with one of my cats, but she might not have been serious. "We have cats of all ages and backgrounds," I began, walking her around the space. We were constantly updating our décor. I wanted the space to be as inviting as possible, with plenty of places for people to sit. We had comfy couches, a couple of nice chairs, fluffy floor pillows, and even a few meditation pillows. Some people liked to sit and let the cats climb all over them. Everything was done in bright colors—oranges, teals, yellows—and I'd gotten some really fun art for the walls donated by one of our local artists who wanted to help the cats. "We work closely with the animal control officer to bring the cats in."

"Are they all strays?" Maeve asked.

"Some are owner surrenders, some are strays."

"It seems like such a small island to have enough to keep the cafe full," she said.

I laughed. "I wondered about that myself when I was thinking about opening it, but you'd be surprised. We never have a problem being full. Honestly, we've got more cats than I planned to have in here all at once, but it's all good."

Maeve dropped to the floor to talk to one of the cats sprawled out in a fluffy bed. "Who's this?" she exclaimed. "What a pretty cat!"

"That's Cindy," I said. She was right, Cindy was gorgeous. She was a tiger cat, but looked like she might have a bit of Maine coon in her. Katrina had found her hiding in someone's shed. They'd called because they thought there was a raccoon or some other wildlife living in there. The owners of the shed claimed not to know the cat or who she belonged to. She'd been skinny and hungry and had just looked so sad when she'd first arrived a month or so ago. Now she seemed happy. And a little chunky.

"She still feels very betrayed. It will take her some time to trust again."

The voice behind me almost made me jump.

Chapter 18

I hadn't even realized Balfour had joined us. I glanced up at him. "I'm sorry?"

"Betrayed," he repeated, kneeling down to place a hand on Cindy's head. "She had a family who rejected her. Pretended not to know her. She was put outside and told to leave."

I stared at him, not sure what to make of this. Maeve didn't look fazed at all. She was still fawning over Cindy. "How do you know that?"

He looked at me, a small smile playing over his lips. "I'm a psychic, remember?"

"And you can read animals?" I wasn't quite sure what to make of this, but if it was true, how cool would that be? We'd get to know the mystery behind some of our residents.

He nodded. "I can. The ones who want to connect with me. Cindy is eager to tell her story." He paused again, his hand still resting on her head. She arched her back and leaned into his touch, purring.

When he spoke again, his voice was flatter, and he spoke faster, as if trying to get it all out. "Her real name is Hermione, but she prefers Cindy. She prefers living here, actually—it's not just the name. She lived in a house with a family until they got a dog. Then they put her outside. She didn't know where to go, so she hid in a small building—a cabin or a shed?—until someone came and took her away and brought her here. Poor girl," he murmured. "People can be so cruel."

My mouth dropped open. "She told you all that? The ACO picked her up from a shed. The owners said they thought wildlife was living inside it." Then a thought struck me. "Was it her original family who called us? Did they lie about her being a stray?"

Balfour was silent for a moment. I presumed his eyes were still closed behind those tinted lenses. Then he nodded slowly. "Seems so. She didn't go far because she'd never been outside. It makes sense that if she'd found shelter nearby she would just go there."

"I need to tell Katrina," I said. "Those lying jerks."

Balfour looked like he was about to protest, but Grandpa interrupted us with a tray of steaming mugs. "Ethan sent in his famous pumpkin latte," he informed us. "Wanted to make sure Balfour got to try it."

"How lovely," Balfour said, standing and accepting a mug.

"Oooh!" Maeve squealed. "Pumpkin spice is my favorite!" She reached for one, sniffing appreciatively. "This is so nice."

"Thanks, Grandpa." I happily took a mug. Pumpkin lattes were my favorite too, especially the way Ethan made them. No sugary syrup here. I wasn't exactly sure how he did it, but they were ten times better than the processed stuff at most places.

Balfour looked like he was happy about it too as he took a sip. "Delicious."

"You wanted to see the rest of the house?" Grandpa asked. "I'm happy to take you now, as long as you don't mind the mess that comes with two of your grand-daughters and their significant others living under the same roof." He winked at me.

"We're not messy at all," I informed Balfour. "And Grandpa loves having us here."

"I do," Grandpa affirmed. "Because I'm going to have you pay the housekeeping bill."

I laughed. "Funny. I'll join you guys for the tour."

Maeve stood. "I'll tag along too. I'd love to see the house. It looks so beautiful."

"I'll be outside, keeping all the onlookers at bay," Harry said. "Part of my new security detail gig. I'll send the others in when they finish up in the cafe."

"Oh, they won't come in probably. They're not big animal people," Maeve said. "Sharlene is afraid of any-thing with more legs than she has. It took forever for her to get used to Balfour Jr."

See? Weird.

We followed Grandpa and Balfour through the French doors into the main house. "So what do Sharlene and Manfred do for Balfour?" I asked Maeve.

"Oh, they do a bunch of different things. They're ba-sically executive assistants. And drivers. They're the Swiss Army knives of the organization," Maeve said.

"I see. Have you all worked with Balfour long?"

"Yes," Maeve said. "I'm actually the newest addition, and I've been around for almost ten years. Tomas and the twins have been with him for longer than that."

The twins didn't look old enough to have worked for someone for ten years, but I didn't say that to Maeve.

"I can't wait to see the rest of the place," Balfour was saying to Grandpa as we went into the living room. "I

can already tell you have more than just your grand-
daughters and their friends staying with you."

Grandpa and I looked at each other. "What do you
mean?" Grandpa asked.

Balfour smiled. "You have a lot of other family members here too. The ones who've passed on. They're all
around you." He turned slowly in a circle, hands out and
turned up. "It's a little noisy in here. Was your family
very boisterous?"

"The loudest family in town," Grandpa said proudly.

I looked doubtfully at the room around me. All was
quiet. I didn't have any weird sensations or vibes. I
turned back to Balfour. He must've seen the disbelief on
my face, because he smiled. "I feel a very loving presence," he said. "Think of it as added protection from the
Other Side. These are all relatives who have lived here
or were close to those who lived here."

"Like . . . my grandmother?" I asked, glancing at
Grandpa. His gaze was fixed on Balfour like his life de-
pended on his answer.

Balfour was silent again. When he spoke, it was in
that same weird tone as when he was telling us about
Cindy. "There is a strong female presence here," he said
finally in that same flat voice. "She's showing me an image of a"—his brow furrowed a little—"a baking dish of
some sort. With a blue emblem or graphic on the side.
And green beans."

I resisted an eye roll. Green beans? This was our esteemed psychic? I was prepared to dismiss it, but when
I looked at Grandpa I got alarmed. His face had turned
as white as one of Jacob's alleged ghosts. I grabbed his
arm. "Grandpa? What's wrong?"

"Our first big fight," he said, his voice rough.

"What fight?" I asked. "Who?"

"Your grandmother and me. She was upset at me. We'd gone to a holiday party at her work. The inn," he added, glancing at Balfour. "She worked at the inn where you're staying."

"Is that so?" Balfour asked.

Grandpa nodded. "I had some words with her boss. We didn't speak all the way home, and then she laid into me when we got back. Said I embarrassed her. I argued back that he had been out of line—I don't even remember what he'd said—and I didn't feel I should have to keep quiet. She did not agree. And finally she picked up the dish—we'd brought green bean casserole, and the leftovers were on the table—and threw it at me." He smiled at the memory. "Your grandmother had a temper."

Balfour was still, listening closely. Even Maeve seemed intent on not breaking the spell that had settled over the room.

I couldn't believe what I was hearing. I'd never heard this story. "Grandma threw a casserole dish at you? Did it hit you?"

"I ducked, of course," he said. "I was a cop, Maddie. I had good reflexes. But what a mess it made. And as soon as it hit the wall and smashed on the floor, we both started laughing. And that was the end of the fight. We were cleaning up green bean casserole for days."

I smiled at the image of the two of them picking up soggy green beans, laughing about how she'd tried to beam Grandpa with a baking dish. They'd had a whole life I didn't know about, I realized. You never really thought about your elder family members like that. It was a good reminder.

But where had Balfour gotten such detail? There had to be an explanation. Certain dishes that were popular when Grandpa was young or something. I was about to suggest it when Grandpa spoke again, as if he could read my mind.

"There's no way anyone could have known that," he said. "It was one of those stories that meant something to us, but we never told anyone else about it."

Chapter 19

After that revelation, the tour continued. Maeve and I trailed behind as Grandpa took Balfour around the house, floor by floor. Balfour wanted to see it all. Sometimes he was silent, sometimes he asked questions. He seemed to be taking it all super seriously, paying attention to everything Grandpa said. My mind was still trying to catch up to the baking dish story. I felt a little unbalanced, like I'd had a glass of wine on an empty stomach. There was no way Balfour had tuned into my grandmother. Was there? I remembered Alice insisting he was the real deal, but she was his mother. She *had* to say that. Still, Becky—who was one of the biggest skeptics around—seemed to believe in this guy. Maybe there was some kernel of truth to it all.

We finally got to the top floor. Balfour spent a minute gazing at my reading nook. But he didn't drop any other Grandma-related bombs. Finally, he turned to Grandpa. "Thank you," he said. "This was very helpful. I'm booked for a lot of different places while we're here, and sometimes coming into too much new energy overwhelms me. It helps to feel things out beforehand. But your home is lovely. There is very good energy in it."

"Absolutely," Grandpa said. "And I'm looking forward to our reading tomorrow night."

We all traipsed back downstairs. When we reached the cafe door, I turned to Balfour, hoping his mood was good enough to address the contract. "Can I talk to you for a moment?"

I could feel him observing me from behind those glasses. He nodded. "Of course. I'll meet you back in the cafe when I'm done," he told Maeve, a dismissal that she didn't seem happy about.

But Grandpa took her arm and led her back into the cafe, launching into a conversation about the cat costume parade, and she went willingly.

I led Balfour into the living room. He sat on the couch and I took the chair across from him. "What can I do for you?" he asked. "I hope you're not upset about your grandmother."

"Upset? No, I just . . . I'm not sure what to think," I admitted.

He smiled. "That's okay. But she really wants to speak to you. I've felt her presence from the first time I met you. It makes sense that she used to work at the inn. It was very strong there yesterday, when we all arrived. I wasn't sure who it was, but it was clear she was there for you."

I just kind of stared at him. It sounded way too *Sixth Sense* for me and I wasn't sure what to say.

"Is there a sign that you can think of that would make you believe your grandmother was in contact with you from the Other Side?" Balfour asked.

I had to stop and think about that. There had been a lot of meaningful moments in my time with my grandmother, and I wasn't really sure what he meant. "Like . . . Grandpa's baking dish?" I asked.

He smiled. "It doesn't have to be that extreme. It could

be an animal, or a landmark, or a song or scent. I had a client who thought of her dad every time she smelled a pipe and came to recognize that as a sign that he was nearby after he passed."

I thought about that. One vivid memory I had of my grandmother when we lived with her was her love of Ella Fitzgerald. Every night before dinner she would play an Ella record on her old stereo and sing along. My favorite was the song "I Can't Get Started." When I came into the kitchen, she'd make me dance with her. It always made me giggle. But was I really just going to start hearing a classic Ella Fitzgerald song out in the wild?

"Anyway," he said, clearly reading my vibe, "if you ever want to talk more about it, just let me know. Now what did you want to talk to me about?"

I snapped back into business mode. It was certainly easier than processing what he'd just said. "I wanted to tell you about the Halloween event we usually do to get some attention on our black cats, who often get overlooked at shelters." I figured this was the best way to start—get him sympathetic to the cause. I told him about Katrina's event and how we'd been evolving it, and how a shelter cat always took center stage at the culminating Halloween event.

He listened quietly and intently, and when I finished, he nodded. "That sounds wonderful. I'm very supportive of helping cats. Especially black ones, to whom I have an affinity, as I'm sure you can tell. So what do you need? I'm happy to give a donation, if that will help."

I stared at him, slightly puzzled. "Well, I know you wanted to make sure Balfour Jr. was the star of the show, so I wanted to see if we could find a way to have two cats participate. Maybe, a rags-to-riches story about his rescue, and then a spotlight on the shelter cat?"

He'd cocked his head slightly now. Those damn glasses

were unnerving. As if I'd said it out loud, he reached up and took them off, blinking against the sunlight streaming in through the windows. It was the first time I'd gotten a good look at his actual eyes. They were an interesting shade of blue—almost purple in this light—and super intense. Like he could see right through you.

"I'm afraid I don't understand. I'm happy to offer up Balfour Jr. however you need him, though."

"Okay, but with the contract addendum, I wanted to make sure we were able to accommodate what you wanted."

Balfour frowned. "What contract addendum?"

"The one that came by certified mail. About Balfour Jr. being the featured cat at the event?" It sounded absurd even to me, and I love cats.

But the way he was looking at me gave me pause. I was starting to think he had no idea what I was talking about.

"We signed the contract," he said. "At least, that's what my staff told me."

"Right. But then I got an addendum. Monday, before you arrived. Did you not know about the addendum?"

"I had no idea," he said. "Did you sign it?"

"No. I wanted to talk to you first."

"There's no need," he said. "Don't sign it. I don't wish to take anything away from a shelter cat who needs a home. That isn't right."

"Okay," I said, not sure what else to say. "Thank you. But there's definitely room for Balfour Jr. at the event. I know people will love to see him. I don't want you to think we didn't want him there."

Balfour didn't answer. He looked past me, out at the street in front of the house. I could hear a commotion out there, but resisted the urge to turn and look.

"This is going to be my last big event," he said finally.

"I've decided that I don't want to be in the limelight any longer."

"Your last event? Really? Wow," I said. Why was he telling me this? I mean, I didn't know the guy at all. "Does your staff know?"

He shook his head slowly. "I haven't told them. It would distract them. They won't be happy about it. But it's time to settle into a quieter life."

"You mean retire? Like here with your mom?" I asked.

His gaze returned to me. "Maybe. I'm not sure yet. You know my mother?"

I nodded. "A bit. She works with my best friend Becky. She's the editor of the local newspaper. That's who we're meeting with tonight."

"Yes." He looked outside again. "I do this work to help people," he said finally, after another long pause. "It's really all I ever wanted to do. But somewhere along the way, it turned into much more of a . . . business. I mean, I know it needs to be a business if I'm to make a living. But they make me out to be some celebrity, and I'm not that. I don't like being the center of attention. I just want to give people who have lost loved ones some comfort."

I nodded. "That's . . . a noble goal."

"I don't mean it to be noble. It's just what it is. But other people feel they're now in charge of my image, and I'm starting to lose myself. I can feel it happening, and I'm not happy about it. I'd been thinking about this being my last big splash, but now I'm certain. I'm retiring."

The sound of glass shattering made the two of us jump up. I turned to find Maeve standing in a pile of broken shards, the remainder of the coffee mug she'd been carrying during the tour, her eyes on Balfour. I had no idea how long she'd been standing there.

"Are you okay?" I rushed over to her.

She refocused, gazing in dismay at the mess. "I'm so sorry. I can be such a klutz sometimes. At least it was empty, right?"

"Right." I pulled the French doors shut behind her so none of the cats would come in and step on the broken pieces. "I'll grab a broom."

"Thank you. I'm so sorry." She took a deep breath, then turned to Balfour. "We need to go." I could feel a distinct chill in the air enveloping her words. "We have another meeting in an hour. Plus our presence is causing quite a commotion outside." She gestured to the window and I turned to look.

There was a line of cars outside, and the number of people milling around had tripled since I'd last looked. I could see Harry standing at the edge of the driveway, talking to people. Grandpa was out there too. Which must've been how Maeve got back in here when she was supposed to be occupied.

How much had she heard? A lot, I was willing to bet. And almost definitely the part about Balfour quitting.

"Fine," he said. "But first, where's Sharlene? I have a question for her."

"I'll get her," Maeve said. Jaw set, she turned and marched back into the cafe.

"Let me help you with that," Balfour said to me, as I retrieved the broom and dustpan from the hall closet.

"No, really. It's fine," I said, sweeping the remnants of the mug into the dustpan. "I'll vacuum later but just want to make sure no one steps on this." I dumped the shards into the trash, then turned to him. "I think Sharlene was out in the food cafe. We can meet them outside."

I led him back through the cat space and out the side door. Maeve and the twins were emerging from the cafe. Sharlene hurried over. "You need me?" She looked much less like a robot now that she was in direct conversation with Balfour.

"Are you aware of a contract addendum that was sent to Maddie?" Balfour asked her.

Sharlene nodded. "Tomas asked me to do it." She glanced from him to me, then back. "Did I do something wrong?"

Tomas. The cat handler who seemed a little obsessive about his charge. What was he trying to gain? More celebrity status, as Balfour thought?

Balfour shook his head. "No. Thank you for telling me. We're going to void it."

"Okay," Sharlene said. "I'll take care of it."

Balfour turned back to me. "Thank you again. My apologies for the misunderstanding."

"Not at all. Thanks for coming," I said. "I'll see you later on tonight. I'm joining Becky for the interview."

They headed for the van, Balfour waving to people who were shouting for him. This guy was popular. His retirement was going to be quite a shock to a lot of people.

As I turned to go back to the house, I saw a white SUV out of the corner of my eye come flying down the street. It didn't slow down, even with all the people—including Balfour—still crossing. For one terrifying moment, I thought it might plow right into them. I ran back toward the street, yelling something incoherent.

At the last minute, the SUV braked, careening around the pedestrians.

Maeve shouted something at the driver. But as the SUV blew past, I realized with a jolt that it was a Kia. The same one I'd seen leaving the inn. The yellow scarf I could clearly see through the open driver's-side window clinched it.

The driver was the woman who'd been trying to get into Balfour's room at the inn.

Had she followed him here? And worse, was she trying to run him down? Or at the very least, scare him?

Chapter 20

After they left and the cafe resumed its normal activities, I threw myself into getting some work done. But I couldn't stop thinking about Balfour and the white SUV. And his revelation that this was his last event. Maeve had clearly heard that bomb drop, which explained the broken mug. She hadn't expected that. He'd said none of his staff knew, and that they wouldn't be happy. It sounded like he'd made the decision in that moment. But it also sounded like he'd been thinking about it for a while.

It would almost certainly mean their jobs would disappear. I wondered how Maeve was feeling about all this. If they'd talked more when they got back to the hotel. If she knew that the catalyst was the contract addendum I'd told him about, which appeared to be Tomas's doing without Balfour's knowledge. The whole thing was weird.

And who was this crazy woman in the SUV? I'd told Grandpa it had been the same woman from the inn yesterday and given him the partial plate I'd seen when she drove past me in the parking lot. It was probably a rental, but they could still track it. Grandpa assured me that he would look into it, and that he and Harry were taking the security detail seriously. But I was worried.

And tonight we had the interview with Balfour. I wondered what other bombs might drop.

I ate an early dinner and took a shower so I was ready for Becky. She picked me up at five thirty as promised.

"Aaron is meeting us there," she said, referring to one of her multimedia staffers. "We have permission to do photos and video. I'm so excited we get to talk to Balfour. And to get to write some stories again. Did he tour your place today?"

I never heard her talk this much. "He sure did." I filled her in on the visit, leaving out the part about Grandpa and the baking dish—I still wasn't sure how I felt about that—and Balfour's pending retirement. Probably not a good idea to tell the local newspaper about that. So the headline really was the strange twist about the contract and, of course, the white SUV.

"That's wild. You think he's got himself a stalker?"

"Maybe. People seem pretty rabid about him," I said.

"Hmm." I could see her filing the information away as a potential story. "Does he know?"

"I have no idea. I told Maeve about her trying to get into his room. Not sure if she told him. I didn't get to tell her I thought it was the same person today, but I'm sure it was. I recognized the car. And the scarf."

"Wow," she said.

"Yeah." I was silent for a minute. "So Grandpa signed up for a reading. Tomorrow night."

Becky grinned. "Good for Leo. I'm sure Lucille has a lot to say to him. Did he take my spot?"

I ignored the comment about Grandma, but inside I couldn't stop imagining her hurling a baking dish—with food still in it—at his head. It did make me laugh. "No, there was someone else who needed to be fit in. I hope that's okay. They rescheduled you, right?"

"Yeah. I actually took the last reading of the night. It's

all good." Becky turned onto the winding road leading up to the inn. The sky was clear as it faded into twilight. From up here, I could see the horizon where the sky met the water in a brilliant show of colors ranging from rosy pink to lavender to hues of blue. She whipped the car into a parking spot and turned to me. "Ready?"

I followed her inside. Aaron, the photographer and videographer whom I recognized from some stories the paper had done on the cafe, waited in the lobby. He waved at us. Becky went to the front desk, returned a minute later. "Harry's going to take us up," she said.

When Harry came out of one of the offices from the hallway behind the desk, Jacob was right behind him.

"Hello, ladies," Jacob said. "What can we do for you?"

"We're interviewing Balfour," Becky said. "We need an escort upstairs."

"Right." He took a key out of his pocket, handed it to Harry. "What kind of story are you writing?"

I couldn't believe him. I'd just recapped the media plan with them. But Becky didn't seem to mind answering.

"I'm going to get a couple of stories out of it. Event related, a profile, and maybe we'll be able to solve one of your ghost stories too," she added with a wink.

But Jacob did not look happy at that. I couldn't help but think he'd asked the question just to try to pick a fight when he heard the answer. "I'd appreciate you not attempting to sensationalize my place of business," he said. "We had one unfortunate incident here with no explanation—"

"Two," Becky corrected.

He flushed but continued. "It seems that we shouldn't be trying to scare people with the idea that there are bad ghosts. Our inn is not that kind of haunted place. We have kind spirits who are just lonely. . . . And only police solve crimes," he added.

I wanted to point out that I knew from personal experience that wasn't entirely true, but I sensed I shouldn't get involved. Becky didn't need me anyway.

"Not true about the police. And also not true that ghosts are bad for business. I guarantee it'll be even better for business," Becky said. "People like to have the crap scared out of them. Plus, you all wanted a splashy media presence for the event. You're getting a ton of earned media, so probably you should thank me. Come on, don't you want a front-page story? Talk about good publicity!"

She was definitely having fun with Jacob, but it was clearly one-sided. His lips thinned, and I could see he was about to say something that probably wouldn't go over well with Becky. He didn't realize whom he was about to mess with.

Harry saw it too. "Let's get upstairs," he said. "We don't want to leave our guest waiting." He put a hand on Becky's shoulder and guided her toward the elevators. Aaron and I followed her, leaving Jacob standing there smoldering.

Upstairs, Harry knocked on Balfour's door. "It's Harry with your guests," he called.

It was still cold in the hallway. I made a mental note to mention it to Jacob.

Balfour opened the door. He still wore his purple glasses. He was holding Balfour Jr. on his shoulder like one might a baby. "Hello again," he said to me with a nod as he held the door open. "Please. Come in."

I introduced Becky and Aaron, then turned to Harry.

"I'll be in the hall," Harry said. "Have fun."

Balfour motioned for us to take seats in the living area. He let Balfour Jr. free, and the cat climbed onto the back of the couch behind his person. It was the first time

I'd gotten a good look at him. He'd been huddled in his carrier last time I'd seen him. He was definitely a handsome kitty, with long black hair and a regal face. He observed me with curious eyes as I went over to pet him. He purred and head-butted me.

"He knows a cat person," Balfour said.

"He's so sweet." I scratched behind his ears, then sat down next to Becky.

While Aaron set up his video camera, Becky explained what she wanted to accomplish. As she talked, I looked around the room. Balfour had added some of his own touches to the sensational décor, which made sense since he was staying nearly two weeks. He had a small table set up with a purple scarf draped over it. Tarot cards were laid out, and some crystals were scattered around them. I wondered if it was for the photo shoot, or if he read cards too. He had candles burning throughout the room and the lights were low, contributing to the atmosphere. The window was open a bit.

"It was stuffy in here," he said, when he saw me looking at it. "If you're cold I can close it."

"No, it's fine," I said, although I actually was cold again. I usually wasn't the person in the party who was always cold, but this floor just seemed to have a chill.

"Ready when you are, boss," Aaron said, pressing the record button on his camera.

I sat back while Becky launched into the interview. They talked about him personally first. Balfour's story was interesting—the psychic hits he'd been receiving since before he could talk, the fear that he used to have about what he was seeing and feeling, the way he tried to ignore it for years. It wasn't until he met another medium that he realized his powers were not scary, and that they could be used for good, to help people reconnect with lost loved ones. It was also heartwarming to hear about how he connected with people's pets as much as he did with humans.

After she covered what she wanted for his profile, Becky pulled me into the conversation, and we talked a bit about the event, what we were trying to accomplish and how rewarding it was to have such an esteemed guest. Balfour talked about what an honor it was to return to the place he'd grown up and be part of this. As the video recorded, Aaron snapped still shots while we chatted—he got a bunch of Balfour Jr. He was taking close-ups of the artsy reading table when Becky pivoted to what I knew she really wanted to talk about.

"I know you've done some work with cold cases in the past. Can you tell me about that?" she asked.

"Yes. I've offered my services many times and had success," he said. "Some members of law enforcement don't like to get involved with psychics. Unfortunately, there are people who have exploited the role and it affects those of us who can really bring this skillset to the table to help. But I'm working to change that perception." He took a deep breath and his gaze turned to me.

I held my breath. I thought I knew what was coming.

"As a matter of fact, I've decided to retire from the public part of this work and focus solely on helping law enforcement," he said. "This will be my last big event. I'm honored it's here, where I grew up."

Becky's eyes widened as she processed the scoop she'd just gotten. "Wow. That's a bombshell," she said. "How do you think that will be received in your community?"

"I'm not sure," he said. "I'm sure there'll be some disappointment, but it's what I need to do."

"Thank you for letting us know first," she said. "It's honorable, what you want to focus on. And speaking of that, I'm sure you know we have a couple of cases here at the inn that were never solved."

Balfour nodded slowly. "A dead man in an elevator shaft. I've certainly heard of that one."

"And a missing maid who vanished on Halloween night, less than a month later," Becky said. "They found pieces of her Catwoman costume, but she was never seen or heard from again." She leaned forward. "Did you want to stay up here because it's where the elevator murder happened? Do you think you're going to be able to get any insights into what happened with either case?"

For the second time that day, shattering glass interrupted us. Our heads all snapped around to the open window, where apparently the impending storm had kicked up the wind and blown a vase with white lilies off the end table. Balfour Jr. sprang off the back of the couch and made a beeline for his room through the connecting door.

We all looked at one another. "Weird timing," Becky said with a nervous laugh.

"I'll get it," I said. "You two keep talking." I went to pick up the pieces, again worried the cat would step on some glass, but kept my ears trained on the conversation. Becky, like a dog with a bone, had gone right back to her questioning.

"So you were about to tell me what you thought about the cases," she said.

"My team prepped me on them, mostly the elevator shaft incident. It *was* one of the reasons we decided to stay here. And it does feel like someone has been trying to come through. Someone who died here," he said.

"Whoa," Becky said. "How does that work?"

"I'm clairvoyant and clairaudient," he said. "Which means I can feel *and* hear things from the Other Side. And I've been getting a strong sense that there is someone around me up here. But as I understand it, there are other ghosts, so I'm not sure who could validate some of my insights. The man who died. Remind me of his name?"

Becky pulled an old newspaper clipping from her notebook and handed it to him. "Archie Lang. Short for Archibald. He was in town on business with some investor group, but the firm wouldn't say if they were actually meeting with anyone about any investments."

Balfour studied the page for a few moments, then handed it back to Becky. "They were trying to blame the woman," he said.

We looked at each other. "The maid," Becky said. "Yes, there was some speculation."

He shook his head. "It was definitely a man," he said. "The killer."

"You picked that up from just the article?" Becky stared at him. "Did you get a name?"

Balfour smiled. "It's not that easy. But I do think . . ." He trailed off for a moment, closing his eyes. Then he stood and, without another word, walked out into the hallway.

Becky and I looked at each other again. This time I shrugged. She got up and followed. I pondered staying where I was, but curiosity got the better of me and I followed them both out into the hall. Harry and Jacob were talking down by the stairwell door, but Jacob was clearly distracted by Balfour, who walked slowly down the hall, pausing at each of the many photos displayed along the wall.

He lingered in front of one, then pointed to it. "I'm feeling like the murderer has some similarities, at least in physical appearance, to the people in this photo," he said. "I'm getting a lot of images of a very bushy mustache."

Becky and I stepped closer to it. It was the same staff

photo in which I'd first noticed my grandma. There were a lot of people in the photo. The men all had those porn-star mustaches that were popular in the seventies and early eighties, which was clearly the right time frame for the murder. I felt another chill, this one not related to the outside temperature. Had my grandma been close to a murderer?

Becky motioned for the photographer to get a picture of the photo. As he was focusing in on the shot, Jacob zoomed down the hall. "May I ask what's going on here?" he demanded.

Balfour regarded him with that same calm expression. "Ms. Walsh was asking me about the unexplained death," he said. "I was showing her the picture that best described what the suspect might have looked like, based on what I saw."

"What you saw?" Jacob repeated. "Which was?"

"Jacob," Becky began, but he held up a hand to cut her off.

"I'd like to hear what he has to say."

Balfour gave a brief explanation of what he'd told us. "I felt an overwhelming sense that the suspect is a man, and he had a similar look and feel to the people in this photo. Specifically, a mustache."

"That's pretty much everyone at that time," Jacob scoffed.

"Maybe so," Balfour said. "But your suspect will have something the others didn't."

"What's that?" Becky asked.

"Ties to organized crime," Balfour said. "And a long, successful life here on Daybreak Island."

Chapter 21

"And then Jacob almost lost his mind. I'm guessing it's not going to be much better when he sees how everything hit the news."

It was opening night of the haunted inn tours and Balfour's first private readings, and Grandpa, Lucas, and I were on our way back to the inn. We were talking about Becky's interview with Balfour and his dramatic review of the photographs in the hallway.

Which, of course, had blown up, along with the bombshell news of his impending retirement. I kind of wondered if he regretted mentioning that. Becky hadn't even been sure of which story to lead with. In the end, she'd run two stories this morning—the profile, in which she'd led with the retirement and the shorter, newsier clip about the elevator shaft murderer potentially still living on the island. The respective video clips had run last night on the *Gazette*'s social media accounts—TikTok, Instagram, YouTube. I assumed his fans were freaking out—but his staff was probably freaking out more.

Not to mention Jacob. It promised to be a wild night.

Everyone was going to be here tonight—the entire committee, my whole family (even my dad), and likely half the town. Along with all our out-of-town guests, of course. There were multiple tours beginning at six p.m., just after it started to get dark. Grandpa had made us reservations for a later tour, after his reading. The tours were going to be held every night through Halloween, and the paper was actually following one of the tours to capture it on video. Much to Becky's chagrin, some other media outlets had come to town. Which was probably why she'd been so aggressive about her coverage and getting interview clips out so fast. The *Boston Globe* was here, surprisingly, but I guess that meant Maeve was good at her job. They were supposed to be interviewing Balfour and Alice together. Becky, not to be outdone, was doing an in-depth profile on Alice.

"But why did he almost lose his mind?" Lucas asked. "It's not like Balfour incriminated him as a murderer."

"He's been so cranky about this whole thing. I guess he just doesn't want the inn's reputation tarnished."

"Do you really think Balfour can tell who the murderer is?" Lucas looked enthralled by the concept.

"I don't know. I mean, if it was that easy, there'd be no unsolved cases left, right?" I glanced at Grandpa Leo. He'd been quieter than usual during this story. "Grandpa. Do you think psychics can help solve cold cases?"

"I honestly don't know, Maddie. I've never seen it done successfully myself," he said.

"Why do you think Jacob is so uptight about this? Did people really think evil spirits killed that guy and made a maid disappear?"

Grandpa smiled. "I don't think evil spirits were ever the problem. I didn't work the murder. I was still on patrol at the time. But I remember it. It was obviously a big deal at the station. The working theory was that whoever had done the guy left the island the same night, before anyone discovered the body. He was here with some convention. A bunch of investors, if I remember correctly."

"That's what the article said. Investment bankers. But also, Balfour said the killer had a long, successful career here." Which was a little freaky.

"I wish he'd told Balfour his name, in that case," Grandpa said, tongue in cheek.

"Right. But if someone had left, wouldn't you know from the guest roster?"

Grandpa glanced at me with a smile. "My granddaughter, the detective at heart. The theory was that someone came in from the mainland, went to the hotel, met with Archie, killed him, then left."

I frowned. "Then what about the ferry roster?"

"It's my guess that they ran down as many people as they could, but remember, resources were constrained and there weren't many murders out here at that time," Grandpa reminded me. "The force didn't have the experience. And the logs weren't computerized then, so it would've been very easy to simply not log a name in."

"Do you think the investigation was mishandled?"

"I didn't say that, Madalyn." His tone had the slightest hint of annoyance, which was very unlike him. It made me even more curious.

"So they never thought it was anyone who worked at the inn?" I kept thinking about Balfour pausing at that photo. He'd been clear that he hadn't been pointing the finger at someone in the picture, just the general idea of what the killer had looked like, but I couldn't help but wonder.

"They interviewed everyone who was around that night," Grandpa said. "The staff all had alibis. The people staying at the inn denied knowing anything, and most of them had each other as alibis. Which is never a good alibi in my mind, but no evidence to suggest otherwise was ever located, from what I'd heard. Hence the theory that some-one had come in, done the deed, then left." He pulled onto the street leading to the inn. The road was lined with cars on both sides, which meant the parking lot must be full already. I could see flashing lights ahead, which meant the police were here directing traffic. I wondered how Jacob could be unhappy at all with this turnout and the attention the inn was getting. It seemed counterintuitive at best.

"Let me drop you both off at the front door and I'll park," Lucas offered.

"No need, son," Grandpa started, but I cut him off.

"Thanks, Lucas. I don't need to be climbing the hill in these shoes." I motioned toward the high-heeled boots I'd broken out for the occasion. "Besides, you have a reading soon, Grandpa. You don't want to be late."

That was true. He didn't. Outnumbered, Grandpa pulled up at the entrance to the inn, and he and I got out. Lucas slid behind the wheel and headed off to park. I grabbed Grandpa's arm before we went inside. "I didn't mean to upset you," I said. "I wasn't insulting your de-partment. It was before you were in charge."

He sighed. "You didn't, Maddie. Look, could they have done things differently? Sure. But I wasn't in the chief's head. And when I took over the detective's unit and tried to reopen the case, I got a lot of pushback and ultimately had to let it go. I wanted to look into it when I became chief, but I didn't want to involve too many of the detectives, and it was time-consuming to work on myself."

"Who pushed back?"

"Andrew Blair," he said.

"Jacob's father?"

Grandpa nodded. "This is between us. Not for Becky or the newspaper. But he was very closemouthed about the whole thing."

"I wonder if he knows something," I said. "Maybe that's why Jacob is so touchy." I suddenly remembered the story Grandpa had told when Balfour was over, about Grandma and the casserole. He'd said he'd "had words" with Grandma's boss. Which had to be Andrew Blair.

"That's reaching, of course. We have no idea. It's just that his behavior was a tad suspicious." He broke off as my parents rushed up to us, before I could ask him.

"You're here!" Mom exclaimed, giving Grandpa a hug.

"Hi, Maddie." My dad gave me a kiss on the cheek.

I was happy to see him. We hadn't been able to spend a lot of time together lately, with my crazy schedule. "Hi, Daddy. Looking forward to the haunting?"

He smiled. I didn't think this was really his thing either, but he was here for the town, and to support Mom—and his daughters—who'd all been working so hard on the event. "Can't wait," he said.

"Maddie." My mother slipped her hand into mine. "Everything looks great inside. Have you heard from anyone?"

"Not yet," I said. "First tour starts at six, and Balfour started doing his readings this afternoon." I thought of Lilah, who had likely already snuck in the back door for her reading as Jane. I'd had to arrange that on the downlow with Maeve. Apparently Manfred would be the one to let her in the back and lead her upstairs through the delivery elevator, then up the special staircase since that was the only way in and out of the top floor. "Is Sam here?"

"She came with us. She was talking to the man who takes care of the cat. Odd guy," my mother added in a low voice.

She wasn't kidding. "How are the rehearsals coming?"

"Great! A week until the show." My mother beamed. "It's going to be a hoot."

A man dressed as a sea captain opened the door and rang a bell. A loud one. As conversation died down, he announced, "First tour begins in ten minutes! Those with reservations, please line up in the lobby."

I saw a guy with a camera snapping photos of the crowd. "Becky must be here already too."

"She is. I saw her inside," my mother said. "She's in her glory. She has a reporter, two photographers, and video people with her. Alice is here, of course. She looks proud as punch. Come on, let's go in. We're booked for the next tour."

"I have to wait for Lucas. He's parking. You go ahead, I'll catch up." I waved them in, then sat on one of the benches out front. I hoped he hadn't had to park too far away. People streamed past me as I waited, talking excitedly, some dressed in costumes, others not. Maybe Salem refugees—people wore costumes there all season long. I wondered how Lilah was going to disguise herself. She'd have had to park far enough away too. I assumed I'd get a phone call about that soon enough if she was displeased. I hadn't heard from her though, which I hoped meant things were going swimmingly.

I wondered if the crazy lady in the white SUV would make an appearance tonight. Worse yet, I wondered if she'd set up a reading with Balfour. Maeve would have all that under control. I hoped. But no sign of her that I'd seen yet, and no white SUVs—so far so good.

I saw Donald Tunnicliffe and Sal Bonnadonna walk by, deep in conversation. Donald caught my eye and lifted his hand in a wave. Sal glanced my way but didn't acknowledge me.

I felt someone sit down next to me and glanced over, realizing with a start that it was Sharlene, one of the Creepy Twins. She lit a cigarette, tossing her long hair over her shoulder, and gazed at me with those blank eyes.

"Hi," I offered. "Maddie. I picked you up from the airport?"

She took a drag. "Hey," she said finally.

First word she'd spoken directly to me. It was progress. "How are things going?" I asked.

"Not bad," she said. "A little tense."

"Because of Balfour's announcement," I said, not really a question.

She acknowledged that with a slight tip of her head. "Everyone was already mad at each other anyway." She gave a wave of the hand with the cigarette.

"How are you doing? Like, with his news?" I asked.

Sharlene didn't look at me, just kept staring ahead into the darkness. "It stinks," she said finally, then lapsed into silence again.

"How long have you been with Balfour?" I tried.

"Like, twelve years." Her voice choked up a little. "He saved us. Me and my brother. We lost our parents. They died. He connected us with them and they told us it wasn't our fault. Manny was driving the car when they . . . died."

Wow. She'd gone from not speaking to me to spilling her guts. "Your brother," I confirmed.

She nodded. "All four of us were arguing, and someone hit us, and it was bad. We always felt like it was our fault and it was messing with us, you know?" She took a long drag, then blew the smoke out her nose. We both watched it fade into the night. "He offered us jobs. We were just kind of floundering until then. But he helped us get on a good path. And now . . . I don't know what we'll do. We'll be lost without him."

"I'm sorry," I said. "But maybe he'll need your help

in another capacity. It sounds like he's going to be doing some really important work."

"Yeah, well." She tossed the butt and stood, grounding it out with the heel of her combat boot. "I guess we'll see, right?"

I saw Lucas approaching and stood. Sharlene followed my gaze, then flicked her eyes back toward me. "See you," she said, then turned and headed inside.

"All set?" Lucas asked, slipping his hand into mine.

"All set," I said, following him inside. I scanned the room for Sharlene, but didn't see her anywhere. Like a ghost, she'd managed to vanish into thin air. I still found her a little creepy, but she felt more human now. And I felt sorry for her. She seemed very dependent on Balfour, and I couldn't help but wonder—what *would* happen to her and her brother if he didn't need them anymore?

Chapter 22

When Lucas and I got inside, the first tour group was off and running and the second group was already gathering in the lounge area. The tours were scheduled about half an hour apart. Of course, they ended in the inn's gift shop, where there were tons of souvenirs available for purchase, including books written by local authors about the history of some of the inn's ghosts. People were coming early to check out the decorations and soak up the atmosphere. No one wanted to miss the chance of a ghost—or a Balfour—sighting.

I saw my parents already in line. They waved. Sam was across the room talking to Jacob, who didn't look happy. I turned the other way to avoid him seeing me for as long as possible. I assumed I'd catch some flak for the newspaper stuff.

There was a food spread in the lounge that Val had orchestrated. I knew she'd gotten Ethan to do the desserts. I didn't see her, but figured she was buzzing around somewhere making sure everyone had plenty. Other committee members milled around—I saw Sal with a beer in his hand, talking to some guy I didn't recognize. Ellen was at the tour check-in desk, welcoming everyone and getting them organized.

So far, everything seemed to be going right along. "Let's go see Harry," I said to Lucas. "He's still doing security up at the check-in area."

"Security? Sounds serious," Lucas said.

"Yeah." I hit the button for the elevator. I hadn't gotten a chance to tell him about the white SUV lady. I gave him the abbreviated version in a low voice while we waited for the elevator to arrive.

"Wow," he said. "You think she's a stalker or something?"

"I have no idea, but they requested security, so I'm thinking either this happens a lot in general, or they know who she is."

The elevator dinged its arrival just as Becky hurried down the hall. "Hey, wait," she called.

Reluctantly I let the elevator go. "Hey. How's it going?"

"Oh my gosh. So much stuff." Breathless, she appeared to be about to launch into a story, when an angry voice stopped her in her tracks. We all turned to see Jacob storming down the hall waving a newspaper. Uh-oh. Here it came. I braced myself.

"Ms. Walsh! May I speak with you." He caught up to us, barely glancing at me.

"Sure, Jacob," Becky said. "What can I do for you?"

I expected him to rant about the photo and Balfour's commentary about the murderer and started preparing a secondary defense.

"I have a bone to pick with you. Your newspaper printed proprietary information from this inn!"

She frowned. "What do you mean? Balfour's interview—"

"I'm not talking about that drivel," he interrupted. "I'm talking about this!" He thrust the paper at her.

She took it, glanced down at it then back at him, her brow furrowed with confusion. I peered at it, trying to get a glimpse of what he'd handed her. "I'm sorry, I'm not following," she said finally.

"That cleaning trick. In your Helpful Hints column," he said through gritted teeth. "That is proprietary."

"This?" Now Becky laughed. "I didn't know there was such a thing as a proprietary cleaning recipe."

"There certainly is. Where did you get it?"

Now she was starting to look annoyed. "Our columnist wrote it."

"Well, please print a retraction."

"A retraction to what? Sorry, we lied, it's not two tablespoons of vinegar?"

I stepped in between the two, trying to moderate. "Look. Maybe we can talk about this tomorrow," I suggested to Jacob. "It's such a busy time tonight—"

"My father will be beside himself if he sees this. I will come to your office tomorrow and we'll rectify it," Jacob informed Becky, then stalked off.

We all looked at one another.

"Is he kidding me?" Becky said finally.

"Yeah, that was bizarre," Lucas agreed.

"He's been acting bizarre lately. This is just next level." I jabbed the elevator button again. "I have to go see Harry," I said. "Let's catch up later."

She waved and headed back into the fray. Lucas and I went up to the fifth floor and stepped out into the hall where Harry, Tomas, and Manfred were all stationed. Manfred was at a small desk. I assumed he was checking people in. I wondered if Harry was here when Lilah arrived, and how they managed that. Again, no news was good news. I didn't want to know, as long as she was happy. I'd already deposited the check, just in case.

"Hey Harry," I said. "How's it going?"

"Hey, Maddie. All is well," he said spreading his hands wide.

"Yeah?" I glanced at Tomas, who looked, as usual, disinterested in the whole process. He was leaning against the wall and kept checking his watch.

"Yes. We've got everything running on schedule and everyone seems happy. We just had someone check in already for their reading later tonight. She's so excited. Apparently last time she saw him, he was able to talk to her dog she lost when she was seven." Harry smiled. "Her parents told her he ran away, and she thought it was her fault. That he didn't like her. Said she always felt bad about it. And now she knows the truth."

"That's so cute," I said. "Is Maeve upstairs with Balfour?"

"Yes. She's escorting guests and doing the time keeping."

"Sounds like a well-oiled machine," I said. "Okay, then, we're going to head back down. Just wanted to make sure things were all good."

Harry flashed me a thumbs-up. "All good."

"Awesome." I was more relieved than I'd let myself believe. I'd been so worried about this night—all the nights, really, but the first night in particular—not going well. To see everything running like clockwork was a huge weight off my shoulders, aside from Jacob's weirdness.

"Let's get some wine," I said to Lucas, and pushed the button for the elevator. When the doors opened, Grandpa stepped off. "Oh! Hey, Grandpa."

"Hey, Doll. Almost time for my reading," he said. I could tell how excited he was.

"Cool," I said. "They'll get you all checked in over there." I pointed to Manfred at the desk behind me.

"The other person hasn't come down yet, have they?" Manfred asked Tomas.

"No," Tomas said.

"Can you text Maeve?"

Tomas looked a bit put out, but pulled out his phone and sent a text.

Lucas and I stepped into the elevator. "She's not responding," I heard Tomas say as the doors closed.

I couldn't wait for a glass of wine. "I hope the reading goes well for Grandpa," I said. "He's so looking forward to this." I hesitated. "Do you believe in ghosts?" I'd never asked him that, not that it was typically something that would come up in conversation. At least I didn't think so. "I mean, not like the psychic stuff. Like actual ghosts that haunt places."

"Totally. Don't you?" He jabbed the button for the lobby.

I was kind of surprised, I had to admit. Lucas didn't seem like the ghost type. "I don't think so."

"Really? Not even a little curious if it's all real?"

"No. I think it's mostly a Halloween gimmick. Which I'm not saying isn't fun. I'm just saying it doesn't seem terribly . . . real. And I know I'm the outlier in my family. Everyone else is all about it, apparently."

"But you love Halloween."

"I do. That doesn't mean I love ghosts. Other than Casper, of course." It was true—I'd watched the cartoon Casper the Friendly Ghost religiously as a kid.

He smiled. "I liked Casper too. But I really loved visiting haunted places and learning all the stories. My mom loves that stuff too. I guess I inherited it from her."

"Really?" I hadn't met Lucas's mom yet, or anyone in his family, for that matter—something I did wonder about, especially since we were theoretically serious at this point—so I didn't really know what I was picturing, but I'd never thought of him as being from a woo-woo-type family. I'd always wondered what he thought of my mother, who was definitely woo-woo.

"Totally. She lost a cousin when she was a kid and they were super close. She said she always got the sense that he was hanging around her, helping her kind of get through life." He shrugged. "I love the possibilities of that. Like the people you love aren't really gone after they die."

I had a momentary pang for my grandmother, so sharp it almost brought tears to my eyes. I was lucky that I hadn't yet lost many people, but that one loss had been devastating. For all of us, certainly. But I carried some guilt about it because I hadn't been around much in the years before she died. Living all the way across the country and running a business, I didn't have a ton of time to travel back and forth a lot. Which was why after she died and Grandpa wasn't doing so great, it didn't take a lot of thinking about it to know that coming back here permanently was what I needed to do.

"Mads? What's up?"

"Nothing," I said, too quickly, because he gave me that look that said, *I don't believe you.* "Just thinking about my grandmother."

Lucas squeezed my hand tighter, waiting for me to continue if I wanted. I didn't really know what to say, though, so I leaned against him.

"She used to work here," I said. "Being around here so much has made me think about her a lot lately."

"Did she know all the ghost stories?"

"Grandpa said she was really into it. She never talked about them to me." That also made me feel kind of bad. If this place had been an important part of her life for so long, why hadn't she shared more about it? Was it because I never seemed interested?

We reached the lobby and stepped back into the fray. As we headed over to the table to grab a glass of wine, I spotted Becky—and lo and behold, she was talking to Damian. And they looked pretty friendly, which made my heart happy. I'd catch up with her later.

We got to the table and one of the servers smiled at us. "We have wine, red or white, and beer," she said.

"Two reds, please," Lucas said.

As we waited for her to pour the wine, my phone buzzed. I pulled it out and read the text from Harry: *Problem coming atcha*

I frowned. What did that mean? Before I could try to guess, I heard my name being called. I turned to see Tomas running toward me. When he reached us he was clearly out of breath. "Balfour. He's not upstairs. Neither is Maeve. Have you seen them?"

"Have I? No, I mean, I just left you and got down here." I looked around, trying to see if I could spot him. It was virtually impossible in this crowd. "Maybe he's in the bathroom. Did you check the whole suite?"

"Of course I did." He looked offended. "But Maddie. I don't know how he would've gotten out. There's only one exit, and he would've had to walk past us and get on the elevator."

That was true. I opened my mouth to say we needed to go get Jacob.

And then the lights went out.

Chapter 23

The chatter in the room faded into stunned silence. There was a beat where I thought everyone must be wondering if it was part of the Halloween atmosphere, a little live ghost action, but unless Jacob and his staff had planned this without giving us a heads-up, I didn't think that was it.

Didn't this place have a generator? I grabbed my phone and turned on the flashlight. "I need to find Jacob," I said to Lucas. "Be right back."

I started across the room. I kept the flashlight in front of me, dodging the people who were still frozen and waiting to see what would happen next. Just as I reached the front desk, I heard a whirring noise as a bunch of things regained power at once. Lights went back on, but not the full spectrum. The generator must've finally kicked on.

"What's going on?" I asked one of the hotel employees behind the desk.

He shook his head. "Not sure, ma'am. The power went out. Could be weather."

We both stared doubtfully out the window on the far side of the lobby. It was dark by now, but also obvious that there was no weather to speak of. Nor had any bad weather been forecasted.

"Will the generator take care of everything we need?" I asked. "For the tours?"

"We've got lanterns," a man said, appearing from the room behind the desk. "We'll use those. It could be atmospheric." He smiled at me. "Hello. I'm Martin, the night manager."

"Hi. Where's Jacob?"

"I'm not sure. He must be around somewhere," Martin said. "Not to worry. It's all under control."

"Did you call the power company to report the outage?" I asked.

He nodded. "We're on it."

"Okay." There wasn't much else I could do. Maybe people would think it was part of the act. A ghost reenactment or something. I turned to head back to find Lucas, but instead found Tomas standing almost toe-to-toe with me. I jumped back, startled.

"Jeez," I said. "Give a girl some warning that you're standing there."

"Did you not hear what I said? That Balfour isn't upstairs?"

"Right. Okay, well, have you tried calling him?"

"Of course I have!" Tomas screeched, loud enough to draw stares in our direction from the people standing nearby.

Martin watched us curiously. "If I may. Is something else wrong?"

"Balfour. Is. Not. Upstairs." Tomas enunciated each word with a point of his finger at the ceiling. "We cannot locate him."

I raised my eyebrows at Martin as if to say, *Help.*

"Where's Harry?" he asked, grabbing a walkie-talkie off the desk.

"Harry was upstairs in the hall," Tomas said. "We were stationed there. He was called away. I went to my room to get something. I had the stairwell key." He pulled it out of his pocket as if to prove the point. "It hasn't left my possession. Maeve was upstairs with Balfour and she's gone too."

Martin disappeared into the room behind the desk again. I heard the crackle of the walkie.

"Look," I said to Tomas. "Go check again. Maybe he needed some alone time and found a little nook up there to go to." I had no idea if there were any other spaces up there where this could be true, but at least it would keep him busy and out of my face while I tried to think. "Or maybe he went to your room? Or Maeve's or one of the twins? Check all your rooms. And leave me the stairwell key."

His face told me that was almost the dumbest thing he'd ever heard, but he clearly had no better options. He handed me the key, spun on his heel, and headed back toward the elevators.

I called Grandpa. "Where are you?" I asked when he answered.

"In the restroom at the moment, then heading back up to wait for my reading. What's going on down there?"

"No clue. Power outage, but I can't imagine why." At that moment, I heard sirens in the distance and frowned. Uh-oh. Related? Maybe there'd been an accident or something. I hoped they weren't heading here. "Listen. Tomas is freaking out. Says he can't find Balfour. Can you or Harry go look with him? I'm going to leave the key with the night manager while I check around down here."

"Sure. I'll come get it. But I don't know where Harry is. He got a call from Jacob and left."

I handed the key back to Martin, who'd just come out

of the hallway to assure me Harry was on it, and started
doing a sweep of the lobby. I doubted Balfour would be
down here mingling with the crowd—he seemed way too
introverted for that—but you never knew. I tried to not
panic. Everything had to be fine. He probably just got
overwhelmed and needed a break or something. Maybe
Lilah drove him to it.

Lilah. He'd been in a reading with her right before
they noticed he was gone. Coincidence? I was trying to
process the possibilities of that when Sam rushed over
to me.

"What happened?" she asked.

"I have no idea."

"I heard sirens," she said.

"I did too." I didn't want to tell her about the other potential problem. She would probably freak out. "Listen,
can you go make sure Ellen is okay wrangling people so
the tours stay on track? They're still going to do them.
They have lanterns to add to the atmosphere, but the generator should have the lights on most places."

"Sure," Sam said, and hurried off.

The crowd in the lobby had thinned out a bit, so I got
a good look around. No sign of Maeve or Balfour. I went
back over to where Lucas was waiting at the table talking to Val.

"I need to go outside for a minute," I said. "I'll be right
back, but if you see Balfour can you text me?"

"Sure," he said.

"Thanks." I hurried out the front door, almost bump-
ing into Alice Dempsey, who was coming in. She looked
stressed out. "Alice. Hey." I hesitated, not wanting to
worry her, then decided to ask anyway. "You haven't seen
Balfour recently, have you?"

"No," she said. "I haven't. Why?"

"Tomas said he's not in his room. I'm sure it's fine.

Maybe he went out to get some air. I know he really liked the ocean view. Maybe he's around back. I'm just going to go check."

"I'll come with you." Alice fell into step beside me. There was a moon out tonight—not quite full, but nearly, so it gave us some much-needed light once we moved away from the patio area of the inn. "He really liked being out at the cliffs," she said. "He might've gone out there."

I sighed. "Jacob won't like that. They already had a fight about it."

"I know, but my son is . . . headstrong."

We both ignored the signs posted around the property about staying off the path, which was nothing more than a thin line of sand with rocks poking up, that led down to the rocks. Alice seemed tense. She didn't say anything, but I could feel it vibrating off her.

"Did you guys do the interview with the *Globe* yet?" I asked, mainly to fill the awkward silence.

Alice nodded. "This morning."

"How did it go?"

"It went fine," she said, but didn't elaborate.

I decided to concentrate on walking, because my heels were making it difficult the farther we got down the forbidden path. Jacob would lose it if he knew we were out here. No need to make the situation worse by falling off the cliff.

My flashlight caught a glimpse of something shiny on the ground as the path began to narrow even more. Up ahead, I could see a makeshift fence that Jacob must've installed, with more signs proclaiming *Danger! Steep rocks!*

I refocused on the object I'd seen, pausing to shine the light on it.

And felt my heart sink into the pit of my stomach.

Alice paused too, turning back to see what I was

looking at. When she recognized the object, she covered her mouth with her hand.

We'd both recognize those purple glasses anywhere.

"Don't touch them," I said. I reached down and pulled my boots off. "Stay here," I told her. Dropping my shoes next to the glasses so I'd remember where they were, I crept further down the path toward the edge of the cliff. The path was narrower and harder to walk on as I got closer.

When I reached the fence I could see that it was bent, as if something heavy had landed on it. It wasn't much of a fence, to be fair—one of those short, wire gardening fences. Admittedly it would be hard to install any real fencing up here. The rocks would probably start falling if you tried. Strong winds probably took their toll on it, I told myself as I went a bit closer.

But why would it be caved in so perfectly right in one spot, if that were true?

I went up to the edge, risking a peek over the side, shining my phone flashlight, which had a pretty good beam. Had to hand it to Apple. At first all I saw were rocks jutting out of the side of the cliff. Below, the ocean crashed around them. I estimated the drop at a hundred feet or so.

But as the waves receded, I noticed there was something out of place. Something that didn't belong. A flash of color where it should only be black.

Instinctively I stepped back, and almost lost my balance when I bumped into Alice. "Let's go," I said, but it was too late. She was staring over the cliff with her own flashlight, seeing the same thing I was.

A body, splayed below us on the rocks, alternately being covered and uncovered by the rushing waves.

Chapter 24

I pulled Alice back. "We have to call the police. And it's not safe out here." Clearly.

"Is that my . . ." her voice broke before she could get out the word *son*.

She was going to lose it, and I couldn't have her lose it out here. I didn't need two people going over the cliff.

Over the cliff. I felt nausea roil in my stomach. If that was Balfour—and I was ninety-nine percent sure it was, because his glasses were only a few feet away on the ground—how did he end up at the bottom of the cliff when he was supposed to be up in his suite doing readings? Had he been out here looking for a ghost and fallen? Or . . . had something else happened? Why were his glasses on the path? If he'd dropped them and he was alone, why wouldn't he have picked them up?

All these thoughts were running in a jumble through my head. I took what my Zen master friend Cass Hendricks would call a backpack breath—four counts in, hold for four, exhale for four—to clear my thinking. Alice was still frozen but she looked like she might bolt toward the cliff any moment. I held her with one arm and used my other hand to scroll through my phone contacts for Mick Ellory. But when I pressed the call button, it failed.

No service out here. Great.

Then Alice started to scream.

"Alice. Stop. We have to go inside and get help," I said, trying to sound soothing. Really, I was freaking out, and had no idea how to handle a distraught mother, to boot. I ended up dragging her back down the path, trying the call every few feet. Finally it went through. I waited impatiently through three rings until Mick answered.

"Maddie. What's up? I'm in the middle of something. What is that noise?"

"I need you out here at the inn," I said. I could hear how choked my voice was over Alice's cries.

Mick heard it too. "What's wrong?"

I turned away from Alice. "I think . . . someone's dead."

There was a long silence. "Who?" he said finally.

"Just come, please."

"I'm actually right down the street. There was an accident. Someone hit the utility pole. Took the whole thing down."

The sirens. The power outage. Guess I'd been right. "Are they okay?" I asked.

"Not sure," Mick said. "The pole came down on the vehicle. The driver must've been practicing for a NASCAR race." He sounded disgusted. "She's en route to the hospital, but it's not looking good. Anyway, I'll be there in five." He disconnected.

"Come on," I told Alice, whose screams had turned into soft sobs. "The police are coming. Let's get you inside."

She stared at me like she'd never seen me before. I realized she was probably in shock. I couldn't bring her back to the inn full of people. I called Grandpa. "Can you meet me out back?" I said urgently.

Thankfully, he didn't ask any questions. "On my way."

We reached the patio area. Not wanting anyone to notice us, I held back since there were still people milling around outside. Grandpa slipped out a back door minutes later, took one look at Alice, and shot me a look that said, *What is going on?*

"I'll explain later."

"Come on," he said. "We can go inside through the side entrance and get warm." He led her away and I hurried out front to wait for Mick. It wasn't until I noticed people looking at me oddly that I realized I'd never picked my boots back up. I was still in my socks—luckily they were fuzzy and warm—and my boots were still back on the cliff, marking the spot where Balfour's glasses lay.

Mick drove up without a lot of ceremony—no flashing lights or sirens—and parked in the valet area. "What's going on? And where are your shoes?" he asked.

"I'll explain on the way." I led him out back and down the path, breathlessly filling him in on everything that had happened since the power outage, and what I thought I'd seen at the bottom of the cliff.

He remained silent, taking it all in. When we reached the spot where my boots sat next to Balfour's glasses, he stooped to inspect the area, then snapped some pictures. When he had photographed from every angle, he reached into his pocket, pulled out gloves and an evidence bag, and placed the glasses into it. He returned it to his pocket. Wordlessly, he picked up my boots from where I'd discarded them and handed them to me. "Stay here," he said, then continued to the edge.

I held my breath as he examined the fence, taking pictures of that too, before finally turning his gaze over the side, keeping a careful distance back from the edge. He used his phone to zoom in and take some more pictures, then put it to his ear and made a call. I couldn't hear what he said.

Finally he turned back to me. "Let's go," he said curtly. "No one should be out here."

I hurried to keep up with him as he strode back down the path. "Did you see . . . Was it Balfour?" I asked.

"There's a body down there. I have no idea who it is," he said. "I've never seen Balfour. And it's impossible to tell from up here. Also, retrieving the body from down there is going to take a while."

Maybe it wasn't him, I reasoned with myself. My flashlight wasn't that good from such a distance. Maybe he'd dropped his glasses when he'd been out here earlier and couldn't see to find them. Or maybe they were just cheap accessories and he had more pairs, so it wasn't worth looking for them.

Maybe when we went back inside, he'd be back at his little table doing readings and this would all be one big mistake.

But then who was at the bottom of the cliff?

Mick turned back to me to make sure I was keeping up. "You can't discuss this, Maddie," he said. "We need to work the scene and it's going to take a while."

"If it's him, it's going to be pretty obvious," I said. "What are we supposed to do?"

"Right now, nothing. I need to get a team out here to retrieve the body. I called for backup. We need to talk to Jacob. Can you bring me to him?" Mick asked.

I nodded, registering faintly that Jacob was going to lose it.

Then I remembered Alice. "His mother," I said.

Mick looked at me. "Sorry?"

"Balfour's mother. She's with Grandpa. She saw . . ."

Mick sighed. "I'll need to talk to her too. Where are they?"

"Grandpa took her inside."

I could hear the sirens now, racing up the street. No one was being quiet and stealthy any longer.

"I've got to start securing the scene," Mick said. "Go find your grandfather and Jacob and wait for me."

I nodded, but didn't move.

"Maddie," he said. "Are you okay?"

"I . . . don't know. What do you think happened, Mick?"

He didn't answer. "Go find them," he said again. "I'll meet you inside."

I turned and started for the inn, dreading the next few hours.

Chapter 25

I wanted to avoid the crowd I figured would be out front, so I tried the back door of the inn, but it was locked. There must already be people securing the scene. Probably Grandpa had done it in anticipation of what was happening. I could call him, but I didn't have the energy. I turned to walk back around to the main door, vaguely aware that my feet were freezing and now wet. The spray from the sea must have soaked the rocks and the grass, because the night was still clear and calm. It seemed like a cruel paradox to everything that was going on right below.

As I came around the side of the building, one of the side doors opened, nearly slamming into me and a large, dark figure rushed out, pausing when he realized someone was there.

"Oh. Maddie. Hey."

It was Sal. "What are you doing out here?" I asked him.

"I heard some commotion. Wanted to see what was going on."

I searched his gaze in the darkness, but could barely make out his eyes. "There's no commotion back here," I said.

He reached up, fiddling with the gold chain around his neck. "Guess I'll go around front and see." He turned to go, then paused. "Something to do with the psychic?"

I froze. "Why would you think that?" I asked carefully.

He shrugged. "What else could it be?" When he saw I wasn't going to respond further, he turned and walked away.

I reached for the door, but it was locked, so I followed Sal around the front of the building. I wondered what he was doing. Why had he been going out back? Was he trying to get off the property without being seen? Why wasn't he jumping in to help as a committee member?

I lost sight of him once we hit the crowd out front. I saw Craig heading inside with three other cops and called his name. He said something to the others and came over.

"Why aren't you wearing your shoes?" he asked.

I shook my head, dismissing the question. "Did Mick tell you what happened?"

"Yeah. Helluva night, between this and the accident."

The accident. I'd nearly forgotten about that. "Any word on the person? Do you know who it was?" I was fervently hoping it wasn't anyone we knew.

"No. Some tourist in a rental SUV. One of those Kias. It folded like an accordion. I'm glad I drive a Subaru, tell you that. But these people drive so fast and they have no idea what these roads are like."

But now he had caught my attention. I grabbed his arm. "You said an SUV? A Kia? What . . . what color?"

He narrowed his eyes at me. "Why?"

"Just tell me," I snapped. "Was it white?"

"Yeah. It was. How did you know that?"

Oh, man. I needed to sit. I managed to make it to the bench—the same one I'd sat on with Sharlene what felt like days ago, but was probably only an hour or two—and dropped onto it. *Don't jump to conclusions*, I told myself. There has to be more than one white Kia SUV driven by a tourist on this island. And at this event. Half the island was here, along with a ridiculous number of guests.

It had to be a coincidence that the crazy woman who'd seemed to have been stalking Balfour drove the same kind of car. Didn't it? And that the car had been racing away from here around the same time that Balfour had somehow ended up at the bottom of a cliff?

"Maddie. Are you okay?" Craig asked, kneeling in front of me. "Do you need some water?"

"Do you know who the driver was?" I managed.

"Some woman. Again, a tourist. It was a rental. Are you going to tell me what's going on?"

"I have to find Grandpa. Mick told me to." I pushed myself off the bench, unsteadily.

Craig grabbed my arm. "Let's go inside," he said. He led me into the building, through the crowd still gathered in the lobby. But now the whole vibe was different. No longer celebratory. Instead, people were whispering among themselves as they tried to figure out what was happening.

Lucas rushed over to me. "Maddie. What is going on?" he demanded, glancing from the boots in my hand to Craig. "Is she okay?"

"I'm fine. Have you seen Grandpa? Never mind, I'll just call him." I pulled out my phone and jabbed the button with a shaking finger.

"Where are you?" I asked when he answered.

"Down the hallway past the elevators. There's a meeting room."

"Mick's here. He wants to talk to Alice." I listened to Grandpa, disconnected, and looked around. "Have you seen Sam?" I asked Lucas.

He shook his head. "I think she went looking for Balfour."

Maybe she hadn't heard yet. "I'll be right back," I told him, then turned to Craig. "Tell Mick to come find us." I repeated the location Grandpa had given me. "I'll wait there until he comes."

"I'm coming with you," Lucas said.

I thought about protesting, then decided against it. Why shouldn't I take advantage of having someone to lean on? "Come on," I said, reaching for his hand.

When we were out of earshot, he tugged my hand to slow me down. "Are you going to tell me what happened?"

I looked around to make sure no one could hear me. I didn't want this getting out yet. "Balfour's dead. At least, I'm pretty sure it's him."

"What?" He looked stunned. "How?"

"Not sure yet. But he went over the cliff somehow. Shoot," I muttered when I saw Becky rushing toward me.

"What's going on?" she demanded. The question of the night. "Why are the cops here? Is it something to do with the power outage? We heard there was a bad crash. Aaron's heading down to see what he can find out."

"Yeah, the crash took down a utility pole," I said. "I can't talk right now, Beck. I'm sorry. I'll catch up with you later," I promised, and pulled Lucas away down the hall. I could feel her eyes boring into my back as we turned the corner.

I found the room with Grandpa in it at the end of the hall. The Hawthorne Room, a little plaque outside proclaimed. It was one of those rooms that could be halved for a small event or left open up for a larger one. He and Alice sat at a lone table in the middle. She stared straight ahead, seemingly at nothing.

My heart ached for her and I fervently wished I'd insisted she not go down that path with me. Granted, it was a long distance down to see for sure, but both of us knew in our hearts it was Balfour down there. Probably her more so than me—a mother always knows, right?

"Where's Mick?" Grandpa asked.

"He'll be here soon. He was getting some things organized." I turned to Alice and touched her hand.

She didn't acknowledge me.

"Has anyone seen Jacob?" I asked Grandpa. "He really needs to know what's going on."

"I haven't seen him, but I've been in here."

"I'll text him. Mick wants to talk to him too." I sent him a curt message. *Need to talk to you ASAP. Hawthorne Room.*

I waited for a few minutes, but no reply. Where was he?

Lucas went to the side of the room where some chairs were stacked and began pulling a few free.

I paced the room, trying to stop my racing thoughts so I could make sense of what had happened. Balfour and Maeve were supposed to be upstairs, but suddenly they weren't. So where was Maeve? Had anyone seen her? How had they gotten off the top floor without anyone seeing them? That was a question for Jacob. Clearly there had to be another exit. The white Kia SUV driven by the stalker woman had been fleeing the scene when it crashed into a utility pole and took the power out. Jacob was nowhere in sight. Sal was creeping around back, and Balfour was at the bottom of the cliff.

How had this thing gone so sideways?

Mick strode into the room a few minutes later. He had his usual cop face on, but I knew him well enough now to know that he was stressed. His mouth turned down at the corners and his hair looked like he'd been raking it with his fingers.

"Leo," he said with a nod, then turned to Alice. "Ms. Dempsey?"

It took her a moment to register that someone was speaking to her. She nodded.

Mick moved to the table and sat. "I'm Lieutenant Ellory with the Daybreak Harbor police. I'd like to talk to you about what happened outside, if that's okay."

Her eyes moved to his. "Alice," she said softly. "It's Alice."

"Alice. Thank you." Mick motioned for me to come over. "You went outside with Ms. James earlier?"

Alice nodded. "We were looking for my son."

"Why were you looking for him?" Mick asked.

"Because he wasn't upstairs," I said when Alice didn't speak. "He was supposed to be doing readings in the suite. On the top floor. Grandpa was next." I stared at Grandpa, realizing he wasn't going to get his sign from Grandma. I felt inexplicably sad about that.

"Maddie?" Mick prompted.

"Sorry. Yes. I had just been to the waiting area. On the fifth floor. Tomas, Harry, and Manfred were there. They hadn't seen him. But I think they'd stepped away. Or at least Tomas and Harry had." I vaguely recalled someone saying that.

"Wait. Who was there?"

I explained who Tomas and Manfred were. "And you know Harry. He was there working security." I glanced at Alice, not sure if she knew about the white SUV lady. "They thought everything was fine because if Balfour had left, they said he'd have to have come out of the stairwell and gotten on the elevator. And Manfred was still supposed to be there."

"Couldn't he have just gone down the stairs the whole way?" Mick pointed out.

I glanced at Grandpa, trying to remember what the inside of that stairwell was like. We'd gone straight up, but I didn't recall seeing the option to go down. It seemed to be a completely separate floor, cut off from the rest of the inn.

"It has a separate stairwell," Grandpa explained. "Just the way the place was originally built. It was the master suite when the sea captain built it. You have to take the stairs down to the fifth floor, then there's a separate stairwell that goes the rest of the way down. Or the elevator, of course."

Mick made a note, then motioned for me to go on. I recounted how the lights had gone out. How Tomas had come down asking if I'd seen Balfour after finding him and Maeve both missing from the suite. "Maeve is his right hand," I explained. "She was upstairs with him keeping things on track."

"And she's gone too?"

"I guess technically, I don't know if she's gone. I haven't seen her. They said she wasn't up there either."

"And then?"

"I went outside. I bumped into Alice, and she came with me. You know the rest."

"You need to find that woman."

All our heads swiveled toward Alice. I hadn't even realized she'd been listening. She'd looked pretty out of it.

"What woman?" Mick asked.

"Maeve Sandler. His *right hand*." She used air quotes around the words. "Or rather, Maeve Ames. You'll find a lot on her if you google."

I frowned, not following. Mick didn't seem to be either. "Sorry, can you elaborate? Is that a married name?" he asked.

"No. Maeve Ames is her real name. She started using a different last name when she went to work for my son because she didn't want anyone to know she had a criminal record."

Chapter 26

I blinked. Maeve had a criminal record?

Mick leaned in, clearly interested in this new direction. "Tell me about that. Where and for what?"

"Well, let's see." Alice ticked off items on her fingers. "Extortion. Embezzlement. And I think there was an assault charge too, but somehow that was dismissed. It happened in Ohio or Missouri or somewhere like that. Before she met my son."

"Who did she assault?" I asked. I couldn't help myself.

"It was the man she was extorting. From what I could tell, he dropped the charges because he was embarrassed that a woman had assaulted him." She turned to Mick.

"Do you think she had the potential to be violent with your son?" Mick asked. "If that was in fact him."

"Of course I do. She was about to lose her golden ticket," Alice spat. "And of course it's him. I would know my son anywhere. A mother knows."

"Okay. Let's not get ahead of ourselves. It would've been hard to see . . . that far down, especially in the dark. Let's take it one step at a time. Tell me what you mean by a golden ticket."

"My son was quitting. Taking down the shingle and going off to do what he really wanted to do—help police departments find missing people." She folded her arms across her chest. "He announced it last night in the newspaper interview, then talked to his team later. Said she was extremely upset. They all were."

"Did Maeve threaten your son?" Mick asked.

"I don't know," Alice said.

"Do you believe he was afraid for his life?"

At this, Alice smiled a little. "No. Balfour trusted everyone. He was a good man." Her voice broke a little. "But I warned him. I warned him about that whole crew. They all had something to lose if he retired."

"And the crew is . . ." Mick looked at his notes. "Tomas, Sharlene, Manfred? Can you give me last names?"

Alice recited all their names as Mick wrote them down. "How long have they worked for him?"

Alice sighed. "A long time. They've all been with him for many years."

I thought back to what Sharlene had told me earlier. "Sharlene told me twelve years for her and her brother. Maeve said ten, I think."

Mick nodded. "I'm going to want to speak to them. But before I do, is there anything else you can tell me about your son's frame of mind? Had he been depressed lately? Troubled or worried about anything? Any history of mental illness, depression, suicidal thoughts?"

Alice frowned. "If you're suggesting my son put himself over the edge of that cliff, you're sadly mistaken, Lieutenant. My son was happy. I actually hadn't seen him this at peace in a long time. Choosing to change his business model was a good decision for him. He was even deciding if"—her voice broke and it took her a minute to regain control—"if he was going to move here."

"Say more about changing his business model," Mick said.

"He was finally realizing the people around him were taking advantage of him," Alice said. "They were like leeches, and he was blind to it for a long time. They only wanted what they could get out of him. He'd started to recognize it recently. Which seems quite coincidental, doesn't it?" A choked sob slipped out of her mouth. Grandpa handed her a tissue. She pressed it to her lips for a minute, composing herself.

"Where did he live?" Mick asked.

"New York City."

"I'll need the address."

Alice recited it. Mick wrote it down. "I'm not sure how long it will take us to retrieve the body. But we'll want to ask you to make an identification," he said. "We can do it in the morning, though."

"I'm staying," Alice said stubbornly. I could see tears rolling down her cheeks.

"Of course." Mick stood. "I need to talk to the staff. Maddie, can you help me with that since you know them?"

"Yep." I got up to follow him out of the room.

Alice called him back. "I want my son's cat," she said.

Mick glanced at me as if to ask, *Why is she telling me this?*

"That person who works for him is going to fight me for him, but he should live with me," Alice said.

"You mean Tomas?" I asked.

She nodded. "He has no right to him. I'm his next of kin."

"There should be no problem getting you the cat," Mick said with a glance at me.

"I'll explain," I said quietly to Mick, motioning to the door.

"Maddie." Grandpa nodded to my feet.

I was still wearing my wet socks. Self-consciously, I peeled them off and laid them on a chair to dry, pulling my boots back on over bare feet.

I led Mick out into the hall. As soon as the door was shut, I turned to him urgently. "You have to find out who the woman was in the white SUV," I said. "ASAP. She might've had something to do with this."

Mick frowned. "How do you know it was a white SUV?"

"Craig told me."

He sighed.

"My fault. Don't be mad at him. The point is, I think the woman driving that vehicle was stalking Balfour." I told him about the run-ins with her, both here at the inn and at my cafe when he'd come for the tour.

"She tried to run him down?" Mick asked in disbelief. "How come you didn't report this?"

"We all kind of brushed it off as a crazy driver. Lord knows there are a lot of them around, especially tourists. Even Craig just said so," I said. "But here's the thing. I think they might know who she is. I told Maeve about her after we caught her trying to get into the room, and I can't be sure but she didn't seem surprised. At the time I chalked it up to him having a lot of rabid fans."

Mick nodded slowly. "And you said the accident happened right after people realized he was missing?"

"That's when the lights went out," I said. "So yeah."

"I should've known this would've turned into a fiasco," Mick muttered. "It always does when you're involved."

"Me? How is this *my* fault?"

He gave me a long look. "I don't know, but you're always involved when something like this happens." He strode toward the lobby.

Before I could think of a good retort, I heard another

commotion in the hall behind me. I turned to see Tomas running toward us, shouting urgently. I felt a stab of
panic. What now?

Mick turned too, and stepped in front of me to ward
off Tomas. "Hey. Slow down, buddy," he said.

Tomas jerked to a stop. "I am not your buddy," he
said indignantly, then looked past him at me. "Maddie.
There's another problem. You have to help!" He sounded
even more hysterical than when he'd chased me down to
say Balfour was missing.

"How can that be?" I asked. "Mick, this is Tomas. One
of Balfour's staff. We were just looking for you," I said
to Tomas. "This is Lieutenant Mick Ellory. He needs to
talk to you. Have you found Maeve?"

"Never mind that! This is an *emergency*." He wiped
his brow with the back of his hand. I suspected he wasn't
used to all this running around.

"What's wrong?" I said impatiently.

"It's Balfour Jr. He's missing too. He was in the suite
with Balfour and now he's . . ." He choked back a sob.
"He's just *gone*."

Chapter 27

I felt a stab of panic. "Are you sure?" Whatever had happened to Balfour, I fervently hoped his cat hadn't been with him. That would be terrible.

Then I realized how odd people would think I was if I seemed more concerned about the cat than the dead man on the rocks below. Although there was nothing we could do for Balfour now. I felt my throat closing up and fought back the tears. I really needed to keep it together.

Mick glanced at me sharply. "His kid?"

"His cat," I explained, ignoring the sound he made at that explanation. "Okay, let's not freak out," I told Tomas. "Why don't you and I go upstairs and look for him. You know cats. He could've been scared and hid somewhere. Cats are such good hiders. Once, I had two kittens find a tiny hole that led into the heating duct work and they both went for a jaunt. Just as I was looking up contractors to come and rip the walls apart, they came back out, looking extremely proud of themselves." I realized I was babbling when I noticed Tomas looking at me strangely.

"Hold on," Mick interrupted. "No one can go up there right now."

"What are you *talking* about? This is *urgent*!" Tomas's screechy tone was back. "He could be in danger!"

"Sorry. No one's allowed up there until we process the room. And if you're part of the staff, I'm going to need to talk to you. Wait here, please." He turned to me. "And where the hell is Jacob?"

I suddenly realized he hadn't texted me back. I checked my phone just to be sure. Nope. Nothing. Where was he? "I don't know. I haven't heard from him."

"Okay. Stay with him for a minute." He pulled out his phone and called someone, walking out of earshot. When he returned, he motioned for us to follow him.

"I am not going *anywhere* until I find my charge." Tomas stubbornly crossed his arms over his chest.

I felt a pang of sympathy for him. He was about to get the full force of Mick's cop persona if he didn't smarten up.

"So you'd rather talk at the police station?" Mick asked. "Fine. I'll have someone bring you there." He pulled out his phone.

Tomas glanced at me, his bravado falling away. "Wait. What?"

I shrugged. "I'd just talk to him here if I were you. All kinds of things can happen down at the station."

"Okay. Okay! Fine. I'll talk to you. Then I *must* find the cat."

"Gee, thanks," Mick said, deadpan. "I'll be right with you."

I grabbed him as he walked away. "How long before we can go up?"

"I need to get my guys to secure his room. We need to process it, see if there were any signs of a struggle or anything that could give us a clue about what happened."

A struggle. Lilah—Jane Cummings—had been the last known person up there. I needed to talk to her. But

I didn't say any of that to Mick. Instead, I nodded and headed toward the lobby to try to find the rest of Balfour's staff. As I did, it occurred to me that Tomas hadn't asked what this was about. Or if we'd found Balfour. He hadn't asked anything, actually, which in itself was odd. The world was clearly crumbling around us, and he didn't seem to recognize it. And Jacob—where *was* Jacob, anyway? I checked my phone again. No message from him. Weird.

Ellen ambushed me as I tried to walk past the check-in desk. "People are here for readings and the police told me not to let them go up," she whispered. "They told me to nix the tours too. What do I do? People are getting angry!"

"Just tell them we're going to have to reschedule, that we're very sorry," I said. "Use the power outage as an excuse."

"Reschedule?" Ellen stared at me. "What is happening, Maddie?"

"I'll come back and talk to you," I promised. "Just keep people down here, okay?" I spotted my parents talking near the front desk and made a beeline over to them, ignoring the hum of the crowd as I passed. I wasn't sure what people knew or didn't know yet, but at this point the speculation had to be running rampant.

When my mother saw me, she immediately pulled me into a hug. "Oh, honey," she said. "Are you alright?"

I nodded as best I could with my head against her shoulder. "Yeah. You heard?"

"I did. Your grandfather let me know. I haven't told anyone else. I wasn't sure who . . . knew yet."

"Yeah. I'm not sure either." I stepped back. "We need someone to make an announcement. Not about that. That tonight is canceled. Where the heck is Jacob? How can he disappear right now? He's always so worried about the inn's reputation. This is the time to worry and he's no-where!"

"I'll find him," my mother promised.

"What can I do?" my dad asked. He looked shaken up, which surprised me. He ran a hospital. People died around him all the time. But I guessed the difference was the environment. It was kind of expected where he was. And he usually wasn't around the dying people.

"Actually, there is one thing."

"Name it."

"You heard about the accident?"

"Yes. A bad one." Dad shook his head. "Tragic."

"I need to know who the driver is."

Dad hesitated. I could feel the HIPAA lecture coming at me and tried to ward it off.

"I know. Privacy. But Dad, here's the thing." I leaned in closer so no one else could hear me. "If I'm right, I think it's the same woman who might've been stalking Balfour. She was showing up everywhere. She even tried to run him down in front of the cafe the other day."

"Run him down?" My dad stared at me. "Are you sure?"

"It looked that way. Although she clearly is a bad driver, so who knows. Anyway, it just seems so coinci-dental," I said. "She was speeding away from here right when he would've been falling down the cliff. You see what I'm saying?"

My dad nodded grimly. "Okay. I'll see what I can find out."

"Thanks. I have to go. I'll catch up with you later."

I saw Becky in the lounge area near the food and did an abrupt turn. I didn't want to start getting questions from her that Mick wouldn't appreciate me answering right now.

I didn't see anyone from the staff down here, so I

slipped into the stairwell and ran up the five flights to where I'd last seen Manfred at his check-in desk. I was as winded as Tomas when I shoved open the stairwell door, which made me vow to get back to a regular exercise routine. Once all the madness was over.

Ha.

Manfred still sat at his desk. Sharlene was with him now. Their heads were so close together as they spoke softly they looked like they were part of the same body. They both looked up, startled, as I burst through the door.

"Hey," I said. "Have you seen Maeve?"

"She's upstairs," Sharlene said. "She's always nearby when Balfour is reading."

"You've seen her?" I asked.

"Not since the readings started," Sharlene said.

So she had no clue? "Have you heard what's going on?" I asked. "Where's Harry?"

"He got a call and left," Manfred said. It was the first time I'd heard him speak. His voice was deeper than I'd imagined it would be. He regarded me with an impassive face. "That was a while ago. Is something wrong?"

I took a deep breath. "The police need to speak to you both. Can you come down with me?"

Sharlene stared at me. "Police? Why?"

"I think Balfour is dead." I didn't think it was possible for the two of them to get any more pale than they already were, but it happened.

"Dead? What do you mean, dead? He's upstairs reading . . . Isn't he upstairs?" Sharlene's voice faltered, and she looked at her brother, her eyes wide with panic.

Manfred jumped up from his chair. "I thought Tomas was just being dramatic when he said he was gone. Balfour is upstairs. He *has* to be upstairs. You're wrong."

I shook my head slowly. "I don't know what happened, or how it happened, but it seems . . . he went outside.

There was some sort of . . . accident. We're not a hundred percent sure it's him, but . . ." I sighed. "I think it is."

Sharlene looked like she was about to pass out. Manfred shoved the chair underneath her and she sank into it, starting to sob. "No, no, no. It can't be. Manny, what are we gonna do?"

Manfred looked at me. "You're wrong," he said again, desperately.

"Can you come downstairs?" I asked again. "The police need some information."

"What information? Why are the police here? What happened to him?"

"We're not sure yet. Come on." I turned to go as Manfred checked on his sister. I hit the button for the elevator. As I waited for the doors to slide open, the stairwell leading up to the suite opened and Maeve stepped out and immediately rounded on the twins.

"What on earth is going on? Where is Balfour?" she demanded. "We're completely off schedule!"

Chapter 28

The three of us stared at her like she was a ghost who'd just appeared in front of us. She looked . . . *disheveled*, was my first thought. Her hair, which was always perfectly styled, looked frizzy and mussed. Her hot-pink blazer was wrinkled, like it had been crumpled up in a ball then hastily smoothed out and worn again. But what stood out the most was her right hand, clutching her phone. Two of those killer nails were broken.

My gaze traveled back up to her face. "Where have you been?" I asked her. "What happened to Balfour?"

She stared at me. "What do you mean, what happened to him? I went to lie down for a bit and when I got up, he wasn't in there. I figured he went out for some air, but it's been a while."

She went to lie down? During opening night? And had somehow lost nails during a nap? That sounded fishy to me. Before I could say anything, though, Sharlene shot out of the chair, sending it crashing to the ground, and flew at Maeve, her tiny fists flying.

"It's all your fault!" she screamed. "He's dead and it's all your fault!"

"Shar!" Manfred reached for his sister, pulling her off

Maeve, but not before one of Sharlene's punches landed right in Maeve's face. We all stared, stunned, as Maeve's hand flew to her nose. Blood started to drip from between her fingers.

"You little—"

Now Maeve lunged forward, and honestly, I wouldn't want to be on the receiving end of her anger. She was twice the size of Sharlene, for one, and she seemed pretty tough. I remembered what Alice had said about an assault charge. Manfred still stood in front of Sharlene, but that didn't stop Maeve. He tried to hold her off, but he probably weighed ninety pounds soaking wet. Sharlene wasn't having it either. She went around her brother, and the next thing I knew the two of them were literally having a catfight. Hair pulling, scratching, punching, screaming, the whole bit.

"Stop!" I yelled, now trying to wedge myself between them. I succeeded only in catching a blow to my own face. I didn't register the ding of the elevator doors until I felt a set of hands pulling me out of the fray, and saw other hands grabbing for the two women who were still going at each other.

"Knock it off!" Craig's voice rang out. He let me go and grabbed for Maeve while the uniformed cop with him restrained Sharlene. It took all of Craig's weight to hold Maeve back—she was strong. It was only when he warned "I'll cuff you if you don't stop" that she finally stepped back and held up her hands.

"No need," she said. "Just defending myself." She shot daggers at Sharlene with her eyes.

The uniform looked at Craig. "What do you want me to do with them?"

"Can you bring those two down to Ellory?" Craig asked, motioning to the twins. "I'll talk to her."

"He's in the Hawthorne Room," I told the cop. He

nodded and motioned for Sharlene and Manfred to follow him. They disappeared into the elevator.

Craig turned to me. "Are you okay? Jeez, Maddie. Your eye."

I raised my hand to the side of my face, which I'd just realized was throbbing. "Great," I muttered. "Just what I needed to top off this night."

"You should probably get some ice for that," he said. He turned back to Maeve. "What was that about?"

"I have no idea. She attacked me. Not her," she said, pointing at me. "Sharlene."

"Why?"

"She started yelling that Balfour was dead and it was my fault." Now Maeve looked at me. "What was she talking about? Not that it matters. She's a flake." She said that in a dismissive tone, as if nothing Sharlene said had any weight.

"Where have you been?" I asked, without answering her.

"I told you. I had a headache and went to lie down."

"But where?" I pressed.

"Maddie. I'll take it from here." Craig shot me a warning look, then turned to her. "Let's go somewhere to talk. Where's your room?"

"Talk about what? Will someone please tell me what's going on here?" Maeve demanded.

"Someone took a dive off the cliffs tonight, and we think it's your colleague," Craig said bluntly. "So we need to talk to the last people who saw him, and I heard that was supposed to be you."

Maeve was shaking her head. "No. Stop it. You're lying."

"He's not," I said.

"That can't be. He's supposed to . . . He's upstairs. Doing a reading," she insisted. "He has to be."

"He isn't up there. Tomas realized he was missing and he couldn't find you either. I went outside to look for him." I didn't finish the story.

"Are you . . . are you sure?"

I looked at Craig. "Come on," he said to Maeve. "Let's go talk. Where's your room?"

Wordlessly she pointed down the hall.

I watched them walk away. Maeve's arms were crossed so she was almost hugging herself. I wondered what she was feeling right now. She'd been upset hearing about Balfour's impending retirement. She'd known the guy for years. Was there something more there? I realized I hadn't been thinking of Balfour as a real person. Aside from Alice, did he have a family? A partner? Did someone else need to be notified? I'd never asked. Or was his staff his other family? It certainly seemed so.

Alice had sounded like she thought the whole bunch of them were just using him for money, or at the very least relying on him for their livelihoods. Which, since they were employed by him, made sense. Didn't most employees rely on their employers in that way? But was one of them too dependent? Unable to imagine a life without him and this business? Would they have lashed out and killed him over it?

I thought of Maeve's broken nails, her disheveled appearance. And again, I asked myself, if she had been napping, how had she broken her nails? I pulled out my phone and texted Craig.

Ask her about her broken nails. At least two were broken before the fight.

Which reminded me of my face. I wondered how bad it looked and figured I should go visit the bathroom and find out.

Chapter 29

When I got back downstairs, I heard a familiar voice coming over the loudspeaker in the lobby. Jacob. My mother had tracked him down after all. I shouldn't have worried.

"I'm terribly sorry for the inconvenience," he was saying. "Given the events of the evening, we're going to have to reschedule the tours for tonight. Not to worry, we'll make sure everyone who had a reservation is accommodated. For everyone else, all readings have been canceled. The booking people will be in touch about next steps."

I could see people streaming out the front door, their disappointment obvious. I knew how they felt. I'd had high expectations for this event. And then I felt like a jerk for having those thoughts when someone was dead. I mean, our guest of honor was *dead*. That was much worse than a tanked event.

"Holy crap. What happened to you?"

Becky's voice startled me out of my thoughts. "You mean this?" I reached up and probed the area around my cheekbone. "Bad?"

"You're gonna have a heck of a bruise. Who hit you?"

"No one. I mean, no one on purpose. I got in the

middle of a . . . disagreement. I need to go see what this looks like."

"Come on." She took my hand and pulled me to the bathroom. Once we were inside, she checked under all the stall doors then turned on me with the full force of her newspaper editor's intensity. "What is going on here? I heard Balfour's dead. It's a lie, right? Some stupid rumor that got out of hand?"

I shook my head.

Her mouth dropped open. Shock and dismay warred for prominence across her face. "Are you *kidding* me?"

"I wish I was. This is totally off the record for now," I warned. "Or Mick will kill me. It hasn't been confirmed it's him yet."

"Yeah, I know. But we're reporting on the fact that there's a body at the bottom of the cliffs. That's been confirmed. I just need the confirmation of who."

"Talk to Alice," I said, before I could stop myself.

"Oh my god. Alice." Becky covered her mouth with her hand. "How awful. Where is she? Is she okay?"

"She's still here. Said she wanted to wait for them to bring the body up to make a formal identification. But she was with me when we saw him. We went looking for him. She knew he liked it out there on the cliffs, even though guests weren't supposed to be out there." I told her how we found his glasses first, and then saw the body.

"Why was he out there, though? He was supposed to be in appointments."

"I know. And no one can figure out how he got out, since there's only that stairwell that goes up to that floor. His staff is acting weird, Jacob was also MIA, and honestly? I'm exhausted." I finally turned to the mirror, staring at my reflection in dismay. "Oh, well that's just great." The right side of my face was already swelling and red. By tomorrow, it would be nice and bruised. If Craig's predictions were right, my eye would be black. "Do you have any makeup, by any chance?"

She rummaged through her bag and pulled out a concealer stick. "Are they sure he was killed?" she asked. "Did they think it could be an accident? Or . . . something else?"

"They aren't even willing to commit to it being him, so no, they're definitely not sure it was murder. But if you're asking that, if it was him, do I think he killed himself? I have no idea. I don't know the guy well enough to have any insight into his mental health. But my gut says no. The glasses on the path were a red flag for me. If he dropped his glasses, wouldn't he have stopped to find them? No matter what his plans were? And Alice adamantly says no."

Becky was silent for a minute. "I don't think he killed himself. I think he knew something."

"Huh?" I was still poking at the bruised spot on my face, trying to see how far the pain spread.

"About the old murder. I think he was on to something, and once it was out that he was talking about it and potentially looking into it, someone got scared."

My gaze met hers in the mirror. "What do you mean?"

"You were there last night. He had a physical description of the murderer!"

"Oh, Beck. He was messing with you to get you off his back." I turned and leaned against the counter. "I think he wanted you to stop asking him questions."

"No way." She shook her head. "He knew something. He was tuning in to whatever had happened. You heard what he said, about the person having a long and successful career here, or whatever. Maybe they freaked and thought they had to shut him up before he learned anything else."

I thought back to the interview yesterday. I had no idea how Balfour "tuned in" to things like that. I'd presumed that when Becky asked about it, he'd put on the show he was expected to put on, gave some vague information that may or may not be relevant, and left everyone feeling good that he was able to swoop in and offer a lead. I forced out a nervous laugh. "That's crazy, Becky. First of all, the guy had a stalker—"

"Wait. *What?*"

"Yeah. The crash? Go look into that. You might find that it was a woman driving a white Kia SUV, who might be the same woman who's been stalking Balfour. Shoot! I forgot to tell Craig that."

I pulled out my phone and fired another text to him.

Also ask her about the woman from the hotel room/ the white SUV. She might know who it is.

"Hold on. He was getting stalked?"

"Yes. And one of his staff allegedly has a criminal record for extortion and assault."

Now she looked like her head was going to explode. "Extortion? Assault? Hello? Were you going to tell me any of this?"

"Alice just told us that one. She seems to think the staff is where they should be looking if it is a murder. And this same staff member was the one who was supposed to be up there with him but was also MIA during all of this. Then she showed up a few minutes ago with broken nails and messy hair and no good explanation. She's the one who accidentally punched me, by the way. And she packs a heck of a punch."

Becky, who was usually so quick on the draw, looked like she was still trying to process all this. "Wow. So you're saying he had a few things going on. Not to mention the clips about him retiring that went viral from our Instagram reel."

I nodded slowly. "There's definitely that too. But which one of those things got him killed?"

Chapter 30

Becky headed out to talk to her photographer. They'd been trying to get photos of the body removal. News was still news, I guess. Lucas texted me to see if I wanted him to get the car so we could head home. I wasn't sure I wanted to leave yet, though. Mick might have some more questions for me, and there was the whole missing cat thing too. I also kind of wanted to know if and when they were able to make a positive ID on the body.

Can you give me a little bit? I texted him back. Then I checked my watch. It was only nine thirty. It felt like it had been days since the lights went out. I wished I could remember where I put my purse, because I needed my own makeup to try to cover up my face, but I had no memory of what I'd done with it. Everything had been a blur since Tomas had rushed into the lobby shouting that Balfour wasn't upstairs.

I called Grandpa. "Where are you?"

"In the lounge with your mom and dad," he said. "One of the officers is sitting with Alice. Where are you?"

"Coming out now."

When I made my way over to them, the three of them

stared at me. My mother jumped up. "What on earth happened to your face?"

I sighed. "I got in the way of a disagreement."

"We need to get you some ice."

"Mom. It's fine. I'll take care of it when I get home. Have you seen Mick?" I asked Grandpa.

"He's still talking to Balfour's crew."

"Should we stick around and wait until he's done? I have to help Tomas look for the cat."

"The cat?"

"He thinks the cat's missing."

"Oh dear," my mother said. "That's not good."

"None of this is good," my dad reminded her.

"True," she said. "Speaking of, the committee is meeting early tomorrow morning, Maddie. We have to regroup and figure out how to handle this."

"Okay," I said, catching sight of Jacob ducking into the office behind the front desk. "I'll be right back." I hurried over.

The woman behind the desk smiled at me. "Can I help you?"

"I need to speak to Jacob," I said.

"I'm afraid he's unavailable," she said.

"I don't think so. I just saw him." I moved past her and rapped on the partially open door, ignoring her protest. Jacob looked up from a file cabinet he was riffling through. He looked . . . shaken.

"Maddie. How can I help? It's fine, Trina," he said when the annoying woman popped up over my shoulder. She gave me a nasty look and walked out.

"Where were you? We couldn't find you anywhere."

"I had to run home for a bit. When I returned, all hell had broken loose. It's truly a tragic day."

"You went home?" I repeated. "On the busiest night of the year?"

He closed the drawer, slowly. "I had something to tend to, yes," he said, an edge coming into his voice. "Is that a problem?"

"Do you know what happened to Balfour?"

"I know that he was where he shouldn't have been," he snapped back. "And because of that, he lost his life. There's a reason why I have signs posted all over that path, and a fence up. Because it isn't safe!"

We stared at each other. Did he really think Balfour just fell? "Have you talked to Mick yet? Because he's looking for you," I said.

"I have not. I'll make myself available when he's ready." His tone was still icy. I didn't care.

"Fine. I'll tell him." I turned to go, then glanced behind me. "Is everything okay?"

"With what?" he asked, exasperated.

"At home. You said you had something to tend to."

"Oh. Yes. I did. And it's fine. Thank you for asking." He turned back to his file cabinet.

I thought about Jacob as I walked back to my family. He'd been opposed to Balfour coming here. He'd gotten very upset last night when Balfour had pointed out the picture upstairs and suggested that the murderer from forty years ago might have a mustache like the people in the photo. And now he, too, vanishes at the same time all this happens?

I wasn't sure I believed in ghosts, but I definitely didn't believe in coincidences. I needed to talk to Grandpa about this.

When I got back to Grandpa and my parents, though, Mick was with them. He did a double take when he saw me.

"I know, I know, my face." I was already sick of hearing about it.

"Who hit you?"

"Maeve and Sharlene went at each other. I tried to break it up. I got hit instead. Definitely Maeve. That chick is strong. How's it going with all of them?"

"They're a strange bunch," he said. "I can't figure out if they love or hate each other. And I haven't talked to Maeve yet. Craig is still with her. I sent Manfred to get me the roster of his appointments, but he gave me the name of the last person who had one before they noticed Balfour was gone. A Jane Cummings. I have to track her down next, see what she can tell me from her appointment, if anything was strange. If Balfour was still up there when she left. But my team just called me. They've retrieved the body."

I worked hard at keeping a blank face. Did I tell him who Jane Cummings was, or did I talk to Lilah first?

Mick was already walking away, so I figured I'd wait. "Hey, Jacob's back," I called after him.

He turned. "Back?"

"Yeah. Apparently he had to go home while all this was happening." I arched an eyebrow to show what I thought of that and pointed toward the desk.

Mick nodded, catching my drift. "I'll grab him when I come back."

Sounded like he was going to be busy for a bit. Maybe I could get upstairs and see for myself if anything pointed to Lilah and Balfour having some kind of altercation. I waited until he was gone, then I went back to the room where he'd been interviewing the staff. Tomas and Manfred were still there. They sat at opposite ends of the room, not speaking. Manfred's head was in his hands. Tomas stared blankly at nothing.

They both looked up when I came in. "Are you both done, or do you need to wait here?" I asked.

"We don't know," Tomas said. "He didn't give us further instructions."

"Well, do you want to try to go look for the cat?" I asked.

He leaped to his feet, his face brightening for the first time. "Yes."

"Let's see what we can do," I said.

But right away when we got upstairs I could tell we were out of luck. There was a cop on the fifth floor, standing in front of the stairwell door.

"Sorry, this area is off-limits," he said.

"But we need to find the cat!" Tomas exclaimed, his voice tipping into the realm of hysteria. I elbowed him. He glared at me.

The cop frowned, clearly confused and probably a little bit amused. "The cat?" he repeated. "We've got a death on our hands, in case you missed it."

"I know. I've been helping Mick find the right people to talk to. Hi there. I'm Maddie James. My grandfather was the chief of police here on the island for many years."

"Leo?" The cop asked, a smile now breaking across his face. "You're Leo's granddaughter?"

I nodded. "I am."

"Wow. He was an amazing chief. It was an honor to work in his department. I'm Sergeant Murphy, by the way."

"Nice to meet you, Sergeant." They had a sergeant watching the door? Mick wasn't fooling around.

Murphy leaned closer. "So what exactly do you need?"

"Balfour—the man they suspect is dead—has a cat. He seems to be missing, and lot of people will be distraught if he isn't found. He was in the room during the readings. This is his handler, Tomas."

The cop gazed at Tomas. I could tell he was trying to figure out what that even meant. Tomas didn't offer any explanation.

"Anyway, we'd hoped that we could take a look around for him, if you've already cleared the room?"

Murphy looked doubtful. "I don't know, Ms. James," he said. "A detective did look around, but Lieutenant Ellory said no one else was allowed in here. He wants to see it himself."

I was betting he didn't want Balfour's staff in there, and I didn't actually blame him. They were all acting suspicious, if you asked me.

"I get it," I said smoothly. "I would've asked him myself, but he was in a rush. And we're just worried because it's been a few hours, and if he's not inside, we need to start searching outside quickly. He's not from around here, so if he got out, it could be bad."

Murphy was about to say no, I could tell. I quickly added, "My grandfather is downstairs. Maybe if he comes up?"

"Leo's here? Well that might be okay, then."

"Great. Let me call him." I pulled my phone out of my pocket and called Grandpa. "It's me. Can you come up to the fifth floor?"

Grandpa was so good. Once again, he didn't even ask why, just appeared in the elevator a few minutes later. "Al!" he exclaimed, clapping the other man on the back. "Good to see you. Under awful circumstances, though."

"I'm tellin' ya." Murphy shook his head. "What a night. Haven't had one like this since that big storm about ten years ago. You remember that one, Chief? We had the three-car pileup and the domestic with the guy holding his family hostage, and power was down all over the island?"

"I do remember that, Al. This is definitely a close second. So what's going on, Doll?"

"Well, you know how I told you the cat is missing?"

"I do," Grandpa said.

"And they're not letting anyone upstairs, understandably, until Mick can get a handle on things."

Murphy nodded. "He's gotta get eyes on all of it."

"But I thought maybe with your supervision, we could take a look around for the cat."

Murphy nodded. "I know the Lou has you helping out on cases a lot. Knows you know how to handle things, obviously." *Lou* was the nickname all lieutenants got on the force.

Grandpa gave me a look that said, *I know what you're trying to do.*

The elevator dinged again and Craig stepped off. "Hey," he said. "What are you two still doing here?"

Murphy looked relieved. "Hey, Tomlin. Are you going up to take a look at the suite?"

Craig nodded.

"Can you take the chief and his granddaughter up with ya? The other one stays here," he said with a look at Tomas. "They gotta look for a cat."

Tomas was about to protest but I dug my elbow into his side again.

"Sure," Craig said with an amused glance. "Booties and gloves, though."

"What am *I* supposed to do?" Tomas demanded.

"Wait here," I said.

This did not make him happy. I didn't much care.

Craig unlocked the stairwell door and ushered us in. "Is there really a cat, or are you just trying to get a look inside his room?"

"There's really a cat," I said. "And he's really missing. At least, according to Tomas. But I was in the room last night, and I thought I could tell if something looked . . . off."

Craig was climbing the stairs, so I couldn't see his face. "We had someone look around up here and they said nothing looked out of place. No signs of a struggle. They got photos and everything, dusted for fingerprints just in case. I'm just coming up to see for myself so Mick doesn't have to. He's a little busy." He pushed open the door to the upstairs hallway. There were two more cops guarding this floor, both uniforms. Craig nodded at them.

"Officers. This is former Chief Leo Mancini. Not sure either of you were on the force when he was running it?"

They both shook their head, but I could tell they'd heard a lot about Grandpa. "Pleasure to meet you, sir," they both said, almost in unison.

"Same, officers."

"We're just here to look for a cat," Craig said. "They're with me."

"Of course, Detective." Craig had recently been promoted. It was kind of cool to see him getting so much respect from the guys on the force.

We followed him down the hall. I could feel that chill settling over me again. Jacob had never fixed the heat, I thought, then realized it didn't matter anymore. Before we got to the door of the suite, I paused, looking for the picture Balfour had pointed to yesterday. When I found it, I lingered for a moment, studying it. The men did all look the same, and they literally all had that same god-awful mustache. I was so glad I wasn't in the market for a guy back then—I wouldn't have been able to get past that.

"Doll?" Grandpa waited expectantly at the door. "What's up?"

"Can you come here for a second?" I asked.

He obliged.

"Do you know any of these people?" I asked, pointing at the photo Balfour had noted. "Aside from Grandma, of course." I didn't want to get too hung up on the picture since Balfour was using it more as a point of comparison, but still.

Grandpa stepped closer and studied the photo. I saw him run his finger gently over Grandma's face. "I know a few of these people," he said finally. "Your grandmother worked with them. Some of the names are escaping me. But this one"—he jabbed at the man standing in the back left corner of the photo, unsmiling under that bushy mustache—"is Andrew. Jacob's father."

I took a closer look. I could see the resemblance now.

"His father," I repeated.

Grandpa nodded. "Why?"

"Just curious," I said. I pulled my phone out and snapped a picture of the photo, then stuck it back in my pocket, just in case I couldn't get up here again.

Was that why Jacob had been so angry with Balfour's comparison? Because his father had been in the photo?

Chapter 31

The uniforms stepped aside to let us pass. Craig unlocked the door, then paused and handed us some gloves and booties to put over our shoes.

"Was the door open or closed when you guys first got here?" I asked.

"Closed, I think, but I'll have to check with the detective who came up first."

I hoped that meant Balfour Jr. hadn't bolted out. If he had, he could be anywhere in this building. Or outside. Even up here just in this hallway, there could be tons of hiding places for a scared cat. The inn was old and this floor had never been redone, which meant a lot of hidey-holes.

I walked slowly into the room. Aside from fingerprint dust all over the place, the table where Balfour had been doing his readings looked normal—at least, normal for his persona. The crystal ball, which he'd told me and Becky was just for atmosphere; a well-worn tarot card deck, which some people requested for their readings instead of a medium session. His chair had a purple scarf on it. The other chair, across the table, was slightly askew, as if the person getting the reading had left in a hurry. Lilah.

I had to talk to her.

I realized Craig was watching me and started calling for the cat, pausing to listen. There was no sound in the room at all. I crossed to the connecting door, which was slightly open. "You guys did your thing in here too, yes?"

Craig nodded.

I pushed the door open and stepped through, calling softly for the cat again. I felt sorry for him—he must be so scared. I wondered if Alice would win the fight to take him. Tomas seemed pretty obsessed.

I went to the refrigerator, looking for his food. As I suspected, no cans of Fancy Feast for this cat. A selection of single-serve plates, all covered and labeled *Breakfast*, *Lunch*, or *Dinner* were lined up inside. I pulled out a dinner one and inspected it. It looked better than the food I made for myself when Ethan wasn't cooking.

I warmed the plate in the microwave, then put it on the raised stand on the floor with two sections for bowls. The other held water. I freshened that too, put the plate down, and hoped he'd smell it and come out. I glanced behind me. Grandpa and Craig were talking in the other room, so I used the opportunity to look around some more. Although since it was the cat's room, there didn't seem to be much to see here. Nothing of Balfour's, anyway. There were some outfits—for the cat—laid out on the table. A purple sweater, a white sweater with black skulls on it, and a little winter jacket, also purple.

I checked all the obvious hiding places I could see. Kitchen cabinets, the bathroom shower, behind and under all the furniture. The closets. The one in the bedroom had a pile of Balfour Jr.'s things hastily thrown in it—his wheelie cart, the carrier, a duffel bag—but there were no sounds, and no sign of him. I went back to the main suite and did the same. No cat, and Craig was right—no sign of any disturbance in the room, at least

that I could see. If Balfour had an altercation with someone, it hadn't started here.

"Nothing?" Grandpa asked.

I shook my head.

"He could just be hiding really well," Grandpa said.
"If he's scared enough. You of all people know how they
are."

I did. Cats were tricky. And resilient. They did what
they wanted on their terms.

"Maybe we need to give it tonight. We can come back
tomorrow," Grandpa suggested, looking at Craig.

"Yeah, good idea. We might need to get Katrina involved too," I said. "She can bring traps."

"You can work that out with Mick, but it should be
fine," Craig said. "We should be able to clear this room."
He looked around too. "Doesn't seem like anything happened up here."

"It doesn't," I agreed.

My phone dinged. I pulled it out to look at it. Lucas
wanted to know where we were.

My dad had texted at the same time. *The person involved in the crash is in critical condition. Still uncon-
scious. Not sure of prognosis at the moment. There's a
cop at the door of her room. She's been identified as
Marybeth Montgomery.*

I let out my breath in a whoosh. Now we had a name.
And apparently Mick had taken me seriously, because
he'd moved fast with the guard at her door. But still, it
wasn't great news. If she had been the one to shove Balfour over the cliff, she certainly wasn't talking right now.

Craig's phone rang. "Yeah." He listened for a minute, then nodded. "Okay." He hung up and looked at us.
"They're bringing Alice to the van to see the body. She
was asking for you, Leo."

"For me?" Grandpa looked surprised.

"She probably needs a friend," I said.

"I'm sure she does. I'll head down there. Meet you outside in a bit."

"You should go home," Craig said as we headed back downstairs. "Ice that eye," he added. "It's looking a little rough."

"Thanks," I said dryly. "So what's next? After Alice . . . identifies him?"

"Well, then he goes for an autopsy. See if the fall killed him, or something else."

I paused. "You think he was killed before he went over the cliff?"

"I don't think anything. I'm just telling you what they'll look for."

When we got back to the lobby, a lot of the crowd had dissipated. There were still people milling around, clearly trying to figure out what was going on and if they'd hear any gossip if they stayed. I wanted to ask Maeve about the woman in the SUV. I couldn't shake the feeling that she'd known who I was talking about when I told her about the incident upstairs.

"Where's Maeve?" I asked.

"I left her in her room."

I wondered if she and Sharlene would go at it again when they saw each other. Sharlene had taken the news pretty badly. But I still wasn't sure what to make of all of them. Was it an act? Either way, tonight didn't seem like the right time to start asking those questions. Plus, Mick was trying to do what he needed to do and I didn't want to get in his way. Still, I was hesitant to leave in case there was anything else I could do—or learn—while I was here.

"Go," Craig said firmly, reading my mind. "We'll be in touch tomorrow."

Before I could agree, I saw Tomas beelining toward me. "I'll just give Tomas an update on the cat," I said to Craig. "And we came with Grandpa, so we have to wait for him."

He gave me a long look. "Stay out of trouble," he said, then headed out into the night.

"Did you find him?" Tomas asked breathlessly as he reached me.

I shook my head. "But we put out food and hopefully he'll come out now that it's quiet. I'll come back tomorrow. Maybe bring reinforcements if there's still no sign." Meaning Katrina and her traps. "So you don't think he got out?"

"Never," Tomas said firmly. "Balfour didn't let him outside, first of all. He wouldn't have brought him, even if he did go out for a walk. And I can't imagine how Balfour Jr. would've found his way out on his own."

"Then he's got to be there somewhere," I said. "Don't worry. We'll find him." I awkwardly patted his arm. He looked truly distraught.

"I hope so," he said sadly. I had a feeling his emotions were more about the cat than his boss.

"Hey, Tomas," I said. "Did you send the contract addendum? About Balfour Jr. and the party?"

He flushed, just a little. "I did."

"But Balfour didn't know."

"He did not, but he didn't know everything anyway. We were in charge of the business," he said, jabbing his chest with his thumb. "Otherwise there probably wouldn't *be* a business."

"What do you mean?"

"That he's not the best businessman," Tomas shot back. "Always doing favors. Not worrying about getting paid."

"It didn't ask for more money."

"No. I did that to get Balfour Jr. some attention. Which

our fans love, and sometimes Balfour forgets." He sighed. "I know he was angry and he canceled it, but I'm not sorry. My job is to look out for this company and the cat."

I nodded slowly. "Where were you earlier? When Balfour would've slipped out?"

His face reddened. "I just talked to the police about this. I went to my room. There was really nothing for me to do at that moment. We only needed one person checking in guests, and that was supposed to be Manfred." He turned to go.

"One more thing," I said. Figured I may as well ask him since he was right in front of me. "Did Balfour have any issues with anyone . . . stalking him?"

Tomas looked at me blankly for a minute, then sighed. "You mean Marybeth Montgomery? She's here too? I thought we'd finally escaped her," he said with a little laugh.

I stared at him, my heart starting to pound. I'd been right. They did know her. And it was the same woman. I couldn't let on that my dad had told me her identity, though. "There was a woman trying to get into his suite the other day when you all were checking in. She was out front of my cafe when Balfour came the other day too. She was . . . driving really fast down the street when Balfour and the others were crossing."

"Sharlene mentioned there was an erratic driver. That was her? I guess I'm not surprised," he said.

"So you all know who she is?"

He looked at me with a raised eyebrow. "Of course. Why do you think we needed the security detail? She's harmless, I think, but a little . . ." He circled his finger around his temple. "Can't take any chances."

"Why was she following him?" I asked.

"She's been coming to him for readings for years. Since her husband died almost six years ago, actually. He was with another woman when he died, and she's been obsessed with finding out how long and whether he was cheating with anyone else." Tomas rolled his eyes. "I say he got what he deserved, honey. I'm sure he's not resting in peace. But some people can't let go."

"But why was she trying to get into his room?" I wasn't getting it.

"Oh. Well, he told her about a year ago that he wasn't going to take her money anymore. That he had no other insights. Essentially, that her hubby had gone dark. She refused to accept that. Became obsessed with getting Balfour to keep trying. Since then, she's showed up at pretty much every public event, regardless of where it's held. We thought she might not come here given that it's not super easy to get here, but apparently we were wrong."

"I told Maeve about it. She didn't seem surprised. That's why I wanted to ask."

"Maeve knew she was here?" Tomas asked sharply. "She never told the rest of us."

I didn't know what to say to that. "Do you think she had something to do with this? She was here tonight."

That caught his attention. "She was?"

"If it's the same woman," I said carefully, "then she was in the accident that took out the power. Hit the utility pole speeding away."

Tomas rubbed a hand over his face. Suddenly, he looked very pale and tired.

"Was she dangerous?" I pressed. "Did she ever threaten him with physical violence?"

"Not to my knowledge," he said finally. "But, it seems I didn't know everything that was going on, so I may not be the best person to ask."

Chapter 32

After Tomas went up to his room, I texted Lucas.

Where are you?

Went out to get the car. Sitting in front. Take your time.

We have to wait for Grandpa. But I'll be right out.

I called Mick again. "Marybeth Montgomery," I said.

Silence. Then, "What?"

"That's the woman's name in the SUV, right?"

He sighed. "How did you know that?"

I ignored the question. "Apparently Balfour and his staff are well acquainted with her. She's been following him for years and is very aggressively trying to get him to contact her dead husband. She sounds like she's got some mental illness going on."

"Okay," Mick said. "She's not awake. No idea if she'll recover. I'm waiting for word from the hospital. Hopefully we'll get a chance to question her."

I hoped so too. "So are you . . . definitely pursuing this as a murder?" I asked.

Silence. Then Mick said, "This is completely off the record, but yeah. There was a fresh bruise on his face. I confirmed with his mother he'd had no bruise when she saw him earlier. And photos from the interview with the *Globe* are out from this morning, and his face is clear. To me that's grounds for a suspicious death."

I reached up and touched my own fresh bruise. Wondered if it came from the same person. "Thanks for telling me," I said.

"Mention it to anyone and I'll cut you off."

"I know. Thanks, Mick." I slid the phone into my pocket and headed outside to meet Lucas. I wasn't surprised at the information, but it was certainly sobering to have my suspicions basically confirmed.

When I got there, Lucas hopped out to open the door for me. Then he noticed my face. "Holy—what happened? Are you okay? Did someone *hit* you?" He looked around, like the person might be nearby and he could tear his or her head off. I had to smile. It was cute.

"I'm fine. I got in the middle of two ladies having a fight."

He reached over and touched the bruise, his fingers featherlight. "A woman did this?" he asked doubtfully.

"Yeah. A strong one."

"We'll have to try to get the swelling down when we get home."

"I know." I climbed in and settled back against the seat. He closed the door and went around to the driver's side, got in, and cranked the heat.

"Where's Leo?" he asked.

"With Alice. She's identifying the body."

Lucas shook his head. "So sad. What a cluster. And that accident? Man, it looked bad. I wonder how fast the car was going."

The white SUV. "Is it still there?" I asked, sitting up.

He looked at me strangely. "Haven't you seen enough disturbing things tonight?"

"I caught a couple of the license numbers the other

day. Wanted to see for sure if it was the same car." Although Mick had pretty much confirmed that it was.

"Oh. No, it got towed already. It was gone when I came back."

We waited for about fifteen minutes until we saw Grandpa walking toward us. He had his arm around Alice, who looked like she was having trouble walking.

"Oh, no," I said, throwing the car door open. "Grandpa?"

"We're going to take Alice home," he said.

"Of course." I met his eyes, a silent question. He nodded.

Guess it was official. I felt a heaviness settle into my chest. Of course I'd known, but having it confirmed was just so *final*.

He opened the back door and started to help Alice in, but she suddenly stopped short, clutching at his arm.

"Where are they taking him?"

He blinked. "Sorry?"

"My son." Her voice choked up again. "Where are they taking him?"

"They'll probably want to do an exam at the coroner's office in Sandwich," he said. "Unless Mick gets someone to come out here. But in the meantime, they'll probably take him to Tunnicliffe's, if he has room. Or the hospital if he doesn't." Tunnicliffe's was the only funeral home in Daybreak Harbor. Which meant Donald was always busy. "I assume you'll work with them?"

"Not Tunnicliffe's," she said immediately.

"They won't do anything to him until you make arrangements, Alice," Grandpa said gently. "It's just to have a place . . . to keep him. You understand?"

She shook her head. "Still. Not there. Promise me." She clutched his arm. "Promise me."

"Of course. I'll talk to Mick," Grandpa said. "Why don't you get in the car where it's warm, and I'll give him a call." He helped her in, then stepped away to make the call.

I got back in and turned to look at her. "I'm so, so sorry, Alice."

"I am too," she said, her voice shaky with tears. "Someone killed my beautiful son."

Lucas and I were silent. The only sound in the car was her weeping until Grandpa got back in.

"All set," he said. "They'll take him to the hospital until you decide what you'd like to do."

"Thank you, Leo," she said, dabbing at her eyes with a tissue.

"Of course." He leaned over the front seat and gave Lucas the address.

We drove to Alice's in silence. She lived in a neat little house right downtown, around the corner from the newspaper offices. Her front gate was surrounded by flowers, a cheery spectacle that didn't fit the current moment.

Grandpa walked her to the door, made sure she got inside safely, then returned to the car, looking exhausted.

"Poor woman," he said once he was back in the car. "No one should have to lose a child."

"I know. Is there a father in the picture?" I asked.

"You know, I have no idea," Grandpa said. "Alice has never mentioned him."

I turned back to look at him as Lucas pulled out of the driveway and headed toward our house. "I have something to tell you, but you can't tell Mick yet."

"Oh boy," Grandpa said.

"I know Mick's got his hands full with Balfour's staff, but he did mention wanting to talk to the couple of people who had readings already. Especially the last person he saw."

"Right," Grandpa said. "And?"

"So, the last person was Jane Cummings."

"I have no idea who that is," he said.

"That's because she doesn't exist. At least, that name doesn't exist. It's made up."

"I see. And who made it up?"

"Swear you won't tell anyone." I glanced at Lucas. "That goes for you too."

He raised his right hand from the steering wheel. "I probably wouldn't know who you were talking about anyway."

I turned back to Grandpa. "Lilah."

I barely ever saw Grandpa surprised—it came from years of perfecting his cop face—but he couldn't hide it this time. Then he started laughing. "Gilmore? You're kidding."

"No. But Grandpa—why are you laughing?"

"Because the idea of Lilah Gilmore consulting a psychic is probably the funniest thing I've heard in a while. I mean, maybe years. But how do you know?"

"Because she asked me to set it up for her with the fake name."

"Is that why she came over the other day?"

I nodded. "She was very stern about not letting anyone know it was her. Made me promise to not even tell Sam, and to just work with Balfour's person. And then she asked for an alternate way into the inn so she didn't have to go through the front."

Lucas glanced at me. "That seems like an awful lot of trouble to go through to get your tarot cards read. Couldn't she have just said she was supporting the town?"

"That's what I thought too!"

"But that's not how Lilah operates," Grandpa said. "You know her, Maddie. She's all about the optics. Can't have people gossiping about her. She's the queen of gossip. She sees herself—and others see her—in a certain light, right? She's got a reputation to uphold. I'm sure she thought that if anyone found out she was engaging in such frivolity, they'd be shocked." He smiled a little. "I'm putting words in her mouth, and that's certainly not my perspective, but you get my point."

I did. Lilah Gilmore considered herself above the fray of mere mortals. She was the type of woman who served tea in the afternoon on fine china, had garden parties at her old-money home, and was a Daughter of the American Revolution. Her husband had made all his money in finance and she'd been the perfect corporate wife until they'd retired to their second (massive) home out here where her family had ruled for generations, yada yada yada. Her circles would probably pooh-pooh psychics. But really, was it that big a deal?

"I know, but still. It seemed just a little too weird. What could she possibly have to hide related to a psychic?" I asked.

"Madalyn. Don't you know by now that everyone has secrets? Even the people who seem least likely to have them? Those are usually the ones with the biggest things to hide," Grandpa said.

"I'm going to go talk to her tomorrow. Tell her that Mick's going to figure out who it is anyway, and that I wanted to give her a heads-up. I just wanted to see if you had any ideas why she might've gone to see him, Grandpa."

"None at all," he answered. "And maybe it was nothing. Maybe she was trying to connect with a dead relative and was embarrassed to let anyone know. I honestly can't say, Maddie. But you're going to have to tell Mick."

"Absolutely," I said. "I just figured I owed it to her to talk to her first, since I promised."

"Uh-huh," Grandpa said. He didn't sound convinced. He knew me too well.

Chapter 33

I fell asleep with an ice pack on my eye and dreamt of my grandmother.

In the dream she was young, like in the photo I'd seen on the inn's wall. She looked beautiful and I just wanted to hug her. But she was talking to me from behind the front desk, and though I could sense her words were urgent, I couldn't hear her. And when I tried to get closer, she seemed to be even farther out of reach.

I woke up feeling unrested. And my face was sore.

When I got out of bed and checked my reflection in the mirror, I saw with some dismay that the ice pack hadn't made much of a difference. Walter sat next to me in the bathroom as I observed the pretty colors that now made up the area from my cheekbone all the way up to my eyebrow. At least it wasn't swollen, but it was definitely a shiner. Maeve sure did pack a punch. I couldn't help but wonder if she had enough strength—and motivation—to push Balfour off a cliff. The guy looked like he'd weighed less than me. He wouldn't have been any match for her if she was mad enough.

Walter barked.

"I know, bud. We're gonna go outside," I told him.

Lola heard the ruckus and wandered in too, tail wagging. I abandoned the mirror—not much hope there anyway—and sat down on the floor with the dogs, thinking about the day ahead. I wanted to call Mick to see what, if anything, new he'd learned last night. I needed to ask my dad if there were any updates on the crash victim—Marybeth Montgomery, as I now knew. I had to look for the cat and maybe get Katrina involved. I needed to go see Lilah, and we had an emergency committee meeting in . . . shoot. I checked the calendar on my Apple Watch. In an hour. Great. "Seriously?" I groaned.

Lola licked my face.

"What's wrong? Your eye hurt?" Lucas stuck his head into the bathroom, holding out a mug of coffee. "Will this help?"

"It doesn't really hurt, it just looks bad. And yes, that will help, thank you. I just realized the committee meeting is soon and I have to rush out." I got to my feet and took the mug. The coffee was, as usual, amazing. "But the dogs need to go out."

"I already took them," he said.

I gave him a kiss. "You're the best."

"Any idea what you're going to do about the rest of the event?" Lucas asked.

"I mean, people are here. I think we have to give them as much as we can. The tours of the inn can still continue. Maybe we can get a replacement psychic in." That was something I'd just thought of when I woke up, although I had no idea how one went about getting a replacement psychic at the last minute, especially one with a name big enough to rival Balfour.

"Well, don't stress yourself out too much," Lucas said. "None of this is your fault. You don't have to save the world, you know."

"I know." But I felt responsible, whether it made sense or not. "I'm going to take a shower. You heading out?"

"Yeah. I'll bring the dogs with me again."

"Thanks." I gave him a kiss. "Sorry your first week living here got overshadowed by all this."

"Hey," Lucas said lightly. "I've learned to not be surprised by anything that happens around you."

I wasn't sure if that was a compliment or not.

When I got downstairs, JJ was in the kitchen dressed in his Sherlock Holmes costume. Grandpa grinned at me. "I wanted to cheer you up. Figured you weren't in the best mood."

"Why? Because of Balfour, or the fact that I had to use an entire bottle of makeup on my eye and you can still tell I got punched?" I sighed. "Either way, he looks cute."

"I thought the nursing home residents would like it too."

"The what?" I asked.

"The nursing home. Remember? Today's JJ's visit."

"Oh man." I stared at him. I'd totally forgotten. Why on earth had I scheduled this in the middle of the event planning and execution? Probably because I'd set the visits up pretty far in advance and I hadn't realized. I made it a point to take JJ once a month to the local nursing home as well as the senior center so he could visit his adoring fans. JJ was probably the biggest celebrity on the island. Everyone loved him, and he had friends everywhere.

"Don't tell me you're canceling," Grandpa said. "I'd do it, but I'm on the schedule today and you know how Adele gets when people don't stick to the schedule." He grinned. "Plus I have some stuff to do for the costume parade."

"I'm not. I just have to figure out how to fit it in. No

worries. I'll make it work." I downed the rest of my coffee, hoping there was more.

Grandpa handed me a travel mug, already filled. "Here you go."

It was lovely to have people around who truly knew me. "You're a lifesaver. Where's Val?"

"She left already. I think she had some things to do before the meeting. When are you going to Lilah's?"

"I don't know. I have the committee meeting now, then I'll hit the nursing home. Probably after that. Adele is here, right?" I had a moment of panic about the cafe. I'd barely been around to run it. The truth was, Adele really was the one running it lately.

"She is. I'm here too. Everything's under control," he assured me. "Let me know what happens with Lilah. And don't forget you need to tell Mick."

"I promise. Hey, Grandpa? What exactly did Grandma do at the inn?"

He looked surprised at the question. "She started out doing housekeeping. It was her first job, actually. We were still dating." He smiled a little at the memory. "But she really loved it. She moved up from housekeeping staff to server at the events they had. That wasn't full time, so she did some reception desk work, answering the phone and such. And then she was promoted to assistant to Jacob's dad."

"Really?"

Grandpa nodded. "Before assistants had any credibility. And she was doing it all. Scheduling his meetings, managing his calendar, organizing staff meetings, and even doing some Human Resources–type work."

"Did you like him?"

"Andrew?" He shrugged. "Not really the type of guy I'd hang out with."

"Did Grandma get along with him?"

"Of course she did. Your grandmother got along with everyone," he said. "Why do you ask?"

"Just curious." I glanced at the clock. "Shoot. I have to go."

JJ trotted behind me to the door, squeaking. He knew we were going out, and he stopped obediently at the door to let me put on his harness and leash.

But when I pulled open the door, I was startled to find two women I'd never seen before standing there, about to ring the bell.

The one in front looked about my age, with stunning red hair that brushed her shoulders. She wore a long, lacy purple skirt, a tight black leather top, and purple combat boots. And so much crystal jewelry that it must have added up to twenty extra pounds. Rings, necklaces, earrings, bracelets. The other woman had a mop of curly hair that looked like it hadn't been tamed in years. She wore a dress that looked like it belonged on one of Jacob's ghosts but was also super stylish. Vintage but still very cool. Maybe it was the lace-up boots she'd paired with it, or the velvet headband that tried to hold back all that hair.

"Hi," the redhead said with a bright smile, handing me the newspaper that had been tossed on the steps. "Sorry to surprise you. I'm looking for Maddie James."

"I'm Maddie James," I said. "What can I do for you?"

Her face relaxed. "Oh, good. I'm Violet Mooney, the crystal vendor. And this is Sydney Santangelo, my manager." I could see Violet noticed my eye, but she didn't say anything.

"Hi," the curly-haired woman said, lifting a hand in a wave.

The name rang a faint bell. Right. Sam's crystal supplier. But what was she doing here? "Nice to meet you," I said. "Do you want to come in?"

"Thank you." They followed me inside.

"Look at the cat," Violet squealed, catching sight of JJ in his outfit. "Is that not the cutest thing ever?"

"Sherlock Holmes?" Sydney asked.

I nodded.

"Nice," she said.

"I have an orange cat too." Violet crouched down in front of him. JJ sniffed tentatively. "Is he from the cafe?"

"That's JJ," I said. "He's mine. The cafe's in the other part of the house."

"If I'm completely honest, that was why we decided to come out here instead of just calling. I wanted to see the cafe." She grinned.

"You shouldn't let her see it. She'll move in," Sydney said. "She's got two cats already and she's obsessed."

I grinned. Maybe the crystal chick and I would end up hitting it off. "Well, I've got plenty more who need homes," I said. "So what can I do for you? Sam isn't here but I can call her."

"No, we're here for you. I'm terribly sorry to show up at your door like this, but we just came from the inn where we were supposed to stay," Violet said. "And, well, there was some scheduling mistake or something. There are no rooms."

I frowned. "The Inn at Lighthouse Point?" I knew Jacob had set aside a bunch of rooms for the vendors. Had they had to close down some rooms because of last night? I couldn't imagine why. Nothing had happened inside the inn.

Violet nodded. "We got confirmations and everything, so I'm not sure what happened. But they told us to come see you and you could help."

See me? We weren't a hotel. I could feel my teeth gritting and forced a smile. "That's so odd. But don't worry, we'll get this figured out. Please, sit." I waved a hand at the living room, checking my watch. I was totally going to be late.

"Thanks. I would've figured it out myself, but I thought it might be better to let you handle it since everyone says you're the boss of this event."

Now I laughed out loud. I wasn't sure how I'd gotten that title—my mother was literally the head of the committee—but somehow I always ended up in charge of things around here. A pitfall of a lot of people knowing enough about you to be dangerous.

Grandpa walked into the living room at that moment. "I thought I heard voices. Hello, ladies. Leo Mancini."

"Grandpa. Thank goodness," I said, relieved. He'd help me figure this out. I introduced Violet and Sydney and explained the dilemma.

"They should stay here," Grandpa suggested. "We have plenty of room." He looked at them. "If that works for you, of course. We have lots of cats, and a cafe on-site." Grandpa loved company. Someone had asked him recently if he'd ever thought about making this place a bed-and-breakfast and I swore he was thinking about it.

Because that was just what we needed.

"We would love to," Violet said immediately. "Right, Syd?"

"I'm in," Sydney agreed. "As long as it's no trouble."

Grandpa waved that off. "The more the merrier, right?"

I hesitated. We certainly could have them stay, but what happened if the next vendor who showed up didn't have a room either? I guess we'd have to cross that bridge if we came to it.

"I guess it's settled, then," I said brightly. "Thanks, Grandpa." I gave him a hug. "You're the best. But I have to go."

"I know, you're late. Not to worry. I'll get them all settled. Right this way, ladies," he said.

"Thanks, Maddie!" Violet gave me a hug. When she pulled back, she looked at me closely. "Hold on one second," she said, and hurried to her purse. After riffling around for a moment, she finally dumped the contents onto the coffee table. I watched in astonishment as probably another five pounds of crystals poured out, along with her wallet, keys, and other purse stuff. She picked through the pile, then with a triumphant "Aha!" brandished a small pink stone with darker spots throughout. "Take this. It's a rhodonite. Good for bruising," she said with a wink. "You can put it on your eye and it should help."

"Um. Thanks," I said, accepting the stone. Was I supposed to walk around holding this on my face?

"Of course." She patted my arm, then turned and hurried after Grandpa and Sydney.

I pocketed the stone, scooped up JJ, and headed out. Thank goodness for Grandpa, saving the day again.

I got in the car and realized I was still holding on to today's paper. I didn't even want to look. I risked a glance at the headline above the fold.

ESTEEMED PSYCHIC DEAD
BALFOUR DEMPSEY FOUND AT THE
BOTTOM OF THE CLIFF OUTSIDE THE
INN AT LIGHTHOUSE POINT
By Becky Walsh

The Daybreak Island Haunted Halloween Festival took a deadly turn last night when the guest of honor was found dead.

Balfour Dempsey had just kicked off the ten-day festival with private readings at the Inn at Lighthouse Point when staff were alerted that he was no longer in his room. After a brief search, a body was discovered at the bottom of the cliff. Police later identified Dempsey, forty-one.

Ugh. I tossed the paper aside without reading the rest of it. It was making my stomach hurt. And now I was really going to be late.

As I put the car in gear, I happened to glance in the rearview and winced at my reflection. With a sigh, I pulled the crystal out of my pocket and held it against my eye as I drove. Couldn't hurt, right?

Chapter 34

When I got to the funeral home, the parking lot was already full. I hurried inside, past a family making arrangements in the office. I could hear someone crying softly, and winced. I reached the conference room and shoved the door open. All heads turned my way.

"Maddie," said Donald, rising. "Welcome. We thought you weren't coming. And JJ. Just look at that costume!" Everyone oohed and aahed over JJ appropriately. He squeaked and preened for them. I had to admit, the costume was adorable. I loved the little hat that came with it, and was surprised that JJ was allowing it to stay on his head.

Donald pulled out a chair for me, then peered at my face. "Look at our heavyweight champion," he said admiringly. "You can see it, Maddie, but it's not as bad as they said it was."

Jeez. Was everyone talking about how I got punched in the face when we had a dead guest of honor on our hands? "Um. Thanks, I think." I sat, self-consciously moving my hair in front of my shiner. "Sorry I'm late, but I had two vendors show up at my door this morning because they found out they suddenly didn't have rooms at the inn." I looked pointedly at Jacob.

"You tell 'em they got the wrong holiday?" Sal asked, deadpan.

Aside from Ellen's nervous giggle, no one laughed.

"Oh no. Which vendors?" Sam asked.

I ignored her, keeping my eyes on Jacob.

He looked appropriately sheepish. "I know. It was a terrible development in an already stressful week. But I have no rooms left. I'm not sure what happened. There must have been a miscommunication with the bookings team."

He looked kind of bad. Like he hadn't slept at all. I wondered how much of a wringer Mick had put him through, then remembered Jacob hadn't exactly been super helpful or forthcoming last night. I gritted my teeth, trying not to let my annoyance come through. "Did you try to find them another place?" I asked.

"Which vendors?" Sam asked again.

"I did, but I'm afraid everything is full," Jacob said. "I'm very sorry, Maddie."

"We aren't a hotel, Jacob," I grumbled. "Grandpa offered to make it work, but still. Is this going to happen with any other vendors? Because we don't have that many rooms. And it's our house. We live there. Preferably not with a bunch of strangers."

"I know," he said again, apologetically. "And I'll certainly offer them a comped room should they wish to come again, but aside from kicking someone out, I really don't know what to do."

"Is anyone going to tell me which vendors!" Sam's voice rose. We all turned to stare at her. I didn't think I'd ever heard my little sister raise her voice. At least not since we were kids and she used to get upset when Val and I ganged up on her. She must be overly stressed about Balfour. Who could blame her, really.

"Your crystal friends. Violet and Sydney," I said.

Sam turned on Jacob. "You don't have a room for Violet? Are you serious?"

My mother cleared her throat. "It sounds like Maddie has it sorted. Shall we get started? We have a lot to cover today." Everyone nodded. The mood in the room was subdued, to say the least. "First, let's just take a moment to address what happened and offer up some positive thoughts to poor Alice. This is just terrible."

We all sat in silence for a moment, a unanimous show of respect for Balfour. Sal broke the silence first. "It's too bad and all, but the guy was probably on drugs. Had to be, with that line of work. I'm sure he just got high and fell over the cliff. People do stupid things like that when they're on something."

The entire table fell silent in genuine astonishment. Why would he even say something like that?

"Sal!" My mother was the first to recover, and she did not sound happy. "What's gotten into you? You should not be making assumptions like that. And especially not saying them out loud with no validation. If that got out, it's harming someone's reputation. And no matter what happened, it's tragic." Her eyes flashed with anger.

He closed his mouth, but didn't look properly chastised.

Donald cleared his throat. "Speaking of assumptions," he said, clearly changing the subject. "Do the police . . . know what happened yet? Was it an accident?"

"They're still looking into it, as far as I know," I said.

He shook his head sadly. "It's very sad for Alice. I need to reach out to her about arrangements. I'm presuming he'll be sent here."

I had a sudden flash of memory from last night that

I'd forgotten about until now—Alice's urgent request that Balfour be sent to the hospital to await whatever happened next, and her determination that he not end up at Tunnicliffe's Funeral Home. Why had she been so adamant about that? And what was she planning to do with his body? Was she sending him off-island? If so, where and why? I had no idea if they had other family. Maybe Balfour had a father somewhere who needed to be consulted. Come to think of it, I didn't recall ever hearing anything about his father. Was Alice divorced? I wondered if Becky knew. I made a note to ask her. I shook off the thoughts and turned my focus back to the matter at hand—our festival that was now in danger of completely tanking.

"So. What's the plan for the rest of the Daybreak Island Haunted Halloween Festival, now that we're missing our headliner?" I said, trying to get things back on track, and maybe lighten the mood a bit. I didn't want to keep talking about Balfour with this crew. Especially not with Sal's reaction, which had seemed particularly curious to me. Both he and Jacob were so against Balfour, it seemed a little beyond a simple disbelief of psychics, at least in my opinion. I filed that away to process later. "Is there any chance we can get . . . some kind of replacement for him?" I asked.

"Maybe we can get a tarot reader," Damian said. "Balfour did some tarot, right?"

I nodded. "Do you know anyone?"

"There's someone in Boston I heard was good. I can look into it."

"Thanks," I said.

"I don't know any other psychics, at least not of his caliber," Sam said. "And it's awfully short notice. But I was thinking, maybe we can ask Violet to help. She does crystal prescriptions at her store. Maybe she can offer them here. I don't know what she's brought with her for stock, but that might be an option. I mean, she's already here."

"What's a crystal prescription?" Sal asked.

"She sits with people and diagnoses what healing crystals they need for their particular problem," Sam said.

We were all waiting for Sal to scoff. Surprisingly, he didn't. Instead, he shrugged. "So, ask her. Not sure what else we can do at the moment."

Sam looked like she was waiting for the punchline. When none came, she nodded and asked if there were any objections.

No one had any. Thank God. "I'll go talk to her as soon as we're done here," Sam said. "If she's agreeable and wants to start tonight, we'll get to work on the marketing."

"Are we keeping the tours running?" I asked, looking at Jacob. "I think we should. And we need to make sure the people from last night get put on new tours."

"Yes, we'll keep them going. I can add a few extras to recoup what we missed last night."

"Great. I talked to Grandpa Leo and we can do a second round of the cat costume parade this weekend—we can add one on Sunday. Just to fill some time. But we need a new judge," I remembered somberly.

"That would be wonderful," Ellen said. "I have cats on a waitlist! And I keep getting inquiries. I'm sure we can find a judge very easily."

"A waitlist? Wow. I didn't know we had one," I said. "Well, good. We'll make that happen, then. Grandpa will handle it." I hoped. "Everything else still on schedule?" I looked around expectantly. "What's going on with pumpkins?"

"Well, I'm pleased to tell you I have some good news," Leopard Man said.

"We're in desperate need of some, so that's great," I said.

"We have a shipment of pumpkins arriving tomorrow. So pumpkin carving can commence Sunday as planned. That should help." He looked so proud of himself. And maybe he was right. Maybe all we needed was some good, old-fashioned pumpkin carving and scary movies. At least you could turn those off when someone was murdered.

"That's amazing. Thank you," I said.

"Why don't we have the pumpkin carving contest here?" Donald suggested. "That way we can take some of the pressure off Jacob." Originally, the contest was going to be held at the inn. "We have the whole west viewing room available, so there will be plenty of room to set up tables."

"That's a great idea," Jacob said, clearly relieved.

"Agree," Ellen chimed in. "Let's do it. Thank you, Donald."

I kept my thoughts on this to myself. Everything else was moving forward on schedule, so we ended the meeting. As we got up to go, I noticed Mick Ellory standing in the doorway.

"Morning, everyone," he said, moving into the room. "There's a few of you I still need to speak to that I didn't get to last night. Hope you can spare a few moments." He smiled easily. "Donald, Sal, mind sticking around for a bit?"

"Of course not, Detective," Donald said.

"It's lieutenant now."

"Is that right? Got a promotion? Congratulations." Sal went over and clapped him on the back.

Mick frowned and moved away. He took a seat at the conference table.

Everyone else made a beeline for the door, but I hung back for a second. "One quick thing?" I asked Mick.

"One second," he told the men, then got up and followed me out of earshot. "What?"

"I need to go back and look for the cat today. Can I get up there without a whole big production?"

"Yes. I cleared the area last night, but did ask that Jacob not let Balfour's staff up there. I don't want any problems with them taking his stuff and running before Alice gets to it. We'll have to figure that out once she's ready to address it."

"Fair enough. What *about* his people?"

"They're here for the duration. I'm not done with them yet."

I waited, but he didn't elaborate.

"Is that all, Maddie? Because I have work to do."

"One more thing." I took out my phone and scrolled to the Notes app where I'd captured the numbers from the white SUV's plate. "I got these from the license plate on the SUV the other day. Just wanted to make sure it's rented to Marybeth Montgomery. You should be able to find out from the rental agency, right?"

"Send that to me. I'll compare it. Gotta go, Maddie. I have to talk to these guys before our press conference at noon," he added.

I wondered if he'd have any developments by then. If so, it looked like I wasn't getting a heads-up.

Chapter 35

I hurried to my car before anyone could shanghai me into a conversation—or worse, into an additional chore, which usually happened at these things—but the coast was clear. I called my dad as I pulled out of the parking lot.

"Any news on the crash victim?" I asked when he answered.

"I'm afraid not. The situation is unchanged," he said.

"Do they think she's going to recover?"

"It's still up in the air." My dad sounded subdued. This had been a pretty serious accident, from the sound of it.

"Thanks, Dad. I'll call you later." I disconnected and looked at JJ. "What do you think? Nursing home first, then Lilah?" It was still kind of early, barely ten. Our meeting had been pretty efficient. Probably because everyone was still in shock.

JJ squeaked his agreement.

I stopped by the Bean to grab a coffee and a bagel with smoked salmon that I knew I'd end up sharing with JJ, then headed to the nursing home. I planned to do an abbreviated visit today—I'd make up for it next month.

We'd hit some of JJ's favorite friends, then head to Lilah's. I called Becky as I drove.

"You heard there's a press conference today?" I asked.

"Yeah, they just sent the email."

"Good. I just saw Mick. Couldn't get any previews from him."

"No, but he gave me the scoop last night that they confirmed his identity before anyone else published." I could hear the satisfaction in her tone. I knew she'd been concerned about getting out in front since the *Globe* and some other off-island papers had hit the scene. Becky was personally sad about Balfour, but I knew she was a journalist at heart.

"I'm heading back over there today to look for the cat," I said.

"What cat?"

"Balfour's cat. He's apparently missing."

"Oh no," Becky said. "That's awful."

"Yeah. Don't put that in the paper," I cautioned. "Last thing we need are people swarming the inn trying to find him, or steal him if they do. I'll call you later."

I hung up, pulled into the Haviland House Assisted Living parking lot and found a spot right near the door. JJ, recognizing the building, squeaked in anticipation. He loved coming here. He loved going anywhere he got attention, which was basically everywhere, so it was kind of a no-brainer.

We headed inside. Lisa, the front desk receptionist, let out a squeal when she saw us. "Oh. My. Goodness. Would you look at that cuteness?" She sprang up from her chair and came around to us, crouching in front of JJ. "A little Sherlock Holmes. That is the best. Hi, Maddie."

"Hey, Lisa."

"Did I know you were coming today?" She stood,

straightening her skirt. I noticed it was a black lacy skirt with fake spiders climbing it. Gotta love the Halloween spirit around here, even in the midst of tragedy.

"I don't know," I admitted. "My schedule is all off with the Halloween event . . ." I trailed off as the smile faded from her face.

"Yeah. I can't believe what happened. I was scheduled for a reading with him! I'm so sad."

"I know," I said. "It's unreal."

"Do they know what happened yet?" She lowered her voice and stepped closer to me. "All the old timers are saying it's because he stayed up on that haunted floor. That the spirits up there are super evil."

I resisted an eye roll. "Really?"

"Really," Lisa said with a nod. "You've gotta remember, most of the people here grew up with those stories. And people love unsolved mysteries. And ghosts. There are probably a hundred different theories about the man who died in the elevator shaft." She smiled a little. "Some of them are a little over the top. It used to make Mr. Blair annoyed. He had his own opinion about what happened to that man. Of course, now, he's not always at his best to debate the subject."

I paused. "Mr. Blair. Do you mean—"

"Andrew Blair, the family that owns the inn, yes. He's been here for a few years now."

"Jacob's dad," I said slowly.

Lisa nodded. "Yes."

I could hardly believe my luck. Maybe I'd even get a chance to drop in on Mr. Blair today. I'm sure he could use a little cheer from a cute orange cat dressed up like a detective. "Oh, that's amazing," I said. "He's like a celebrity around town!" I had no idea if this was true, but if I gushed a little, maybe she'd point me in the right direction.

"He is," Lisa agreed. "I mean, imagine owning a haunted inn!"

"So you mentioned that he's not always at his best," I said.

Lisa glanced around to make sure no one was listening. "I'm not really supposed to talk about patients, but it's not really a secret. He's got Alzheimer's," she said. "It's not debilitating yet, but it's settling in slowly."

"That's sad."

"It is. But he still has a lot of good days, honestly. He knows his family most of the time, and remembers our names. You know, medicines are getting so much more effective."

"Does Mr. Blair like cats?"

She grinned. "I think he'd love a cute cat to cheer him up. I know he was upset last night after he heard the news."

I frowned. "Last night?"

"Yes. Jacob came over and talked to him. I'm assuming he told him, because Mr. Blair was distraught afterward. I wasn't sure exactly what happened—I think he was mixing up stories a bit—but I heard the terrible news this morning. I'm not sure why Jacob felt the need to upset his father with the story, but they've always been a close family." She shrugged. "Maybe he was anticipating his dad would get questions and wanted to tell him what he knew."

Last night. When Jacob had been MIA. He'd been here, telling his father that someone else had died at the inn. And he'd disappeared long before Alice and I had found Balfour's body . . . how had he already known? My stomach twisted into a knot. Jacob had been so resistant to Balfour. I'd chalked it up to general New England uptightness, but maybe it went beyond that.

Could Jacob have wanted to get rid of Balfour enough

that he'd push him over a cliff? It would have been easy enough for him to do. He knew the land like the back of his hand. Knew how dangerous those cliffs were. And he knew that he could say he'd warned everyone about it and Balfour still ignored those warnings and went out there.

Though on the other hand—my mind continued to race—why would it have been so important to update him at that moment? Surely if he was the murderer it would have been smarter to stay at the inn and act natural. Was there another reason for his visit? I tried not to let my anticipation show, in case it aroused Lisa's suspicions about why I wanted JJ to visit Andrew Blair.

"Well, if you tell me where to find him, I'll put him on our visitor's list," I said brightly.

"Oh, sure. He's in wing one. The studio apartments down that way." She pointed to a hallway. "I know you don't usually visit that wing when you're here, but you shouldn't have any problem getting in. Have them buzz me if you do."

"Thanks." I headed down to the main wing to hit a few of JJ's regular friends so it wouldn't be so obvious, but as soon as I could I headed to wing one. I assumed all the memory care residents who needed more supervision were in this wing.

JJ trotted along, eliciting gasps and chuckles from the staff as we walked the halls. I pretended to just be walking along looking for a taker, but I was checking all the names on the doors as I went by. Mr. Blair was, of course, in the last apartment on the left.

I looked around to see if anyone was paying attention, then knocked. "Come in," a deep male voice called out.

I opened the door and stuck my head in a small but classy studio apartment, putting on my brightest smile. The man I assumed was Andrew Blair sat in a recliner facing a big-screen TV watching a golf game. The room consisted of a small sofa, a bed in the corner near the window, and a door that I presumed led to the bathroom. And there was a little galley kitchen though I didn't see a stove. Probably not allowed.

"Hello! Mr. Blair?"

"That's me. I think." He laughed. "Old folks' home joke. Who are you?"

"I'm Maddie James. This is JJ. We visit here every month and I realized we've never made it down to this wing, so here we are."

Blair gazed at JJ. "What the hell is he wearing?"

"That's a Sherlock Holmes costume. You know, for Halloween," I added.

"Yes, young lady, I know it's almost Halloween. Well, come in. James, you said? As in, the hospital James?" He peered at me closely now as JJ and I entered the room. JJ squeaked, went over, and started rubbing on Blair's legs.

"Yes. My grandmother was Lucille Mancini. She worked with you."

Blair's face brightened. "Lucy! My best employee," he declared, then looked at JJ and nodded. "Well, he's a cute cat, costume aside."

Someone wasn't in the Halloween spirit. "Thanks," I said. "So, Mr. Blair. I'm helping with the Halloween event this year in town."

"With my son?"

I nodded. "Yes."

"That one." Blair shook his head. "Gonna die before me, at this rate. Always giving himself an ulcer about something."

I smiled. That was an accurate depiction of Jacob. "Well, to be fair, he did have a lot to deal with last night." I glanced around to make sure no nurse was going to come up behind me and throw me out for having this conversation. "Did you hear what happened?"

Blair frowned. "Of course I did. He came right over and told me. But they'll find her."

"Find . . . her? I'm sorry, who?"

"The maid," he said, exasperated. "Catwoman. What's her name. She probably just partied a little too hard. She was a little vixen, that one," he said with an old man's leer that made me recoil. "She'll turn up eventually."

"The maid," I said slowly, feeling my heart sink. Though he appeared lucid, Mr. Blair was clearly having a moment of living in the past. So much for hoping to get his take on why Jacob had been so upset about Balfour coming to the inn in the first place. Maybe Jacob hadn't come over to tell his father about Balfour. Maybe Lisa had simply assumed it had something to do with Balfour's murder when she read the papers the next day.

But the moment he'd gone back to was interesting. "You know her well?" I asked casually.

"Of course I know her! I know all my staff," he said proudly. "I'm not one of those bosses who doesn't care about his people."

"So you don't think something bad happened to . . ." I searched my mind for the missing maid's name. "Theresa?" I crossed my fingers that I had it right. Heck, at the very least I could tell Becky that I tried to help with one of her cold cases.

Mr. Blair shook his head slowly. "I don't think so. She's a scrappy little thing. I mean, she liked the boys for sure, but she can also handle herself. Wouldn't put it past her to scratch someone's eyes out if they made a wrong move." He cackled now. "That's what cats do, right?"

"If the situation calls for it, I guess so," I said.

Mr. Blair shrugged. "Maybe she took off because of that guy."

"What guy?"

"Ah, I don't remember his name. The one everyone said the ghost threw down the elevator shaft." Blair rolled his eyes. "Ghost stories are great and all, but the things people believe are just silly sometimes. Heck, I wouldn't be surprised if Ms. Theresa got rid of that guy herself. I saw him sniffing around her when he thought no one was looking. Throwing money at her. Remember, Lucy? You were worried about it too."

I froze. He thought I was my grandmother? I guess reminding him of her had jogged his memory. But was he just mixing a bunch of memories and talking nonsense, or was he telling me that he suspected the missing maid and the dead man were related?

And also, was there a particular reason he was going back to that moment in time? Possibly because he knew something and had held on to a secret for so long?

A knock at the door startled me. One of the staff members. She smiled, looking at me curiously. "Sorry to interrupt, but it's lunch time, Mr. Blair. You want to come down to the cafeteria today and see your friends?"

Blair thought about this, then finally nodded. "Sure, why not," he said. "It's a good day to talk about ghosts." He turned back to me. "Lucy. Please let me know when they find her, okay?"

"I will," I said, then scooped JJ up and left.

Chapter 36

I loaded JJ back into the car and got in, but didn't drive away immediately. Instead, I unwrapped our uneaten bagel and handed JJ some salmon, then took a bite while I thought about what Andrew Blair had said.

I knew that I couldn't put a lot of stock into the conversation, since he was clearly having trouble recalling faces and time frames. But that didn't mean that his actual words didn't have some kernel of truth to them. I grabbed my phone and called Becky.

"You'll never guess where I just was," I said when she answered.

"Where?"

"The nursing home. With Jacob's father." I filled her in on the conversation.

"You're kidding," she said excitedly. "See? I told you."

I remembered her insistence last night that someone who thought Balfour knew something about the past had done this. "Hold up," I said. "He didn't say anything about Balfour. He was talking about the maid and the guy who died. Said he was sniffing around her and throwing money at her. It also sounded like he had a crush on this girl." I shuddered. Nasty. Andrew could've been her father. "But does that mean he was behind that theory about the cases being related? And what does it have to do with Balfour? He said the killer was a guy."

"Andrew has to know something," Becky said, sounding super sure of herself.

"He might, but his memory isn't at peak," I said. I waited for her to answer, but there was silence. "Beck?"

"Sorry, I'm a little distracted. Watching the press conference."

"Oh, that's happening now?" I glanced at the clock on the dash. "Did the police have anything new to add about Balfour?"

"No. They didn't even say they have a definite person of interest. Who do you think they're looking at?"

Maeve's face flashed through my mind, along with Alice's insistence that her son's team was using him. "I don't know," I said finally. "They'll probably pursue the retirement angle and who stood to lose the most from that."

"Even if someone did have a lot to lose, wouldn't they lose it anyway if he died?" she pointed out.

"Perhaps. But who knows how the company was set up? I'm sure Mick will be looking into all of that."

"Well," she said. "Come by the paper later. Maybe we can come up with a theory about the cold case connection that Mick likes. See if we can find out anything about old Andrew Blair."

"I will. I have to go back to the inn in a bit and see about this cat."

"Good luck."

I disconnected and pulled out of the nursing home parking lot, heading for Turtle Point. Time to talk to Lilah.

When I pulled into Lilah Gilmore's driveway a few minutes later, there was a lot of activity going on. Her landscapers were out in full force, cleaning up leaves from the great lawn, probably the last cleanup of the fall. I hoped she was home. The cars were probably in the giant three-car garage.

I wondered what Ethan could do with a garage this big. The unattached garage at Grandpa's was now our cafe, and it was literally half the size of this one. I'd already been sensing an expansion request coming. When the weather got cold and we couldn't put tables and chairs outside, we were short on space.

I turned to JJ. "I don't think you'll be welcome, so I'll leave you here with the salmon, okay?"

He squeaked.

I opened the windows just a tad, spread the salmon on a napkin on the seat, then got out and locked the doors.

Lilah answered the door immediately, already dressed for what looked like a day out at a fancy club, hair perfectly done and pearls in place. She didn't look surprised to see me. She had to have heard the news. Lilah knew everything pretty much before anyone else, so even if by some weird timing thing she'd missed the excitement last night while she was at the inn, she had to have been the first one to get a call.

"Good morning, Maddie." She didn't immediately open the door wide enough for me to come in. "What can I do for you?"

"Sorry to show up unannounced," I said, "but I need to talk to you. Can I come in?"

Her hesitation was so brief no one else might've even noticed it, but I'd been around Lilah Gilmore for enough years that I could see it. Her impeccable breeding meant that she would always be pleasant and welcoming, no matter the occasion. So her hesitation could mean only one thing: she knew why I was here.

"Of course," she said. "Would you like some coffee?"

"I'd love some," I said promptly. Even though I'd

already had three cups, I justified another by admitting my head was spinning from my conversation with Jacob's father.

"Right this way." She held the door open. I stepped inside and paused, looking around. I hadn't been to Lilah's house in a while. It was larger and grander than I even remembered. It almost looked like a museum, with its marble foyer and expensive-looking trinkets.

I much preferred our cozy, full, lived-in house.

She led me into the four-season sunroom with its giant windows and motioned to the sofa. A woman appeared noiselessly in the doorway. "Coffee please, Elsa," she said, and the woman disappeared just as quietly. Lilah looked at me expectantly.

"Did you come to the inn last night?" I asked. "For your appointment?"

Lilah glanced behind her, as if she expected someone to be listening. No one was there. "I did," she said.

"Can I ask—how did you arrange getting inside? I know you didn't want to advertise that you were there."

"I made arrangements with the staff to come in the side door."

"And how did you get upstairs to the suite?"

She smiled. "I'm afraid that was just the old-fashioned way. Up the steps like everyone else. There is no other entrance."

I nodded. "I'm sure you heard what happened," I said bluntly.

Her eyes never left my face. "I did. It's a tragedy."

"The police are looking for Jane Cummings. Since she was the last person to have an appointment with Balfour before he ended up at the bottom of the cliff."

I had to give Lilah credit—she didn't flinch.

"Do you think they'll find her?" she asked.

I almost smiled. It was her way of asking me if I'd

said anything. "They probably will later today," I said. "What happened when you saw him?"

"Nothing happened. He did my reading. It didn't take the full time. I left the same way I came in."

"Who was in the waiting area downstairs when you left? On the fifth floor?"

"No one," she said. "Maybe they had taken a break since the next reading wasn't due for another fifteen or twenty minutes, but no one was there. I took the other staircase down to the first floor, and that was that."

"What about the woman on his staff? The one up on the top floor with him?"

"She was there when I went up, yes. I didn't see her again. I did hear her raising her voice to someone at one point. Probably on the phone. And a bit of a ruckus, like she'd dropped something in the next room. I didn't see her when I left."

I studied her. She had no reason to lie, at least not that I knew of. And I can't imagine Lilah Gilmore would suddenly turn murderous, lure a man she didn't know out to the edge of a cliff and push him off.

Although stranger things had happened.

"Can I ask you something?" I said finally.

She lifted her chin slightly, a grudging permission.

"Why all the secrecy? The assumed name, the spy entrance? Who would care if you went to see a psychic medium to support the town event?"

She looked like she was debating the best way to answer that question when I heard her name being called from somewhere inside the house. A man's voice. Henry, her husband.

"Yes, dear," she responded, giving me a warning look that I instinctively understood meant *Don't talk about this in front of Henry.* "In the sunroom."

He appeared a moment later, wearing what I supposed

was a casual outfit for him. I didn't know Henry Gilmore well, but he had always struck me as uptight, not very nice, certainly not warm and fuzzy. I couldn't imagine being married to someone like that. He was always dressed to the nines—like Lilah—and everything just seemed to be about the optics. The houses, the gardens, the cars, the clothes, the job he'd had before retiring. I knew this old-money generation was like that, but I still didn't find any of it appealing in any way.

He peered at me curiously. "Oh. Hello. I didn't know we had company," he said in a reproachful tone.

"Maddie just stopped by on a whim, dear," she answered. "You remember her. Brian and Sophie's oldest."

"Yes," he said with a nod at me. "Hello, Maddie."

"Nice to see you, Mr. Gilmore," I said.

He didn't reply in kind and turned back to her. "I'm heading to the golf course."

"Of course. Have a nice time," she said.

With one last glance at me, he headed back into the main house. I waited until I figured he had to be out of earshot, then looked at Lilah again.

"So?" I said finally. "Was there something specific you wanted to ask Balfour?"

Lilah stood, signaling that the conversation was over, that she didn't intend to answer me. "I appreciate you coming by, Maddie. When do you suppose the police will discover Jane's identity?"

I stood too. "I have to tell Mick—Lieutenant Ellory—today. It's only right."

She gave a nod. "Then you'll do what you have to do. Thank you for coming by." She walked to the front door and held it open for me. "Do give my regards to your parents," she said.

"I will."

I had barely stepped out when she shut the door

behind me. I stood on the porch for a moment, watching Henry's fancy Jaguar maneuver out of the garage and back into the street before rolling silently away, and wondered why Lilah didn't want to tell me why she'd gone to see Balfour.

Chapter 37

I drove home slowly from Lilah's, trying to make sense of that bizarre visit. I hated to jump to the worst-case conclusion, but Lilah's reticence to tell me why she'd been so adamant about seeing Balfour—and doing it undercover—was hard to explain away. I was having a hard time buying the idea that it was all about her reputation. Since when had getting a tarot card reading become so controversial?

No, there had to be more to it. And the fact that she could have been the last person we knew of, at least inside the inn, to see him alive couldn't be ignored. Could Lilah Gilmore, a pillar of our town, really have had something to do with Balfour's death? I couldn't believe it, but I'd been surprised by people before.

That was, of course, if Maeve hadn't returned from wherever she'd disappeared to. Lilah said she heard her yelling at someone and some kind of "ruckus." What had that been about? I needed to tell Mick.

But first I was going to stop and get lunch, since I'd given JJ most of my bagel. Then I had to call Katrina and ask her to come to the inn with me.

I was going to go home, but as I passed Strike 3, I

found myself swerving into the parking lot. Vince, the owner, still worked the day shift at the bar, and maybe he'd be open to a chat about our unsolved mystery. I parked out front and pushed my door open as my phone dinged with a text: Tomas.

I am still not allowed upstairs. When are you coming to look for Balfour Jr.? They said you were the only one allowed to do so. He could be hurt!!

I rolled my eyes. So dramatic.

I'll be back in a bit with reinforcements, I responded.

JJ and I headed inside. Vince was working the bar, like always. Vince had curly dark hair shot through with gray and a nose that sat sideways like he'd had it broken in the boxing ring a few times too many. He waved and motioned us in. I loved that JJ could basically go any-place on this island and not be thrown out. I was about to go sit at the bar when I saw Harry at a high-top table, finishing his lunch. I headed over. "Hey. Want some company?"

"Hey, Maddie. Sure thing." Harry cleared some space for me. I wrapped JJ's leash around the chair leg. He curled up under the table and fell asleep. "How's that eye?"

I touched it self-consciously. "It's fine. Looks worse than it is."

Harry nodded. "What are you up to?"

"I have to head back to the inn and look for the cat. But Harry . . . last night. Right around the time Balfour must've left the suite. Were you still stationed in the hall?"

"I had to step away for a bit. Jacob asked me to go downstairs and check on something."

"Jacob asked you to leave the security detail?" That was interesting.

Harry nodded. "Yeah. Well, he asked Manny to tell

me. I guess they were texting. He said someone reported a woman lurking around out back near the guest entrance. He thought it might be the stalker woman and asked me to check it out."

"Lurking," I repeated.

"His words."

"Who saw her? Does Mick know?"

"I'm not sure. I don't know if anyone even remembered that happened, after everything else," he admitted. "But I went down there. I didn't see anyone, but then again, I didn't know exactly what she looked like. He gave me a description, but it was a little generic." He shrugged. "But the only person I bumped into was Don."

I frowned. "Why was Don out back near the guest entrance?"

"I didn't ask," Harry said. "Just asked if he saw some woman lurking around. He said no."

"And why doesn't the inn have cameras?" I asked. "It would've made this so much easier."

Harry laughed. "I know. But we're a low-level security organization. As in, you're looking at him. We've never had much going on, honestly. Maybe it's naïve, but Jacob always thought that could be intrusive to guests."

Or helpful if there was a crime, I thought, but resisted saying it out loud. "So when you left the hall to go check this out, who was there?"

"Manfred. His sister had taken a break. He said he was staying put, so I figured it was okay to leave."

That must've been when I saw Sharlene out on the bench. But Manfred didn't stay put. So where did he go?

"Why?" Harry asked.

"Well, that must've been when Balfour left. Sounds like Manfred took a break then too, but just didn't admit it." Maybe he was worried about getting in trouble. Or maybe it was something else.

"Ah, jeez." Harry sighed. "I feel awful now."

"Why? You did what you were asked to do. It's not your fault."

"Do you think Manfred . . . ?"

"I have no idea. But there definitely was a lot going on. Thanks, Harry."

He nodded, then glanced at his watch, pushing his empty plate away. "I have to get to the inn, speaking of. Sorry to run."

"No worries," I said, waving him off. "I'll see you later, I'm sure."

After he left, I decided to relocate to the bar. I scooped up JJ and headed over there.

"Maddie. Sorry, we're a little short-staffed today. I was sending someone over," Vince said. Then he peered at me. "Jeez. Someone pop you?"

I reached up and touched my eye again. I was so tired of answering this question. "Long story. And I actually wanted to talk to you."

"To me?" He grinned. "That's not something I hear a lot."

"Yeah, well, this might be an odd question," I warned.

"Hit me. I love odd questions."

"I was curious about the Archie Lang murder from forty years ago," I said. "Do you remember anything about it?"

"Wow. That's out of the blue. Archie Lang. Sure I do. The guy in the elevator shaft," he said. "Defining moment in my life. I'll definitely never forget it. Closest I've ever been to someone who got murdered. I'm kind of obsessed with crime," he added, dropping his voice. "Not in a creepy way, though."

I had to laugh. "You're not alone, believe me. I know he was last seen alive here before he went back to the inn."

Vince nodded. "Yeah, we had a big shindig here. Private party for Green Farm Ventures, as I recall. Didn't do a lotta those back then. My pop was thrilled they picked our place. Course, Sal steered 'em here." He smiled fondly. "He's been a good friend to the family. And I was working the bar. I don't think I was supposed to since I wasn't even twenty-one yet, but it was different in those days. And my dad didn't wanna pay a real bartender. He got me at a good deal," he said with an eye roll. "But can't complain. Great tips. Those guys drank a lot."

"Sal organized the party?" I asked. "Sal Bonnadonna?" I tried to reconcile that in my mind. Sal was about Grandpa's age, so forty years ago he would've been in his mid-thirties. It made sense.

Vince nodded. "Yeah. He and my pops were . . . colleagues of sorts."

"Colleagues," I repeated. "What kind of colleagues?"

He sighed. "Really? You're a cop's granddaughter, Maddie. I'm disappointed. Anyway, my dad was a great man, God rest his soul." He glanced at the ceiling and did a quick sign of the cross. "Sal helped him out when he could so he could get on his feet and outta the other business, even though Sal was still in it. He liked my dad, so he would help him out on the down-low when he could. He set him up with this party. I think he hoped his investor friends would invest in us."

Was he telling me that Sal and his dad were mob involved? "Did they?" I asked.

"Nope. Restaurants weren't their thing. They wanted easy profits, places that could be franchised and make money by basically turning on the lights." He shrugged.

"Like liquor stores."

"Eh," Vince said. "Those places are a dime a dozen too. Nothin' special about 'em. Sal didn't need funding, anyhow. But now funeral homes. That's where it's at."

He grinned. "Dead people are guaranteed business. A real goldmine. Once that idea caught on, they loved it. Course, it took Lilah almost all night to convince them."

I was getting really confused now. "Lilah? Funeral homes? I'm not following, Vince."

"Sorry. It was Lilah's idea they invest in Don's place. Took her a whole lot of convincing to get the higher-ups on board. I heard the whole thing. She sat here with them all night." He tapped his finger on the bar. "Got myself a good lesson in investing that night. I'm telling you, bartenders can get a whole education with this job. I feel like I got more degrees than those Harvard pretty boys."

"I'm sure you do," I said. "So Lilah knew the Green Farm investors?"

Vince nodded. "Sure she did. I think she was the one who brought them to town. She's the one with the old money in that family," he said with a wink. "Don't let Henry tell you otherwise. And her daddy trained her well. She knew her way around that stuff for sure. Anyway, she had a whole business plan thought out for old Don. He needed help and she really jumped in to get it for him."

"Don Tunnicliffe," I said slowly. "He got funding from Green Farm? And *Lilah* brought them to town?"

"Sure did. Saved Don's business. He was about to lose it. And it was all thanks to Lilah, 'cause Lord knows he'd never go after it himself."

"Why not?" I asked.

Vince laughed. "He was still a snot-nosed kid then. Barely twenty-five when his dad died and he inherited the business. Had no clue what he was doing. He's lucky he had Lilah as a friend. She was his guardian angel, lemme tell you."

Chapter 38

After I left the bar I sat in my car with JJ, thinking about what Vince had told me. None of it seemed to be a secret, but I was wondering why none of these connections had come up publicly during the Lang investigation. But one thing he'd said stuck out more than anything—about his father and Sal being "colleagues."

I called Grandpa. "Was Vince Salvatore's father in the mob?"

A pause. "Hello to you too, Doll."

"Grandpa."

"There were rumors, sure," Grandpa said. "He never brought it here if he was, though. Did whatever dirty work he was involved in over on the mainland. Why do you ask?"

"So Sal was too," I said, almost to myself. "Sal is the one with the long history and ties to organized crime."

"What are you talking about?" Grandpa asked.

He was good, I'd give him that. If he knew Sal was mobbed up, he wasn't letting on. "Balfour said Archie Lang's murderer had a long successful history here and also ties to organized crime. Grandpa. Do you think it was Sal?"

Grandpa scoffed. "What connection did Sal have to that guy?"

"Sounds like he was hanging around with that bunch of investors. Whether he was looking for money or not, I'm not sure. But Don Tunnicliffe was. I just talked to Vince. He had a lot to say about the night Lang died."

"I'd be careful about running with that information," Grandpa said. "Vince tends to embellish things. I'm sure he remembers some of it, but it was forty years ago, Doll."

"Well, he remembered Lilah being there."

That caught Grandpa's attention. "Lilah Gilmore?"

"Yep." I gave him the abbreviated version of what Vince had told me. "She got them to invest in the funeral home, allegedly. I knew there had to be a reason she was talking to Balfour. I need to tell Mick."

"Maddie—"

"I'll call you later, Grandpa." I hung up and called Katrina. "Can you help me find a cat?" I asked when she answered.

"I have a ton of cats. How many do you need?"

I laughed. "Nice try. No, I mean I need help finding a missing cat. At the Inn at Lighthouse Point." I filled her in on the events of last night.

"Oh man. Yeah, Mick told me what happened to the psychic. That's so crazy," she said. "He didn't mention the cat, though."

Mick and Katrina had been seeing each other for a few months now, and surprisingly, the relationship seemed to be working out. It had definitely done wonders for his disposition, which I'd found lacking when I first moved back here. Of course, he'd been accusing me of murder then, so that had soured me on him for a while. But I'd had to give him a second chance because of Katrina, and we'd been getting along well. Grudgingly sometimes, but well. And he was—regardless of what he said—starting to see the value I could bring to some of his cases.

"Probably wasn't high on his list of priorities, but the cat handler is losing his mind and Balfour's mother wants the cat too. Which will be a whole other fight, but we have to find him first. So, you in?"

"I'll meet you there in an hour," Katrina said. "I'll bring a couple of traps."

"Perfect." I hung up then dialed Mick. His voice mail picked up right away. I huffed out a sigh of frustration and left a message.

"I need to talk to you about Jane Cummings. Call me."

JJ and I got to the inn before Katrina. When we got inside, the place was a ghost town—no pun intended. Which wasn't totally surprising given that it was the middle of the afternoon, but I expected more activity with the number of guests he had right now.

Unless they'd all checked out, given last night's events. Although if that were the case, Violet would never have showed up at my door, I supposed.

I texted Tomas that I was here and heading up to look for the cat. He didn't respond right away. While I waited, I went to the front desk and asked for Jacob. Luckily it wasn't the same woman from last night. This one was much more pleasant.

"What a cute kitty!" she chirped when she saw JJ in my arms. "One moment." She picked up the phone.

Jacob appeared a moment later. "Maddie," he said.

"Hi. I need to get upstairs to the suite. We're looking for the cat today."

"Oh yes, the cat. I have the key, and Lieutenant Ellory gave me the all-clear, so whenever you're ready."

"Thanks. Just waiting for Katrina. So they aren't letting anyone else upstairs?" I confirmed.

"Only you," Jacob said. "Balfour's staff isn't allowed in there. Lieutenant Ellory said you could have access to look for the cat."

I glanced around the lobby again. "It's quiet in here," I said.

"It is. People are out sightseeing."

"So you didn't have a lot of people leave?"

He looked surprised. "Oh, no. On the contrary. We've had so many calls about people wanting rooms today, it's uncanny. Even some who want to stay in the suite and offered obscene amounts of money to do so." He grimaced. "People are so strange."

I had to laugh, though at the heart of it, of course it wasn't funny. But here everyone was, worried about what this would mean for the inn's and the island's reputation. I guess it goes to show that the old saying that no press is bad press is really true. I debated asking Jacob why he'd gone to see his father last night, but thought that tipping off Mick to that whole thing first would be a better strategy.

Katrina walked into the lobby then, juggling two Havahart traps, which she unceremoniously dropped on the floor to pull out her phone, probably to call me. JJ and I hurried over to her, JJ squeaking in excitement. He loved Katrina.

She stared at me. "What the heck happened to you?"

This stupid eye. "Long story," I said. "Tell you later."

"Then grab a trap," she instructed. "Hi, JJ." She reached down and scratched his ears. "You think the cat got outside, or is he probably somewhere in here?"

"I'm guessing inside somewhere," I said, hoping I was right. But my gut told me he hadn't gone far. "Getting out would've been complicated, unless he went with Balfour. And I don't get the sense that happened."

"It never would've happened," a voice from behind me said.

I spun around to find Tomas standing there. This guy had an eerie way of just showing up.

"Hello to you too," I said dryly. "Tomas, this is my friend Katrina. She's an animal rescuer."

"How do you do," Tomas said, his tone indicating he was holding his nose. I remembered he didn't have the best opinion of animal control. I couldn't say I blamed him—Katrina was one of a kind. "What do you intend to do with those . . . *contraptions*?" He motioned to the traps.

I saw Katrina's eyes narrow. "Well, we're going to set them up in case the cat is just too scared to come out when people are around. We'll put food in them and hope he goes in when it's quiet," she said. "But first, let's go see if we can find him with some snacks."

Tomas was staring at the traps in horror. "He would never set foot in one of those," he said. "That looks awful!"

"He would if he was hungry," Katrina said. "Did anyone leave food out last night?"

"I haven't been allowed up there. No one has," Tomas said reproachfully. "They said it's off-limits to everyone but you. That you're here in an 'official capacity.'" His tone made his disdain for those last few words clear. "We were given strict instructions by that policeman and by the inn owner."

"Well I left food out for him," I said. "And don't worry. Katrina is an expert."

Tomas's expression said he sincerely doubted that, but he wisely kept his mouth shut. "Just find Balfour Jr.," he said.

Katrina was staring at Tomas in fascination. "Balfour Jr.?" she asked.

"The cat. I'll explain later," I murmured.

"I'll wait down here," Tomas said tersely, and flopped onto the sofa.

I motioned to Jacob that we were ready, and he led us upstairs.

Chapter 39

When we reached the upstairs hallway, I braced myself for the usual chill I felt up there. It was probably a good thing that the hotel wasn't using this floor. It was always so darn cold. I trailed behind Jacob and Katrina, wanting another look at the photo on the wall that Balfour had pointed to the other day. But when I got to roughly the spot where I remembered it being, I didn't see it. I went back down the hall a little, figuring I'd miscalculated, but . . . nothing.

It appeared to be gone.

Now that I looked more closely, some of the pictures were separated by more space than those farther down the hall. As if they'd been rearranged to cover up an empty spot.

"Maddie?"

I turned. Jacob had unlocked the door to the suite and waited expectantly. I thought about asking, then decided to wait. "Coming."

I followed Katrina inside the suite, placing JJ on the ground. With a squeak, he started sniffing around. The room looked exactly as it had last night, with the exception of fingerprint powder scattered on multiple surfaces. Jacob grimaced when he saw it. I went to the table where Balfour had been doing his readings. There were still cards laid out on the table. I leaned in for a closer look. A tarot spread, with multiple cards thrown on top. I had no idea how to read tarot, so I didn't know what any of it meant. It had to be Lilah's reading, though. I snapped a picture of the cards.

"Where was the cat when it went missing?" Katrina asked. "In this room?"

"Probably. Or the connecting room, but my guess is he was in here with Balfour."

"Let's have a look in here then." Katrina began checking under furniture, shaking a bag of treats as she moved around, which only succeeded in getting JJ to run over to her.

Jacob watched from the doorway. I went into the bedroom. It was tidy, with a suitcase tucked neatly into a corner. A pair of folded pants were draped over the chair next to the window, like Balfour had decided to change at the last minute and didn't have time to put them away. A quick glance in the closet showed everything in place, shirts and pants and jackets hung in sections. I bent down to check for the cat, even though the view into the closet was clear. No sign.

I checked the bathroom, just to take a cursory look and see if the cat was in the bathtub—I'd had a cat who loved the bathtub and slept in it every chance he got and also took showers—but a quick glance behind the shower curtain yielded nothing. There was nowhere else to really hide in here. I went back into the main room and looked around. Katrina was going through the kitchen cabinets. JJ sat in front of the door leading to the other suite—Balfour Jr.'s room. He saw me come out and squeaked again.

"What's up, bud? Want to check in there?" I went to

open the door, but it was locked. I looked at Jacob. "Can you open this?"

"Why?" he asked.

"Because we need to look for the cat," I said.

"I thought he was in here?"

"We don't know where he is. That's the whole point," I said. "If this room was open last night, we should see if he's somewhere in there. I left food in here too, so I need to see if it's been eaten."

Jacob hesitated. "I'm not sure . . ."

"Do I need to call Mick?" Katrina asked me, coming out of the kitchen area. "Just to reiterate that we have permission?"

I looked at Jacob. "Your choice."

He pursed his lips, then stalked over and unlocked the door.

Katrina and I exchanged glances as Jacob pushed open the door. JJ ran straight through. I followed him, curious. Mick said he'd had his guys in here the other night but there had been no sign of the cat, so I wasn't really expecting to find anything now, but hey, you never knew.

The first thing I noticed was that the food hadn't been eaten—instead it sat congealed in its plate. I grabbed it as JJ made a beeline for it. Didn't need him to get sick from old food. Disappointed, JJ turned and stalked down the hall.

I followed him while Katrina paused to look around. He dashed into the bedroom area, squeaking loudly at the closet door. I frowned and pulled it open. Balfour Jr.'s stuff was still in there—the little cart with the wheels, the carrier he rode in that went on top, the duffel bag that I presumed was full of his stuff. I opened the bag and checked it. Cat supplies, including some clothing and what looked like some bat ears. Not as fancy of a Halloween costume as I expected from our guest of honor. Regardless, there was no cat. I checked the carrier just to make sure. Nothing.

I turned to JJ. "I don't think he's here, bud. You smell his stuff, though."

JJ squeaked again, then started digging at the rug.

I frowned. "What are you doing?" I crouched down next to him, moving aside the cart and carrier. Maybe the cat had had an accident and JJ smelled it? I leaned down and sniffed the rug. I didn't smell anything, but as I leaned on the floor underneath, I noticed part of it felt different. Hollow, almost.

I moved my fingers around, pressing on the floor beneath the rug. The floors up here were not carpeted. They were hardwood, the real thing, and they had fancy rugs covering most of them in the main room and the bedroom. In here, there was a throw rug that looked like one of the property's originals.

And it was over a spot that definitely felt less sturdy than the rest of the floor.

I moved everything out of the way and tugged the rug back. I didn't see the uneven flooring at first because it was cut so perfectly into the floor that if you weren't looking, you would never find it. But on closer inspection, I could see where the wood dipped slightly. I pressed on the boards, gingerly at first, then harder until a square door popped up. I sat back on my heels, mouth open. I hadn't ever seen this in real life. Just on the *Gilmore Girls*, where Lane used to hide her CDs from her strict mother. Although this was much bigger. Big enough for a fairly normal-sized person to fit through.

I looked at JJ. He squeaked as if to say, *Told you*.

"You did," I said. I pulled my phone out and shined my flashlight. JJ stuck his head into the hole. I shooed him away and leaned forward so I could see.

A set of rickety-looking stairs, which creeped me out a little. But, this could explain a lot about what happened last night. When I shined the light around, I caught a flash of black. Black fur, to be exact. Just the briefest glimpse.

I leaned farther in to get a better look.

And there, huddled between the top two steps, pressed as far into the wall as he could get, was Balfour Jr.

Chapter 40

JJ squeaked, trying to get closer to the doorway to sniff the kitty. The poor thing looked terrified, squinting against my light and shrinking away. "It's okay, buddy," I murmured. "I'm going to get you out of there. You must be hungry, huh?"

He meowed, a plaintive cry that just sounded so sad. I assumed he knew what had happened to his friend. Animals were super intuitive—I don't care what non-believers said.

"Katrina," I called.

She poked her head in. "Yeah?"

"I found him. Can you grab JJ?" I asked. I was still holding him back with one hand while holding my phone flashlight with the other, which left me no hands to grab the cat. And I didn't want to have to follow him down those creepy steps if he took off.

Her eyes lit up. "Omg. What is that?" She came forward to join me on the floor, grabbing JJ's leash.

I handed her the phone, motioning for her to hold the light for me. She positioned it over the hole while I leaned over and reached in for the cat. He swatted at me, but I managed to grab him by the scruff and pull him out.

"Nice," Katrina said approvingly. "What the heck is that? A trapdoor?"

"Looks like it," I said.

"How'd he get in there?"

"Someone must've opened it," I said grimly. "Which could explain a lot about last night."

She let out a low whistle. "I'll get him some food." She went out to the kitchen.

I deposited the cat in his carrier. JJ went up to say hello. I watched them sniff each other through the wire door. I sat back and thought about this. There was another way out of this room. A way that Jacob had to know about. So who had used this trapdoor last night? Had Balfour known about it? Was that how he slipped out? Or had someone slipped in? Either way, the door must've been open at some point for Balfour Jr. to get into it. And then someone else must've come in and put it all back to rights without realizing the cat was in there.

Someone knew about this door. Someone who hadn't admitted knowing about it.

I wondered if you could get in from below. And how far down it went. I went back over to the door to examine it. There was no handle on this side—you had to press on the floor to open it. But when I looked underneath, there was a little latch that looked like you could use it to push the door up and open. I stepped onto the stairs, tentatively at first, then went down a couple of steps so I could examine the latch, being careful not to touch much. Mick would want to fingerprint in here, but I just couldn't resist taking a look around—I could always say Balfour Jr.'s rescue had been dependent on it.

It smelled musty down here—that was the first thing I noticed. I assumed it led all the way down to the first floor, although I really didn't want to check it out myself. I shined the light around, trying to see how far the stairs went, hoping no cobwebs were getting in my hair. I had an unreasonable fear of all things spiders. As I turned the light back toward the opening, I saw something I hadn't noticed before. Something yellow hanging off the second step. I moved closer. It looked like a scarf.

With tigers on it.

As I shined the light on it, my heart started to pound. I recognized this scarf. The stalker lady had been wearing it when I saw her that first day. I'd noticed it because it was so unique. And bright. I snapped a couple of pictures of it, not wanting to touch it.

Katrina came back in with a bowl of food for Balfour Jr., which she put inside his carrier. He attacked it.

"Poor thing," she said, then glanced at me. "What are you doing?"

"Checking to see if you can get in from this side. Which it looks like you can." I wanted to try it, but I knew I shouldn't touch it. Mick would kill me.

"Looks like Balfour could've had an unexpected visitor?" she asked.

"We need to call Mick," I said. "Tell him to come ASAP."

"Roger that," Katrina said, pulling out her phone to make the call.

I hoisted myself out of the hole, using my sleeves wherever I was tempted to touch something, then went out to the other suite to find Jacob. He was on the phone, but ended the call when he saw me coming.

"Maddie. Any luck?" he asked.

"Yeah. We found him."

Jacob brightened. "That's wonderful news! Where was the little rascal hiding?"

"I'm glad you asked," I said. "Can you come here for a second, please?"

He frowned but followed me into the other suite. I led

him to the closet, walked to the little door and stepped on it so it popped up, watching him the whole time.

His face drained of color.

"I'm assuming you knew about this?" I said. "Since your family has owned this place forever."

"Mick's on his way," Katrina said, pocketing her phone. "Should I bring the cat to someone?"

"No," I said, remembering Alice's plea that he go to her. "We might need Mick to mediate that too. Tomas is going to try to get him, but Balfour's mom wants him."

"Oh boy," Katrina said. "Should I take him back to the shelter with me until this gets figured out?"

I thought about that. "Maybe I should bring him to the cafe. It might be less scary. No cages. I can give him his own space, even if it's away from the other cats."

"Even better," Katrina agreed.

"Can you give us a sec?" I asked her.

She nodded and took the carrier into the other room.

I turned back to Jacob. "So? Did you know about the door?"

"I knew it was there from when the inn was built. I didn't know it was . . . useable."

I didn't believe him. "Where does it exit?"

"The basement."

"And can you get outside from the basement?"

A nod.

"Is that basement entry unlocked?"

"It shouldn't be," Jacob said. He looked flustered now. "We rarely have a need to go in the basement for any-thing."

"You better figure it out fast," I told Jacob. "It'll be the first question the police will have when they get here."

* * *

"I'm guessing you found more than the cat," Mick said when he came in half an hour later, glancing curiously at Jacob.

Jacob had retreated to one of the couches in the suite and hadn't spoken another word. He looked almost co-matose.

Wordlessly, I led Mick to the closet and showed him the trapdoor. "The cat was hiding in here. JJ found him. I'm not sure how he got in, but the door must've been open at some point." I'd known Mick for a while now, and I'd never actually seen him surprised. Or with any other expression besides cop face. But when I flipped the door up, his eyes grew wide.

"Haven't seen one of those in . . . scratch that. I've never seen one of those," he said.

"That's not all," I said. "Go look on the second step, in the corner. I didn't touch it."

He took my phone with the flashlight turned on, then got down on his knees and stuck his head in the hole. "Can you hold the flashlight while I take some of my own pictures?" he asked.

I obliged. He snapped a few shots, then reached into his pocket for a glove, slipped it on, and retrieved the scarf. He brought it out to the main room and held it up to Jacob. "Familiar to you?"

Jacob shook his head wordlessly. Mick put it in a small bag he also pulled out of his pocket.

"I've seen it before," I told him.

He frowned. "You have?"

I nodded. "On your car crash victim. Marybeth Mont-gomery."

He gave me a look. "That's not for public consump-tion. We're trying to track down her family. But it seems she's ratcheted up to one of our top suspects." He waved the bag with the scarf at me. "Good find."

"Thanks. I was going to check to see if you could get into the suite from down there, but figured I'd wait for you," I said.

"Good thinking," he said. "Let's try it." He climbed down into the opening until his head was under the floor, then motioned for me to shut the door. I pushed the floorboards down.

We waited.

I heard him grab the latch. He pushed the door up easily and climbed out. "Well, if you could get into this passageway, you could get into the room." He turned to Jacob. "You were aware this door was here?"

"I was. But I didn't think it was actually accessible anymore," he added. *Defensively*, I thought.

"Where does this lead?"

"The basement."

"Was it locked?"

"I don't know," he admitted. "Again, it should be."

"Would you not have checked into that before letting someone stay here? Especially someone high profile?" Mick asked.

Jacob bristled a little. "I was under a lot of pressure to open up this suite against my better judgment. I didn't think of the trapdoor, honestly. I hadn't thought about it since I was a child and my father showed it to me. Even if I had remembered it . . ." He shook his head. "I hardly would have thought someone would actually use it or even realize it was there."

"Well," Mick said, "unless this is fifty years old"—he held up the evidence bag—"it looks like someone did."

"And you think this is how Balfour ended up dead," Jacob said softly.

"I don't know," Mick said. "But I'd say there's a pretty good chance there's a connection."

Chapter 41

I pulled Mick aside as we left the suite, out of Jacob's earshot. "So what's next?"

"I need to get crime scene techs in here to see if there are prints on that door that we can match. You didn't touch anything, did you?"

"Just the floor. Which was how I figured out it was a door."

He nodded. "I need this room closed off again. I'm going to have Jacob take me down to the basement so I can look at the lock situation. See if someone broke in, or what. Where are you taking the cat?"

"To my place."

"Good. We have no idea if there's a will or anything yet, so I'm guessing his property will go to his mother, but I'm not sure."

"Cats are not just property," Katrina reminded him as she walked by with Balfour Jr., giving his arm a squeeze. "His mother should get the cat."

He shook his head, but smiled a little.

"I'll bring him downstairs and slip by the handler," she told me. "I'll let you tell him he was found."

"Thanks," I said to her.

After she disappeared down the staircase, Mick turned back to me. "And you said you needed to talk to me about Jane Cummings."

I nodded. "I do. I know where you can find her."

He waited.

"It's Lilah Gilmore."

He frowned. "What do you mean?"

I explained the whole thing about her stealth reading with Balfour and the lengths she'd gone to conceal it. "I told her I was going to have to tell you."

"Why didn't you tell me last night?" he asked, his tone full of reproach.

"It was so chaotic I didn't think of it until later," I said. I knew he didn't believe me. It wasn't a very believable answer, but hey, at least I was telling him now.

"Why did she use an alias?" he asked.

I sighed. "I don't know. She wouldn't tell me. Grandpa thinks it's because she's just too prim and proper for something like this, but that didn't sit right with me. She definitely doesn't want her husband to know. And there's more." I filled him in on the conversation I'd had with Vince at the bar, about Lilah's presence the night of Archie Lang's murder.

Mick listened. He didn't seem too impressed with that piece of the puzzle. "I'm assuming you talked to her?"

I nodded. "I told her I needed to tell you."

"Did she tell you anything? About last night?"

"No. Said that her reading was over a little early. When she left, everything was fine. But she also orchestrated this elaborate exit and entrance so no one would see her."

"So she went to great lengths to not be seen, is what you're telling me," he said.

"Yeah."

"Great. So she's next on my list to go visit."

"She also said Maeve was up there while she was getting her reading, but then she heard her yelling at someone. She figured on the phone. But she said she heard a ruckus in the connecting room too."

"Which could've been the trapdoor," Mick said.

I nodded. "Do you think she found the stalker?"

"It's a good question. When I talk to her again I'll be sure to ask her."

"When are you doing that?"

"Probably today. At the station. I told all of them I'd need to question them again, but I'm most interested in her."

"Did you look into her other name and the charges against her?"

"I did. But I can't exactly arrest her because she did some shady things over a decade ago."

"Do you think she was doing the same thing again? Maybe trying to blackmail Balfour into not shutting down, and he wouldn't play ball? So she got mad?"

He didn't respond. I took that to mean he had already been considering that possibility.

"Did Craig get an answer from her about her broken nails?" I asked.

Mick nodded. "He said she told him that she was organizing the cat's stuff that Tomas had dumped in the middle of the floor. The cat wagon thing was heavier than she thought and she broke her nails. And then of course the rest of them broke during the fight."

I supposed that was plausible. I'd done that before— tried to pick up something that was heavier than I'd thought and ended up breaking off fingernails.

"So is that it?" he asked finally.

"Actually, there's more, but can I talk to you about it downstairs?" I cut my eyes to Jacob, hoping Mick would get the message.

He did. "Let's go," he said, loud enough that Jacob could hear. "I've got a busy day ahead of me, and this floor is back to being off-limits."

As we headed back down the hall I checked the wall again, scanning carefully for the photo. It was definitely not there. When we reached the stairwell with Jacob, I deliberately asked him about it in front of Mick.

He seemed surprised that I'd noticed, but recovered fairly quickly. "It fell off the wall and broke," he said. "I need to get a new frame for it. You have good eyes, Maddie."

It fell? I tried to keep the disbelief off my face. That was convenient. Next he'd be telling me the ghosts knocked it off the wall. "How did it fall?" I asked.

He shrugged. "I wasn't here when it fell, I simply found it on the floor. Assuming that all the activity up here has jarred certain things loose."

He could have been talking about more than pictures hanging on the walls, I supposed. "It was the only one?"

"It was. Maybe one of the ghosts knocked it down," he said.

I held back a laugh. That had been way too predictable. "Maybe it was the ghost of the man who died in the elevator shaft," I said. "Trying to tell us that Balfour was right."

Jacob's lips thinned so much they almost vanished. "After you," he said, holding the door open for me.

"What was that about?" Mick asked when we got downstairs.

I filled him in on how strange Jacob had been acting about Balfour from day one, his reaction to Balfour pointing out the photo and his theories on what Archie Lang's murderer looked like, and Jacob's oddly timed visit to his father last night during all the chaos.

"How do you know he visited his father? He told you?"

I shook my head. "Jacob didn't tell me. Just said he had to take care of something. No, I took JJ to the nursing home to do his rounds today. The receptionist mentioned it. And when I went to visit his dad, he mentioned it too. But he was confused—thought we were talking about the missing maid from forty years ago. He's in the beginning stages of Alzheimer's," I explained. "But it did make us wonder, if someone is worried about what Balfour could've found out about either of those old cases . . ." I dropped my voice. "Is that worth killing him over? And get this, Grandpa told me Jacob's dad is in the photo. And now the photo is missing. It's the one that conveniently fell off the wall."

"But Balfour didn't say anyone in the photo was the killer, just that he looked like them? Which, quite frankly, means nothing," Mick said.

"I know, but you have to admit that Jacob's behavior is weird. And his father was running the place when both those things happened back then. It's not a stretch to imagine he at least knows something. You have to wonder if there's a reason why that particular incident was what he went back to, right?"

"And you think Jacob was worried that Balfour knew more than he was letting on," Mick said. "And that it would somehow implicate his father?" He thought about this.

"Or maybe his father knew something. Maybe about Sal or Lilah, if they were involved with that Lang guy."

"We need to find out exactly when Jacob left for the nursing home."

"He was definitely gone when all the commotion started. We couldn't find him when the lights went out."

"And that was after Balfour had gone missing?" Mick asked.

I nodded.

"And he told his father Balfour had been killed?"

"He told his father something happened," I corrected. "I don't know exactly what he told him because his dad started talking about the maid being missing."

"I'll talk to him again, but right now I've got to deal with Balfour's crack staff. And now Lilah," Mick said. "I'll talk to you later. I have to go check out the basement and see if someone could've gotten in that way."

I followed him downstairs, veering off into the lobby. I spotted Tomas waiting in one of the chairs near the fireplace. Katrina must've slipped out the side door to get past him.

He jumped up when he saw me. "No luck?" he asked, his gaze traveling to my hands, empty save for JJ's leash. JJ trotted along happily next to me. I could tell he was proud of his find.

"We got him," I said. "JJ sniffed him out, actually."

Tomas let out a shriek. "Where is he?"

"Katrina took him to the vet," I lied. "We just wanted to make sure he was okay."

Tomas's eyes narrowed. "Why? Was he hurt? Where was he?"

"No, but a little dehydrated," I said. It was probably true. He'd been in there since the previous night with no water.

"Well, what are you doing with him after that?" Tomas pressed.

I didn't answer. Instead I asked, "Where were you when Balfour disappeared?"

He frowned. "I already told the police I'd gone to my room. There wasn't much for me to do. Why?"

"Because it's strange that everyone seemed to have cleared the hallway at the same time."

"What are you talking about? Manny was there."

"He wasn't."

"Well, he was definitely supposed to be."

"Supposed to be where?"

We both turned to find Manfred and Sharlene standing behind us. I hadn't even heard them come up. Creepy. They both looked terrible too. The same shade of miserable.

"Checking people in to see Balfour last night," I said.

Manfred's face reddened and his gaze slid away from me.

"Leave him alone," Sharlene said. "He didn't do anything wrong."

"Then where were you?" I asked Manfred, deciding to go with the direct approach. "I know you probably told the police you went to the bathroom or something"— Manfred's face turned even more red—"but I feel like there's more to it. So what happened?" I looked at each of them in turn.

Manfred sank down in a chair. "I should tell her. It doesn't matter now anyway. Balfour's not here to be upset."

"You don't have to, Manny," Sharlene said.

"Okay. I'll just call Mick and tell him you lied. I'm sure he'll be happy to talk about it down at the station." I pulled out my phone.

"No. Wait. Balfour texted me. Told me he needed to go outside to meet someone and not to tell anyone," Manny said. "And said to tell Harry that Jacob wanted him to go check out someone out back."

"*Balfour* did?"

Manny nodded.

"Did he say who he was meeting?" I asked.

"No."

"And you didn't ask?" Tomas interjected. He'd been standing silently the whole time, listening to the exchange.

Manfred's face turned red again. "No. He was the boss. I just did it."

"Did you see him leave? Was he alone?"

"I didn't see him leave. When he told me I could go, I . . . just went. I used the break to go call this girl I met last week at a party." He looked sheepish. "I was on the phone for about fifteen minutes. I'm sorry I didn't tell them, but he told me not to." His eyes dropped to the floor. "Last night I guess I just couldn't think of him as really being gone. I didn't want to betray his trust."

Chapter 42

I told Manfred he needed to come clean with Mick. Otherwise he'd still be floating around in suspect land until this got sorted out. He agreed.

When I got outside, Katrina was waiting at my car with our captured kitty. "Let me know what happens with him," she said. "He's a sweet cat. Keeps head-butting me through the cage door."

"I feel bad for him. He must be so scared. You think I should take him to the vet? I told Tomas you did already."

"It wasn't even twenty-four hours?"

I shook my head.

"I think he's fine. Unless he's not eating or drinking, of course."

"Okay. Thanks for helping me look." I unlocked the car and Katrina set the crate in the back seat.

"Good luck, bud," she said, then with a wave, headed back to her day.

I watched her go, and was about to get in the car when I changed my mind. I was tired and annoyed. My eye hurt and I looked ridiculous. I felt bad for poor Balfour Jr. being trapped in that hole for the night. And I couldn't stop thinking about Jacob—who was supposed to be helping with the festival!—and how he'd done pretty much everything to thwart this whole thing from the start. Now someone was dead and he was still acting all squirrelly.

I was sick of it, and I wanted to get to the bottom of it.

I cracked the windows, locked the doors, and, with JJ still tucked under my arm, hurried back inside. I marched straight behind the front desk to the room I knew Jacob had been working in since being displaced from the offices upstairs and rapped on the door.

"Come in," he called, sounding distracted.

I pushed the door open. He jumped up from behind his small desk. "Maddie. What can I do for you?"

"What's going on, Jacob?" I asked.

He frowned. "I'm not sure what you—"

"Did your father have something to do with one of the unsolved crimes? Is that why you're acting so strangely?"

His face drained of color. "I beg your pardon."

"I know you went to see him last night," I said. "Why? To tell him you got rid of Balfour to protect him? I know you took the photo down because you didn't want your father identified as part of this."

He was staring at me now like he'd never seen me before. "You think—you think *I* killed Balfour?"

"Did you?" I challenged. "You've been against him coming here the whole time. You're acting weird. Not even just weird. You're acting downright suspicious. What am I supposed to think?"

I half expected him to throw me out, call Mick, something—but instead he sat back down heavily in his seat and dropped his head into his hands. "I didn't kill anyone."

"No? Then where were you when Balfour died?"

A staff member walking by glanced in the room, alarmed.

"Close the door," Jacob said.

I reached behind me and pushed the door shut. "So?"

"I did go see my father, but it was before . . . all of that happened."

I looked at him skeptically. "Because you had a pre-monition Balfour was going to die?"

"No! I didn't say anything to my father about him dying because he wasn't dead," Jacob said. "I went to tell my father that he needed to come clean if he remembered anything about the maid, because"—he hesitated—"Balfour was about to reveal that she is still alive and get her to tell her story."

That, I wasn't expecting. "Wait. What? How did you know that?"

"I'd been talking to Balfour all along," Jacob said. "Did you really think I'd let him come in here with no idea what was going to happen? Alice put me in touch with him and we'd been speaking for weeks."

"But . . . why?"

"Because I didn't want him to come in here and drop a bombshell about my family," Jacob snapped. "I'd heard the rumors. I know that maid was reportedly having an affair with an *older man*. I needed to know if it was my father. He would never talk about it and now . . ." He sighed. "Now I never know if what's coming out of his mouth is real or imagined, remembered or fantasy. I didn't want everything we'd built to be destroyed." He looked so miserable.

I put JJ on the floor and dropped into the extra chair in front of the desk. "You think your dad . . . had some-thing to do with the maid?"

"I always thought so," Jacob admitted. "My dad was a terrible womanizer. Even tried to hit on your grand-mother." He grimaced. "Lucille punched him right in the nose and said if he ever did it again, she'd have him arrested. I think he had more respect for her than any other woman in his life, including my own mother. Lucille kept working for him, and he behaved himself with her."

I covered the laugh that threatened to bubble out of my mouth. First the casserole dish and now this. My grandma was badass. "But Balfour tuned in to the maid, and she's alive."

He shrugged. "That's what he said. He wanted to have her come forward. *So I could put all this behind me*, he'd said. I still thought she was going to say my father attacked her, or threatened her or something. I wanted to try one last time to get the truth out of him."

"When was she supposed to come forward?" I asked.

"I wasn't sure. But Balfour told me that night, before the readings started, that she was willing and wanted to get it over with."

"So he'd been in touch with her," I said.

"It sounded like it, yes. And I got very nervous. I needed to speak to my dad. Find out what he'd done before she spoke out and the media swooped in. So I rushed over there. Before everything happened. When I got back, I almost couldn't even get up the street because of the accident, and you were texting, and Martin was calling. I had no idea what had gone on. You can check the visitor's log at Haviland House," he said. "You'll see I was there right when all the excitement was occurring."

Chapter 43

I drove home with one hand, holding Violet's rock against my eye with the other while I thought about what I'd learned. Jacob hadn't killed Balfour. He thought his father had done something to the maid all those years ago. Who was apparently alive and about to come forward when Balfour was killed.

Maybe Becky's theory that this all had to do with the events of forty years ago wasn't so crazy after all. I had to go to the paper and talk to her. I needed another brain to help make sense of all this.

When I got home, I bumped into Violet coming out of the kitchen with a mug of tea. "Oh hey," I said. "Are you all settled in?"

She nodded. "It's so lovely here! I've already been out for a walk today and I'm ready to go for another one. You're so lucky to live on an *island*." She clasped her hands together, starry-eyed. "I'm jealous."

I laughed. "It's got its pros and cons, like anything. So did Sam talk to you about filling in as the headliner for the duration of the event?"

"She did. I'm so sorry about what happened. That is so tragic."

"It really is," I said. "Hopefully they figure out what happened soon. Are you going to do it?"

"Oh yes! I'm definitely happy to help," she said. "I'm going to do the consults here."

"Here?" I repeated.

"Yeah. Since the inn seems to have some bad vibes. I'd rather do them in a happy place. You know?"

"Great. Um, but where are you doing them?"

"Your Grandpa said I could use that little den. Your grandmother's old sewing room?"

"Oh. That's a good idea," I said. "We probably need to clear some stuff out for you. When are you starting?"

"Tomorrow night. Tonight seemed a bit soon after . . . everything. And no need to move things. I can work around them."

"No, really. We want to make sure it suits you," I said. I also wanted to make sure Grandma's stuff didn't get disturbed by strangers. "I'll make sure I go in there and tidy up either tonight or first thing tomorrow."

I grabbed a snack, let JJ in to play with his cafe friends, and headed out again. When I got to the paper half an hour later, the news office was buzzing. Last-minute Friday rush to get the paper out the door in the morning. Casey was on the phone, but she waved and gave me a sad face when she realized JJ wasn't with me. I'd left him home to entertain our new guests.

Reporters were intently focused on their computers, filing stories before deadline as page designers worked on layouts. No one paid any attention to me as I walked back to Becky's corner office. I could barely see the top of her head over the stacks of papers, which looked like they'd grown since the last time I was here.

I knocked on the half-open door. She peered around one of the stacks. "Hey. I've been buried with actually getting the paper out and I haven't had a chance to dig in to anything," she said. "Trying to get as much as we can out on the murder and Balfour. Alice is helping us do a retrospective on his life."

"Wow." I sat in one of the chairs in front of her desk. "She's up for that?"

"I think it's her way of dealing," Becky said. "I feel so bad for her. She's coming in shortly with some photos. Wanted to wait until the staff had cleared out a bit. Anyway, how was your day?"

"Well, we found the cat," I said.

"You did? That's great. Did Alice get him?"

"Not yet. He's at my place for now. But get this." I filled her in on my extremely eventful day, beginning with the trapdoor and the scarf that belonged to the stalker.

"Trapdoor? You're kidding!" Becky stared at me in fascination. "I had no idea there was a trapdoor there."

"Yeah, well, neither did anyone else," I said. "Well, except for the stalker and Jacob, I guess." Which was curious, something that needed to be pondered. "Apparently she was well known in Balfour's circle. Tomas knew exactly who I was talking about when I asked him. But Maeve never told anyone that she was here after I told her."

Becky frowned. "Really?"

"Nope. There's something sketchy about her. Mick thinks so too, but he obviously needs a little more to go on. But if she's into blackmailing people, maybe she tried it on Balfour once she knew he was going to retire. And he didn't go along with it."

"Definitely a possibility," Becky said. "I just called the hospital too to check on the car crash woman. No change in her condition."

Ugh. I really hoped she recovered. It would be so

much easier if she could just wake up and confess. Or point the finger at someone else. Like Maeve, perhaps?

"There's more," I said. "And it plays into your original theory." I told her about Vince's revelations about the party the night Archie Lang died, about visiting Jacob's dad and confronting Jacob, and his bombshell about Balfour and the missing maid. I left Lilah out for now, since I didn't want that getting out before Mick had a chance to talk to her.

"Wait." She stared at me, clearly focused on one piece of information more than the rest. "Are you telling me Balfour found the maid? After all this time? And she's alive?"

I nodded. "According to Jacob, anyway. I mean, there's no way we'll know now. I'd be surprised if anyone comes forward, after he was murdered."

"Hey, Becky?" Casey was at the door. "Sorry to interrupt, but there's a guy asking for you."

"What guy?"

"Damian somebody? Said he's meeting you."

Her eyes widened. "Crap. I forgot."

"Forgot what?" I asked.

"Damian and I are supposed to go out tonight." She looked at me, the panic clear. "I can't go out tonight! I have work to do."

I sighed. "Becky. You can't blow him off. I can stay and do some research—"

"No, there's just too much going on," she insisted. "I'm not even done with my day job, never mind the research you and I are supposed to be doing. And Alice is coming soon."

Casey cleared her throat. "What should I tell him?"

"Send him up," I said, giving Becky a look that dared her to disagree.

"Cool," Casey said, winking at me.

Becky gave me a look. "What am I going to do with him?"

"I don't know, but you made plans. You'll have to figure it out." I pulled out my iPad and thought about who to google first. I doubted Sal's career as a mobster would be waiting for me on Google.

Damian stuck his head in the door a minute later and grinned at me. "Hey, Maddie. New job?"

"Just for today," I said. "The pay is pretty lousy, though. Nice flowers." I nodded at the pink roses in his hand.

Becky stood. "Hey. I'm sorry I didn't call sooner. Things are super crazy here—"

"I figured," Damian said, handing her the bouquet with a flourish. "It's been a crazy week for sure. So what's going on?"

"Uh." Wordless, she took the flowers, sniffing them. "Thank you. They're beautiful. But I have a ton of stuff to still do—"

"Becky is finishing today's paper and I'm looking up Balfour's assistant to see what I can find out about her, since she has a prior record for blackmail and assault." I'd decided to start there and see what else I could find on Maeve," I said.

"You're kidding."

"Nope. And then we wanted to take a look at those two unsolved cases again. It's feeling like they could be related to Balfour's death, but the police are more worried about his stalker, and the fact that his team wasn't happy with him."

"Jeez. Popular guy," Damian said.

"Honestly, he was really nice. Not at all what I expected," I said. "I feel so awful this happened to him."

"Well, let me help." He grinned at Becky. "What do you say?"

"I can't let you . . . work," Becky protested. "I really should have called you to reschedule. I'm sorry."

"You can," he said. "That way we can get done sooner and go out to dinner. And get you a drink, which I'm sure you need after this week. Besides, it would be rude to cancel now that I'm here."

He was being so charming. I couldn't even keep the smile off my lips. He seemed to already know exactly how to handle her. Which was a good sign.

Casey came back to the door. She held a vase. "Found this for you, boss. Want me to put those in water?"

"Thanks, Casey." Becky handed them over. Her face was bright red. She clearly didn't know what to do with herself right now.

Damian took the other free chair. "I saw the video of Balfour pointing out the photo of what the murderer could look like. I remember reading about that when I first moved here. I thought it was fascinating."

Becky frowned. "You were reading about it?"

"Totally. I'm kind of a true-crime junkie. All crime, but especially any near where I live. And cold cases are even better. Of course I figured this area would be full of that stuff, so I studied it before I moved here. I'm partial to haunted things too."

"Seriously?" I asked. The things you find out about people that don't come up in normal conversation.

"Yeah. Why, is that weird?"

Becky was grinning. I felt like he'd just won her over. "No. It's kind of cool."

Damian looked pleased with himself. "I even found a website dedicated to unsolveds that may be related to hauntings. Your two cases were on there."

"You're kidding," I said.

"Nope. Although I don't think it had anything to do

with ghosts myself. I think it was plain old bad human behavior. Anyway, I'll show you. It's pretty interesting."

"You know," Becky said thoughtfully, "Maddie got some good intel today about the investment firm that guy worked for. It's worth looking at more."

"On it," Damian said.

"Perfect." She handed him a laptop off a pile on her desk. "You can use this."

Chapter 44

The three of us were so engrossed in what we were doing that none of us realized someone was at Becky's door until he cleared his throat.

"Oh, hey Rick," Becky said. "I didn't know you were still here."

Rick was Becky's big boss—the executive editor. I didn't see him much. Probably because Becky ran practically everything.

"Yeah, busy day. Hello," he said, nodding at Damian and me. "Got a second?" he asked her.

"Sure."

She followed him out the door, closing it behind her. I raised my eyebrows on her way by. She gave a silent shrug.

"Who's that?" Damian asked when she'd walked out of the room.

"Her boss. The executive editor."

"Uh-oh. She in trouble?"

I laughed. "I highly doubt it."

"Good. So here," he said, turning the computer screen so I could see it. "This is the site I was telling you about."

"'Ghostly murders and ghoul-related mayhem,'" I read. "Awesome."

Damian clicked a photo of who I now recognized as Archie Lang. The page that came up had a summary of the case, theories from the website owners, and supporting documentation. I scrolled the documents, pausing when I saw a copy of the police report. "Is this the real police report?"

Damian nodded. "I checked it out myself. They had photos," he explained. "I wanted to see them. Not to be morbid, but I was trying to imagine the elevator shaft, and, well . . ." He trailed off sheepishly.

"Hey, you don't have to apologize to me. I want to see them too." The two of us crowded around the computer as I clicked through the pics. The first was a pdf of the police report that I enlarged so we could read it. Nothing new there—it was all the same info from the original news story. However, the coroner's report was interesting. It confirmed that there were bruises on Lang's throat, which suggested he'd been in an altercation with something or someone, though ultimately he died from the five-story fall down the shaft. The rest of the links were pics of the crime scene, with the exception of the final two photos—the front and back of the pocket watch that I remembered reading about in the story, the item that was always on Lang's person. The back had his initials in a cursive script.

"Probably ended up in a pawn shop in Boston," Damian said.

"Probably," I agreed, handing him back the laptop.

Becky marched back into the office, looking annoyed and muttering to herself. "Honestly, with everything going on and all the things that could be a problem around here, it's a recipe for a cleaning solution?" She started digging through the papers on her desk, flinging the ones she didn't want onto the floor.

I had a vague recollection of the other night at the inn, before everything had gone sideways, when Jacob had accosted Becky in the hall on a similar topic. I leaned forward. "What happened?"

"Jacob!" She glanced at the door to make sure her boss wasn't around. "He's out of his mind. He contacted Rick about Alice's column. Insists it's a proprietary recipe we should not have printed and of course told him he tried to bring it to my attention and I blew him off. I mean, it's not like there was a murder going on or anything. I swear to God, that man has lost his mind." She looked disgusted. After tossing a few more papers, she found what she was looking for and pulled it out. "And what, now I'm supposed to call a woman whose son just died and demand that she tell me if she plagiarized a stain remover? Are they kidding me? You know, Rick's great, but he cares *way* too much about what the lawyers think." Still muttering under her breath, she got up and marched out of the room with the paper. I saw her head to a copy editor's desk.

Damian risked a glance up from his screen. "A cleaning solution? Man, the newspaper biz can be weird. So I found some stuff on Green Farm. It's now defunct, but there are still some old stories and stuff about it." Damian passed his laptop over to show me what he was looking at. I hit pause on my Maeve search—which hadn't yet yielded me any great revelations, aside from a recap of the story Alice had told me and a couple of followups from the court case, which had ended up being dismissed—and leaned over to read.

It was an old *New York Times* article that mentioned a bunch of venture capital firms that were focusing on small businesses around the country. Green Farm was featured as a New England–based firm that mainly looked to back New England companies. I scanned the article, pausing when I saw Daybreak Island mentioned. Apparently, it was a major area of focus, as were the other islands off the Cape. One of the company's founders lived part-time on Daybreak, the article said, and had personally vouched for the hardy business owners who would be great candidates for funding.

Could they be talking about Lilah? Had *she* founded Green Farm?

I went back through the article, searching for the name of the founder who lived here part-time. I didn't see it mentioned anywhere, though, which was odd. I scanned the photos accompanying the article and almost missed it, but when I saw it, my eyes widened. "Holy crap," I said. It wasn't Lilah after all.

"What?" Damian asked.

I pointed to the photo I was looking at of three men sitting around a table. Their faces were all partially obscured, and I probably wouldn't have recognized him anyway. But the caption read *Adam Vine, Shel Weitzman, and Henry Gilmore at an early meeting of Green Farm.*

"Henry Gilmore," I said. "He's one of the founders."

"Who's that?" Damian asked.

Becky walked back into the office, still looking annoyed. "I have to print a retraction of a Helpful Hints column and give Blair credit. Because the newspaper doesn't want to get sued. Can you believe—"

"Beck," I interrupted. "Look." I showed her the photo.

She scanned it. "What am I looking at?"

"Henry Gilmore was one of the founders of Green Farm."

She sat in her chair. "Really. That could be something."

"It's definitely something." I hadn't told her about

Lilah's presence at Balfour's murder yet, which raised a lot of other questions after reading this. But aside from that, there were all kinds of red flags. Like why wasn't Henry identified as part of the company after the story of the murder broke? Why didn't he come forward? He must've known the guy who died.

Or maybe that was precisely why he hadn't come forward. And why Lilah was so adamant that she speak to Balfour without anyone—especially her husband—knowing.

What had happened that night, after she convinced the firm to invest in Don Tunnicliffe's business? Did Archie Lang want a favor she wasn't willing to give? Had something happened?

Was she trying to find out if Balfour knew it too? And was she trying to keep him silent, if he did?

"Hey, Alice, come in," I heard Becky say.

I turned to see Balfour's mother, looking old for the first time I could remember. And just . . . sad. I flipped the cover on my iPad and stood too, going over to give her a hug. She squeezed back. "Thank you, Maddie."

"I have good news," I said. "We found Balfour Jr."

Her face brightened, just a little. "Oh, thank goodness! Is he okay? I was so worried he might have gotten out through the . . ." Her voice trailed off.

"Through the what?" I asked.

"Nothing. I don't know what I'm saying," she said, brushing it off. "But is he okay?"

"He's fine. We brought him to my place for now, but he's all yours when you want him."

"Oh, that's wonderful. I can't wait to get him." Her smile faded. "I did want to come to the parade tomorrow, but I'm not really . . . feeling so festive. I wonder . . ."

"How about I bring him over after the parade?" I asked.

"You'd do that, dear? You're lovely. Thank you." She reached over and gave me a hug.

"Hey, Alice, I need to talk to you for a sec," Becky jumped in. She came around her desk and led Alice out of the office. They walked back toward Alice's desk, heads close together as Becky relayed the cleaner story. I watched them go, wondering why Alice was worried about the cat getting out.

Was it possible she'd been about to say *through the trapdoor*? There was really no other way the cat could've gotten off that floor on his own.

But how would Alice know about that?

Chapter 45

I was helping Adele put the finishing touches on the cafe decorations for the parade early the next morning when I heard voices outside, then Ethan came in with Mick.

"You've got a visitor," Ethan said, raising his eyebrows. My family was getting used to the cops coming to see me, but it was still a little jarring for them.

"Thanks for coming," I said, hopping down from the ladder where I'd been putting up Halloween streamers. "Let's go to the kitchen."

I got him some coffee and we both sat.

"Thanks for filling me in on your conversations yesterday," Mick said, and I couldn't tell if he was being sarcastic or not. "I confirmed through Tomas's phone records that he was indeed occupied when Balfour went outside. He'd managed to wrangle himself a job interview and that's where he'd snuck off to during the time all this went down."

"A job interview?"

"Yeah. For a job in Salem, which I suppose fits. With a woman who says she's a witch who's opening a cat cafe."

That was almost funny. I wanted to ask if he'd gotten

the job, but Violet walked in at that moment. "Who's a witch?" she asked with interest.

"Oh, no one here," I assured her. "Someone from Salem. That's where the witches hang out, mostly."

She grinned, eyes twinkling. "Is that so? Sounds fun. Sorry to interrupt. Just grabbing a snack before I head over to the marketplace. Also wanted to let you know I'm stepping in to judge the cat costume contest and I. Cannot. Wait." She raised her fist in a fist pump, grabbed an apple, and then, spying the bowl of chocolate on the table that Grandpa must've left out—he had a giant sweet tooth—took a handful and hurried out of the room.

I had to laugh as I watched her go. She was an interesting character.

"Sorry—who's that?" Mick asked.

"She's the crystal girl. Sam found her. She came as a vendor but she's taking over as the headliner. Doing crystal consultations. You probably don't want to ask," I added.

"I definitely don't. I also told Tomas that Balfour's mother is taking the cat," he said.

"And how'd that go?"

Mick shrugged. "He wasn't happy. He also didn't seem surprised. He didn't say anything about legal recourse, so I'm guessing he knows he doesn't have any. So you're clear to give the cat to the mother."

"Oh good," I said, and decided not to tell him I'd already told her I would.

"He did ask if he could see him one last time," Mick said. "I told him I'd talk to you and Alice. Unless you think he's going to do a grab and run?"

"I have no idea," I said. "But I'm sure it will be fine. He can come here. I'll let Grandpa supervise. Maybe Tomas can come to the parade." I was starting to feel bad for the guy. He was odd, but he loved the cat. And how could you fault someone for that?

"I'll let you arrange that," Mick said dryly.

I nodded, pulling out my phone to text Tomas before I forgot. "And Jacob's alibi?"

"He's on the camera at his dad's place, along with the visitor's log. He got there probably right at the same time that the woman took out the utility pole."

I nodded slowly. "So our suspect list is dwindling."

"Narrowing," Mick corrected. I was just pleased he hadn't corrected my use of *our*.

"So what else did you find at the inn? Did you check the basement door?"

"It was locked when I went down, but the lock looked almost new," he said. "Like someone realized pretty recently it was broken and had it replaced. I had it dusted for fingerprints, but didn't get anything."

"And Maeve's in the system, so her fingerprints would come up," I said.

"Technically yes, if she left enough of them."

"And her alibi is still that she was lying down."

"Yeah. Not a great one."

"Not at all," I agreed. "How about Lilah?"

"I'm on my way over there shortly. We've got patrol cops coming to deal with the parade, and I'm going to try to get back for it myself. Make sure no one else winds up dead."

"That would be great. Hey, Mick. Are you going to talk to Lilah about her and Henry's relationship to Archie Lang?"

"Maddie. I'm trying to solve this week's murder, not one from forty years ago. At least not at the moment. Maybe after this one, okay?"

"But what if they're related? What if Lilah had

something to do with Balfour and it was because of this old murder?"

"Look, I know everyone believes this guy was down-loading information from spirits or something, but I'm following the evidence because I'm a cop and that's what we do. So yeah, I'll ask her about it, but unless it's directly related to what happened here this week, that's a problem for another day."

"I don't think he was downloading—"

"And I just don't see Lilah Gilmore running around the cliffs, punching Balfour and throwing him over the edge. I know she's a formidable woman, but she's also, what, pushing eighty? And in the meantime, I have a suspicious staff member who stood to lose a pretty good salary once her boss retired, and a woman who was—according to you and his staff—stalking him and had been for years. Both of them are looking like more-viable suspects to me right now." He drained his mug and put it on the table. "Thanks for the coffee."

I walked him to the door. I couldn't help but feel he was being shortsighted about this. Maybe Lilah hadn't pushed Balfour over the cliff, but my intuition was screaming at me that Archie Lang was the key here.

But no one was talking.

Grandpa wasn't kidding when he said that everyone was interested in our cat costume parade. The participating cafe cats (friendly adults only, no kittens) were all costumed up and ready to roll, and aside from them, we had enough of an outside turnout that they didn't all fit inside the cafe. We had to move operations into the main house to take photos and kick things off. I hoped it wasn't competing too much with the vendor marketplace, but that was open all day and people could come and go. Violet's manager, Sydney, was selling their wares there while Violet helped out here. Those two were definitely bailing the event out, and I was grateful. From the sounds of it, Violet had lined up a lot of appointments, so it seemed like people were glad to have her services.

And the parade was going to be to-die-for cute. Each cat was adorable. Costumes ranged from more traditional (witches and pumpkins) to extremely creative (a homemade Yoda, Tinker Bell, and even a basketball player). I personally thought JJ's was the cutest, but I was biased. Plus, he wasn't eligible to win. It wouldn't be right, since everyone in town thought he was the cutest anyway.

The parade went from the cafe down the main street, which had been closed off, to Damian's place (which I'd checked in on earlier and found decorated to perfection, complete with a platform for our esteemed judges to preside on when all the cats had arrived). Damian's enthusiasm seemed to be buoyed by his date with Becky. Apparently, the wait had paid off and they'd had a great time. He promised details later. I hadn't even heard from Becky, which I intended to give her crap about when I saw her.

But even as I went through the motions of the day, my mind was on Balfour. I was itching to know what Lilah had told Mick. I wondered if he'd talk to Henry too. Had Henry really been hiding his involvement with Green Farm for some nefarious reason? Or had he just not wanted it to be common knowledge that he'd brought investors to the island who'd wanted to disrupt the status quo? Because while it could be a good thing for some business owners to get funding, there was usually a price to pay for that, especially in a small, localized place like this.

Either way, Mick hadn't arrested Maeve yet. I'd seen her standing outside the cafe, watching the cats pass by, her gaze almost wistful. I remembered her saying she really wanted a cat. Tomas was there too, and Grandpa had kindly suggested he walk Balfour Jr. in the parade, escorted by Harry in case he was thinking about staging a catnapping. The poor guy was in tears the whole time.

The parade took about a half hour for everyone to get down to the restaurant. Lucas and I had the rear, me walking JJ and him walking another one of our cats. All our regular volunteers were walking two cats each, plus some other friends from the community who had volunteered to help out for the day since we had so many cats in the cafe.

Katrina was at the restaurant with our featured kitty, Sylvester, who was dressed, appropriately, in a Tweety Bird costume, waiting for the festivities to begin when everyone arrived. The judges were also there—Leopard Man, Ellen, and Violet, who had the center seat. When she saw Lucas and me come in with JJ, she left her post and hurried over, dressed to kill as usual in a black velvet dress and purple knee-high boots.

"I hope you know I just want to vote for JJ," she said. "I adore that costume so much!"

"You're very sweet, but please don't. We can't win this," I said. "We're not really in the running. We're just showing support. JJ is the sponsor."

"I figured, but I wanted you to know you had my vote." She winked at me and hurried back to her seat.

Lucas grinned. "She's a trip."

Ellen stood up and began her spiel, thanking everyone for coming and explaining the judging process while Damian's people hurried around bringing drinks and refilling appetizers in the hot bar. I caught sight of Becky across the crowd and she didn't even look like she was working, which was nice to see. I was debating trying to get over to her for all the juicy date deets when I felt a hand squeeze my arm. I turned to find Craig.

He leaned in close to my ear so I could hear him over the din of the crowd. "Mick wanted me to tell you that he's heading to the hospital. The car crash woman? She's awake."

Chapter 46

I really wanted to go to the hospital, but I knew Mick would never let me sit in on the conversation. Craig was heading over there too, and he promised to tell me what they found out. I wondered what shape she was in—good enough to have a real conversation, or just awake enough to be considered conscious.

Could this possibly be over this afternoon?

I had to admit, I was hopeful. My head was spinning with the people still left in the suspect pool: Maeve. Marybeth Montgomery. Lilah. Henry? I wasn't sure who was completely innocent, at this point. But Jacob, Tomas, and Manny all had alibis. The twins didn't seem to have any reason to kill Balfour. On the contrary—they seemed like they'd been completely dependent upon the guy.

There were too many moving parts with this murder, and some that might or might not be related. I had no idea which direction was the right one or who was even the most suspicious suspect at this point.

As soon as the judging got underway and no one seemed to need me anymore, I went over to retrieve Balfour Jr. from Tomas, who seemed resigned that he had to say goodbye. He gave the kitty a hug and a kiss, told him it had been his honor to be his guardian, then hurried to the bathroom weeping.

I was feeling sorrier by the minute for him.

Lucas, JJ, and I slipped out with Balfour Jr. to get him packed up and ready to bring to Alice.

"You sure you don't mind coming with me?" I asked Lucas once we had everything in the car.

"Mind? It gives me a chance to hang out with you," he said. "You've been a little busy."

"The understatement of the year."

"Do you think they're going to be able to find out what happened from that woman?" Lucas asked.

"I have no idea. I hope so. I'm going to be on pins and needles until we hear something."

We drove the short distance to Alice's tidy little house. As we passed Damian's, we could see the party was still in full swing. I hoped people were having fun and forgetting some of the bad stuff.

Balfour Jr. cried the whole way over to Alice's. I felt sorry for him too. He'd had a rough couple of days, and he must be so confused about where his person was, poor guy.

Alice waited at the door, and she looked both nervous and happy when we showed up.

"It's like getting my grandson," she said, accepting the carrier and motioning for us to follow her inside. "Thank you so much for bringing him over. You're really too kind."

"Not at all," I said. "Happy we could do something, even if it's small."

I watched as Alice placed the carrier on the floor and attempted to coax Balfour Jr. out. He remained huddled in the back of the carrier.

"He's scared," I said. "It's been a lot for him. Let's leave him be for a few. He'll come out on his own."

"Good idea. Let me get you some tea," Alice offered. "Please, sit."

"That would be nice." I sat on the couch. Lucas sat next to me. Alice went into the kitchen and I heard her puttering around, filling the kettle and retrieving mugs. I used the time to look around her tidy living room. There were photos of her and Balfour and photos of Balfour solo at various ages. He'd looked pretty much the same as a kid. I got up to look more closely at one of the pictures. Balfour had to be four or five. Alice was dressed in some kind of nurse's uniform. Balfour looked like he was about to cry, but she had an impish smile on her face that belied the rest of the scene.

"I can barely look at those," she said, coming back into the room with a tray filled with three mugs, creamer, and sugar.

"I'm sure," I said, returning to my seat. "I don't even know what to say."

Alice placed the tea service on the table and busied herself adding sugar and cream. As she worked, the sleeve of her shirt, which was loose, fell back, exposing her forearm. My eyes were drawn to a black mark, faded by time and maybe something else, on her inner wrist. I peered closer, unable to make out the design. "What's your tattoo?" I asked, leaning closer.

Alice snatched her arm back, pulling her sleeve down. "Just a youthful indiscretion I tried to remove," she said.

"Oh. My friend did that. It sounded pain—"

I was cut off by a retching sound. We all turned to see Balfour Jr., who'd snuck out of the crate, throwing up a giant hairball or something equally as disgusting in the middle of Alice's beautiful cream-colored rug. We watched in horror as he gave one final cough, then he turned and bolted up the stairs.

Alice looked like she wasn't sure if she should go after him or clean the stain. "I'll get him," I said. "You take care of that."

I hurried up the stairs, calling for Balfour Jr. I checked the small bathroom at the top. Not in there. I made my way down the short hallway. A room that was probably a guest bedroom was next. It was neat and tidy but had no personal touches in it. I scanned the room, then dropped to my knees to check under the bed. Sure enough, there he was, huddled right in the middle, in between some storage boxes.

I pondered leaving him there, but knew it would be better if we could shut him into a smaller room for the night so he could start getting used to the place. With a sigh, I dropped to my stomach and started to shimmy underneath, stretching my arm to see if I could reach him. "Come here, bud," I coaxed.

He shrank even further back into the shadows.

As I propelled myself forward with my toes, my knee hit a shoebox and jostled the cover off. Cursing, I shoved it aside and reached one more time, managing to grab Balfour Jr. by the scruff.

Triumphant, I scooted backward with my prize. He kicked out his legs to try to stop me, managing to stick his foot in the shoebox. It tipped, spilling its contents, and I ended up dragging it out along with the cat.

"It's okay, bud," I said. "Don't be upset. I just didn't want you to get stuck anywhere else." I brought him to the little bathroom, deposited him on the rug, then closed the door behind me and went to put the room back to rights.

I reached under the bed for the shoebox cover and was about to stick it back on when something flashy caught my eye. It must have spilled out when Balfour was doing his Rockettes' act. I reached for it and was about to toss it back in the box when I realized what I was holding.

A pocket watch.

I studied it, then turned it over.

In the back, in cursive script, were the engraved letters A.L.

Chapter 47

I was frozen to the floor. This couldn't be the pocket watch that had been missing from Archie Lang's personal effects. Could it? And why did Alice have it? Had Balfour found it somewhere and given it to his mother for safekeeping until he decided what to do? Had he figured out who the murderer was?

Were Becky and I right that that was the real reason he was dead?

Or, had the mysterious maid had it all along, and Jacob was telling the truth that Balfour had found her? Maybe she'd had the pocket watch after all. Maybe she really had taken it, and had given it to him to prove who she was.

But why did Alice have it, then, packed away in a shoebox under her bed? If he'd just given it to her, it seemed like she might have put it somewhere more accessible for safekeeping—her nightstand drawer, somewhere down in her office, perhaps. To be packed away like this suggested it had been here for a while.

I reached in my pocket for my phone, trying to remember the name of the website Damian had showed me last night. When I finally pulled it up, I clicked through the photos that went along with the story until I hit the ones of the pocket watch.

I zoomed in on the engraving and compared it with what I held in my hand.

It was the same.

Holy moly. I dropped my phone and stared at the piece of jewelry, reaching into the recesses of my brain for what this could possibly mean.

What if Balfour hadn't given it to her at all? What if she already had it?

What if . . . Alice was the missing maid from the inn?

I let the possibilities roll around in my head. The pieces were certainly fitting with that theory. The cleaning solution, for one. If it had been a proprietary inn recipe, she would've had access to it, especially as someone who cleaned, which could explain how it had ended up in her column. Then there was the tattoo on her inner forearm. She'd definitely tried to have it removed, whatever it had been. The tattoo the maid reportedly had was a Catwoman tat. The maid had reportedly been obsessed with Catwoman—it had been her costume the night she vanished. That would have been a definite identifying mark, and one she'd need to address if she wanted to keep her identity a secret.

I did a quick search on my phone for a photo of Theresa St. Clair. The young girl who stared defiantly into the camera did not remind me of Alice, but it was forty years ago. If they were the same person, she'd gone to great lengths to change her appearance. Her hair, for one. Alice's hair was lighter, a brownish red, and much shorter. She also had green eyes, but those could be contacts.

How was I going to find out?

"Oh, dear," Alice said from behind me, in the doorway. "Where in the world did you find that?"

I froze, then slowly looked up. She stood there, a look of concern on her face. I had a brief moment of panic. If she was the maid, had she been Archie's killer, as some had speculated? What would she do to keep her secret? And, oh God, what had she done with Lucas? The only thing that kept me from completely freaking out was a sense that my grandma had known—and actually cared for—this woman. That made me feel a strange sense of peace, like there was nothing to be afraid of. That maybe she was watching over me.

But Alice moved farther into the room and dropped down onto the floor next to me. "I haven't seen that thing in a long time," she said. "Where did you find it?"

"I . . . Balfour went under the bed and he kicked a box over," I said. "I wasn't snooping."

"Where is he?"

"I put him in the bathroom. You should keep him in a small space tonight," I said, wondering why we were having this inane conversation when I'd just found evidence in a forty-year-old murder case.

"Poor thing must be just so scared. May I see that?" Alice reached for the pocket watch.

I hesitated for a moment then handed it to her. "Where did you get this?" I asked softly. "Is it Archie Lang's?"

Alice studied it for a long moment, then nodded. "It is. I took it from his room that night. The night he was killed."

I sat back on my heels. "You were the maid," I said. "Balfour didn't need to find you. You were right here the whole time."

Alice nodded. "Yes, I was. Theresa St. Clair." She smiled a little as she tried the name out on her lips. "It's been a long time since I've said that name out loud."

"You . . . you knew my grandma."

Alice's eyes filled with tears. "I did. And I miss her every day. She's the reason I came back to the island."

"Did Grandma know who you were? What happened? Why did you vanish? Where did you go?" I had so many questions.

"Why don't we go downstairs and have that tea," Alice said. "Your boyfriend will be wondering what happened to us."

A few minutes later, we were ensconced in the living room with tea and cookies. Lucas was completely confused about what had happened upstairs, but I convinced him to be quiet and let Alice talk.

Which she did. A lot.

"I'd only been here a few months, really. I was still getting my feet under me. My friend's parents had taken me with them on vacation here when I was young and I fell in love with it. As soon as I could scrape up the money to come back, I did. And the inn was the first place looking for help. So I became a maid. It was grand at first. So glamorous, I thought, even though I was cleaning up people's messes. But the inn was amazing and I loved the ghost stories. And your grandma . . . well, she was like a mother to me. And I didn't have a family, so that was very attractive.

"But then things started to get complicated. Mr. Blair . . . well. He would've been an HR nightmare today. Always hitting on us. I had to put him in his place. I thought he was going to fire me, but eventually he left me alone. I think your grandma knew what was going on too and she said something. He was scared of Lucy." Alice laughed just thinking about it.

"Jacob said the same thing," I said. "Good for Grandma."

"She was wonderful," Alice said. She trailed off into silence, turning her teacup around and around in her hand.

"Alice," I said gently. "What happened to Archie Lang?"

"I didn't kill him," she said, finally looking at me.

I nodded, relieved, even though it occurred to me she could be lying. "Do you know who did?"

"I don't know for sure. I . . . was there. I heard everything, but I was hiding."

"Under the trapdoor," we both said at the same time.

"I knew you were about to say that. When we were talking about the cat, I got a sense that you almost said you hoped he hadn't slipped out through that door," I said.

"I did almost slip," Alice admitted. "I used that trapdoor a lot when Archie was staying there. I was the one who showed it to him. And it became a game—a way for me to sneak up and see him without getting in trouble."

"You were seeing him?" That, I wasn't expecting, although it made sense.

"I was. In retrospect, he was a complete slimeball, but at the time it was exciting to be courted by an older man in the finance world." She smiled ruefully. "At least at first. He had money, and I liked it. He wasn't even that much older, come to think of it. But I saw him every time he came to the island. He always stayed at the inn."

"He'd been there before?" I asked, surprised.

"Oh, yes. You see, he wasn't just seeing me. He was seeing Lilah Gilmore too. Although she was still Lilah Fitzgerald back then. She was engaged to Henry at the time."

Now that I really wasn't expecting. I glanced at Lucas, who sat quietly fascinated by what was unfolding. "Wait. So . . . how do you know that?"

"Because he told me, dear," Alice said. "He had quite

the story concocted about how he was seeing Lilah for her money, and her soon-to-be husband's funding for their company, but yet he really loved me. You know how men are. No offense," she added to Lucas.

"None taken," he said, holding up a hand.

"In any event, he wasn't a good man. He rubbed elbows with gangsters, he had a string of women, despite having a family at home. You know the type. By the time I realized what he was all about, well, it was too late. I was already pregnant."

"Wait—he's Balfour's *father*?" This story was getting wild.

"Yes. And he'd become very nasty. I knew I needed to get away without him knowing where I was, or that I was pregnant. So I decided to steal the cash I knew he'd stashed in his room. Cash that Lilah was giving him to invest in her friend's business."

"What friend?"

"Donald," she said, and her voice twisted with disgust at his name. "By this point, I'd realized that it was Lilah herself behind the funding. Henry was just the face of it. Apparently it would've hurt his ego if anyone knew that his wife had the purse strings back then, so she had to contribute anonymously. And I'd also realized Archie had been stockpiling money he should have been investing. It was cash, so he saw an opportunity to take some—or maybe all—for himself. Anyway, I had it all planned. I snuck into his room that night when I knew they'd be out at the party and took the money. This too." She held up the pocket watch. "It was on the desk, which was odd because he usually wore it. I figured I could pawn it as well, get some more money. But before I could get out, I heard him coming back—and he wasn't alone."

"Who was with him?"

"I didn't see anyone," she said, which I thought was

a bit of a nonanswer. "I didn't have time to leave so I hid under the trapdoor. I was going to just sneak down and get out of there, but then I heard the argument start. I knew the voices." She paused. "It got very ugly. And then . . . I heard a scream."

I hadn't realized I was holding my breath until I went to speak again. "Is that when he fell?"

She nodded. "It got very quiet. Then I heard one of the men say they needed to get out of there."

"Who were they? Do you know?"

She didn't answer. "I decided I needed to get out of there too. I went down through the basement and back to my room and stayed there for a whole day. Then I put a plan in place. I couldn't leave right away because I knew I'd be blamed for the murder, but I knew I still had to leave. I wanted that money, and it was stolen twice over. I had an unborn child I needed to care for. So I bided my time. I staged my disappearance for the Halloween party, when I knew there would be a lot of chaos on the island in general. Made it look like a worst-case scenario. Then I slipped onto the ferry with the last big crowd that left that night. No one caught me. I didn't even need a ticket. I ended up in a small town in western Mass and used the money to fund dental hygienist school. There was quite a bit of cash in that bag," she said with a laugh. "I hadn't realized how much, but there was a hundred thousand dollars."

Wow. That was a ton of money forty years ago.

"It was," Alice agreed when I said as much. "I was set for a while. Once I had the baby and my degree, I decided I really wanted to live on the island again. Really, I craved family, but I didn't have my own. Your grandmother was the closest thing I'd ever found, and I wanted to be close to her. But I couldn't go back as Theresa, of course. So I changed my name and my look, created a fictional dead husband, and bought us this little cottage." She shrugged. "I had a good job working for Dr. Hadley all these years."

Dr. Hadley was the island dentist.

"Then Balfour was kind enough to help me retire when he had the means to do so."

"And no one ever figured it out," I said.

"No. The only person who knew, because I told her, was your grandmother." She smiled. "She babysat Balfour for me, and kept my secret. She understood. I was scared, and desperate."

It sounded like she wanted to make sure I understood too.

"Did my grandmother know about Lilah?" I asked.

"We never discussed that," Alice said. "It wasn't my business. By the time I came back, she'd married Henry and their connections with Archie and Green Farm were never spoken of again, as far as I know."

I tried to absorb everything she was telling me and put all the pieces in place. "Did Balfour know about you?" I asked. "Jacob said he did."

"I didn't tell him all these years. I was going to, during this trip. I thought he might figure it out anyway, given his line of work. Having him come here and do this was a risk, and I thought it was time to come clean. But then Lilah came for a reading."

I frowned. "How do you know that?"

"I saw her," Alice said. "She was with Donald the night of Balfour's death."

"Tunnicliffe? Thursday night—you're sure?"

"Positive. I've heard his voice in my nightmares for years now. He's not a good man either, Maddie. That's why I didn't want my son's body brought to his funeral home."

"Why do you say that?" I was super curious. Aside

from his creepy line of work, Donald had always seemed so . . . vanilla.

Alice paused, and seemed to steel herself before continuing.

"Because he was part of the whole thing. He was in the room the night Archie died. I knew his voice. And the other's. It was Sal Bonnadonna."

Chapter 48

I digested that. I could feel Lucas tense beside me and squeezed his hand. I wasn't really sure what to do with that information at the moment. "How did you know them?" I asked.

"They were around a lot when Archie and his colleagues were in town. They spent a lot of time having meetings at the inn."

"And that night. They didn't know you were there?"

She shook her head. "No clue. I was quiet as a mouse. I was actually terrified of what would happen if they found me."

"So tell me about how you ended up telling Balfour your secret."

"He called me with the questions after the reading. Lilah had said a lot about what she thought happened that night. See, she was afraid her husband killed Archie," Alice said. "She was trying to get Balfour to tell her if it was true."

"That's why she was so intent on seeing him and not letting anyone know," I said. "My God. She's been wondering for forty years if her husband had murdered someone?"

"That's what he said. But Lilah also mentioned she knew Archie was seeing 'a maid' too. My sensitive son felt there was more to the story and that it involved me. So I confessed—I'd been planning to anyway, after all. I told him it was me, but that I wasn't hiding for the reason he might think."

"He couldn't have thought you were the killer," I said gently.

"I hope not." She took a deep, steadying breath. "He wanted to talk about it more, and I asked him to meet me outside. Out back, where I knew he liked to go anyway, down by the cliffs. I knew this conversation would require privacy. But he never showed up. At least, I thought he didn't. But it turns out he'd already been there. The next time I saw him . . ." She swallowed. I knew what she was going to say—*he'd been at the bottom of the cliff.*

"Alice," I said. "If Sal and Donald were in Archie Lang's room when he died and they thought Balfour knew about it . . . they're likely his killers too. Even if there were other people in the room the night Archie died and someone else did the pushing, they at least knew about it and covered it up."

"I can't think about that," she said. "I can't think that they had something to do with my son's death. That would mean it was my fault."

"Your fault? Why on earth would you think that?" I asked.

"Because I didn't come forward to the police. About Archie. They've been free for forty years, and if they felt threatened now, well, of course it's my fault." Alice started to cry, quietly.

And then my phone rang. Mick was calling.

Lucas and I left Alice's little house in silence. We didn't speak until we got in the car and had driven halfway down the street. We were on our way to the police station. Mick had asked me to come. Said he needed some help, oddly enough.

"Whoa," Lucas finally said. "That was quite a story."

"You can say that again," I said. "Do you think she's telling the whole truth?"

Lucas was silent for a minute. "I don't know her well enough to really be sure," he admitted. "But it sounds like she doesn't have a lot left to lose, with her son gone."

"Yeah. I think so too." I leaned my head back against the seat. "So the question is, which one of them killed Archie Lang, and does that mean they killed Balfour too? And how much does Lilah know about all of it? Had she found out Archie had been stealing from her?" Another thought struck me. "Was it a crime of opportunity— Balfour was supposed to meet Alice at the cliffs later, after all—or did someone else lure him to his death somehow? What if all three were involved?"

"Lilah?" Lucas shook his head. "How? If she left and Balfour called his mother, sounds like she was already out of the picture."

"What if she was waiting for him downstairs? Somehow got him to go with her? She was with Donald. Alice saw them."

"Why don't we wait and see what Mick has to say. He said he has news, so maybe we'll get an answer." Lucas squeezed my hand.

We drove the rest of the way to the police station in silence.

When we got there, Becky was in the waiting room. She looked as surprised to see me as I was to see her. "What are you doing here?" I asked.

"I was just about to ask you the same thing," she said. "Mick asked me to come down."

"Me too." Lucas and I sat. I couldn't wait to tell her

what I'd just learned. Alice said she was going to sit down
with Becky anyway and give her the exclusive story, but
she wanted to get ready for the police, who were certainly going to want to question her. When we'd told her
we were going to see Mick, she'd said if I wanted to give
him a heads-up that she'd be calling I was welcome to
do so.

All in all, it promised to be an interesting conversation.

Mick made us wait another ten minutes before he sent
someone out for us. The cop led us down the hall to a
conference room, motioned us inside, then left us there.
Mick and Craig came in a minute later. Craig and Lucas
eyed each other, but didn't say a word. They still didn't
really love each other.

"Thanks for coming down," Mick said.

"What's going on?" I asked. "Did you talk to Marybeth?"

"Yeah. She was still a little out of it, but she asked
for a lawyer." Mick rolled his eyes. "But then she started
talking anyway. Thought she was gonna get busted on
stalking. Apparently, that was the confrontation she had
before she got in the car and split. With Maeve. She didn't
seem to know Balfour was dead."

"Maeve? She talked to Maeve before the accident?
Do you believe her? Is she even able to remember everything, after her injury?" I asked.

"I talked to the doctor. She definitely had a concus-
sion, but she's coherent and she's testing well, they said.
Lying? That I'm not sure, but she did seem surprised he
was dead."

"Maybe she just didn't remember," Becky said. "Head
trauma and all that."

"I thought the same thing. So I brought Maeve in to
the station again after I talked to Marybeth. Told her

she was awake and that she'd confessed everything." He smiled. "That actually got her talking."

"Slick," I said.

"The oldest investigation technique in the book," Mick corrected. "Tell them you know everything without actually saying what everything is, and see what they cop to. Her version of the story is that she was in the connecting room that night, and she heard a bunch of noise coming from the bedroom. She went to investigate. Found the trapdoor and the woman hiding in it and threatened her. Said she chased her down the passageway and outside, where the woman took off. But Maeve chased her to her car. Get this—with a taser." Mick shook his head. "Anyway, when she got in the car, Maeve said she was still yelling at her. Threatened to call the cops. Marybeth took off like a bat out of hell and that's when she got in the accident. Maeve said she freaked out when she heard. Thought she would get blamed for it so she snuck back inside and pretended she'd had a headache and slipped away to lie down. But Balfour had gone out by then."

"Did anyone see their altercation?" Becky asked.

"I have to imagine someone did," Mick said. "But what I'm more concerned about is what Marybeth Montgomery said she saw when she left through the basement door."

"What?" I asked, leaning forward in my seat.

"She saw Balfour with 'some guy.' Said *they* were having an altercation, and when she busted out of the door, Balfour took off. Toward the cliffs. Said the guy followed him. She remembered him being a big guy, but couldn't describe him better than that."

Becky and I exchanged looks. "Sal," I said slowly. "Do you know anything about Sal's past?"

Mick nodded. "Yeah. He's got some unsavory connections. He was a known associate of the Patriarca family back in the day."

"Holy crap," Becky said.

"Yeah. Not a big player. Just a grunt, from what the Boston PD told me. But he's got a file."

I thought about Balfour's words: *Ties to organized crime and a long, successful life here on Daybreak Island.* Maybe there was something to this psychic stuff after all.

"So what do you want from us?" I asked finally.

"I know you two were looking into what happened forty years ago," Mick said. "I need whatever information you have. And Becky, I need you to put out to the public that you're writing a story about it."

She frowned. "A story?"

"Yes. Do one of those video teasers you do to follow on to what Balfour said the other day. Make it look like you got the whole story and you're putting it out. I need to see if it shakes someone loose."

She laughed. "Not if I can't guarantee a story."

"Hold on," I said to her, turning to Mick. "What did Lilah tell you?"

Mick shook his head. "Nothing. She said that she and her husband might have been at that gathering but she really can't remember, it was forty years ago, blah blah. Insisted her interest in Balfour was purely for fun."

"What about Henry? Did you talk to him?"

"I did. Separately. Said he did know Lang, it wasn't a secret. He'd told the cops that back then. But he didn't know why the sudden interest in this. He was very blasé about the whole thing. But Lilah . . ." He shook his head. "She tried to play it cool but I sensed something was up."

"Do you believe Henry?" Becky asked.

Mick shook his head. "I'm not sure what to believe at this point. But I need to find out who knew what, and if whoever that is is afraid the story is going to come out, then it might trigger some movement."

"Still," Becky said. "I can't promise an exposé I can't deliver on."

"Well," I said. "I may be able to help you out with that."

They both turned to look at me.

"It might not be the exact story you want, but it's pretty close." I took a deep breath and told them about the conversation I'd just had with Alice.

Becky almost fell off her chair. "Alice is Theresa St. Clair? She's been working for me this whole time? You've got to be kidding me! How was that not the first thing out of your mouth?!"

"I'm not kidding. I was trying to give her the space to tell people on her terms. But she definitely said she recognized the voices in the room with Lang that night. She says she heard Donald Tunnicliffe and Sal Bonnadonna."

"Whoa," Mick and Becky said at the same time.

"She's not sure if anyone else was there or what actually happened. She was hiding in the space under the floor and only heard everything." I looked at Mick. "But since it sounds like your plan won't work without this, we probably need to move on it."

Mick seemed just as floored as Becky at this news. "I'm going to need to talk to her," he said.

"Of course. She knows that. But maybe we let her do the story first. Remember, she's a victim," I reminded him. "She got played by an abusive older man."

Mick thought for a minute. "I'd like more than an untrustworthy eyewitness account—in this case more like earwitness—from forty years ago before we bring in Donald and Sal." He turned to Becky. "So, okay. There's your story. We still on for my plan?"

Becky nodded. "I have to clear it with my boss, but I'm sure he'll be all over it. Unless the lawyers have an issue." She rolled her eyes, clearly remembering the cleaning solution incident.

"Let me know."

She stood. "I will. Maddie, can you catch him up on what we found out? I'm going to go call Alice."

"I sure can," I said. "In fact, I already started to."

Mick sighed. "Yeah, yeah. You can be right later, once we catch a killer."

Chapter 49

Sunday

"Do you think one of them is going to come clean?"

Grandpa, Lucas, and I were in the living room watching the teaser video that the *Gazette* was running across all its social channels, promising a huge revelation in a forty-year-old murder case. Lucas and I had barely slept after all the adrenaline from yesterday, so we'd gotten up early. Grandpa, of course, was already up, so we'd caught him up on everything we'd learned and Mick's plan to try to flush out the murderer. He looked really troubled about the whole thing. I knew he'd known Sal and Donald his whole life, and he was probably struggling to wrap his mind around them being part of something like that.

But I was leaning toward Sal, because if the stalker woman had been right and had seen a "big guy" in Balfour's face, that was definitely not Donald. He was average all around, and would certainly never be described that way. And I'd watched enough *Sopranos* to know that the mob ties were a huge red flag for me.

"Maybe we should cancel the event today," Grandpa said.

"The pumpkin carving? Why?"

"It's at Donald's place," Grandpa pointed out. "That could be a recipe for disaster, yes?"

"I think it would be suspicious to not have it," I said. "That might be worse. Mick would probably object."

Grandpa still didn't look happy about any of it.

"There's going to be tons of people there," I said. "And Sal himself probably won't even be there. I'm sure he's going to lay low. Mick has people on his house and store anyway . . ." I trailed off as Violet came into the room. I didn't want her to hear any of this and freak out about our town having murderers in it. I could only imagine what the poor woman would think of us.

"Hey," I said to her. "Are you going to be able to come to the pumpkin carving? Will Sydney mind if you leave the marketplace early?" Her new duties as the headliner included making an appearance at all the big events.

"Yes, of course! I'm looking forward to it," she said. "Syd is great. She's already over there setting up. She's got this." She peered at me. "Your eye looks way better. Been using the crystal?"

I had, actually. And she was right. It was almost completely healed, which was wild. Lucas had even noticed. I wasn't really sure what to make of it, though. I mean, could a rock really heal my face faster? Sam would tell me yes, but I hadn't wrapped my mind around that possibility yet. I didn't say that to Violet, however. "I have been," I said. "Thank you so much."

"You got it," she said. "I'll see you over at the funeral home later, then."

I was on pins and needles the rest of the day, but literally nothing happened. We were on our way over to the funeral home to make sure everything was set up and ready to go when Becky called to say she and Alice had been working on the story that would reveal her identity and drop the bombshell on what she knew from that night forty years ago. "I'm not going to put the names in since she didn't actually see them, but hopefully it will panic them enough that they come forward."

"That's great, Becky."

"I'm sending someone over to cover the event. But let me know if anything weird is going on, okay?"

I truly hoped nothing weird would go on. I'd had enough weirdness in the past three days to last me a lifetime. But I promised and hung up.

When I got there, my mom, Leopard Man, and Ellen were all there, helping Donald and his wife, Susan, set up. Leopard Man had definitely come through on the pumpkins—one of the viewing rooms had two tables full of them, all sizes. There were other tables set up as carving stations, as well as snack tables. This place would be mayhem in a couple of hours when all the kids and parents got here. It seemed surreal that we were doing all this in a funeral home, but no one else seemed worried about it.

I tried to act normal as I let Susan direct me to the kitchen to help get the snacks ready. I wondered if she knew anything about what was going on. She seemed bubbly and enthusiastic about the event, and didn't appear to have a care in the world. If she was worried about her husband, she wasn't showing it.

People started lining up outside early. I hoped we had extra pumpkins in case there were more people than had RSVP'd. Lucas had jumped right in and was helping kids pick out their pumpkins and directing them to places where they could carve. I hoped no one had any carving accidents—that was just about the last thing we needed right now.

But once the first wave of people were in and working, the spooky music was playing, and the newspaper photog was taking lots of photos, I started to relax. There was no sign of Sal, which was for the best since I didn't think I could look at him right now. I kept my eye on Donald from across the room—he was being a gracious host, but I was avoiding him too. I had no idea how to act around him, honestly.

Sam showed up with Violet in tow just as the second wave was about to come in. "Sorry I'm late," Violet said, looking flustered. "The market was so busy! It's been so great for sales. So where do you want me?"

"Are you going to do consults?" I asked.

"I definitely can, or I can just mingle and judge the pumpkins when you're ready. Whatever you want me to do."

Sam and I both opened our mouths, presumably to suggest consults. Before we could speak, another voice behind us chimed in.

"Let's have her do consults." We all turned at the voice eerily in our ears. Donald had come up behind us and stood there, smiling. "People will like that."

"Sure," Violet said. "Just tell me where to go."

"We'll get you set up over there. Let me just grab some chairs." As he hurried away, Violet wrinkled her nose.

"Something wrong?" I asked.

"He has a weird aura, that's all. I also read auras," she explained. "I usually don't do it unless people ask, but sometimes I can't help myself."

I didn't really get what that meant, but it sounded like it might be pertinent to whatever was going on. I was about to ask her more when Donald came back with the chairs and ushered her away. With a sheepish wave, she followed him.

My mother came up to me. "How's it going?" she asked. "Everything okay?"

"Good, yes, fine," I said. "How about you?"

She didn't answer. "I saw the *Gazette* video. Do you know what that's about?"

"Kind of," I said. "But I can't really talk about it right now."

"Have they made any progress on Balfour? I heard the woman who hit the pole is recovering."

"She is. She was creeping around that night, but doesn't look like she did it."

"Does Mick have another top suspect?"

"I think so. Hey, Mom—Leopard Man needs you." I pointed across the room to where Leopard Man was waving madly at her.

"Uh-oh. What now? I'll catch up with you later." She squeezed my hand and hurried off.

The flow of pumpkin carvers was nonstop. Everyone seemed happy—and hungry. I noticed Susan trying to keep the snacks refilled and took pity on her. "Can I help?" I asked, joining her at the table.

"Oh, Maddie, wonderful. I have more, but they're down in the storage area," she said. "Would you mind terribly going down to get them? I have bags of chips and candy down there. Lots of them."

"The storage area?" I asked doubtfully.

"Yes. Go out this door, then take a left. The first door in that hall and down the stairs."

Ugh. If it was near the morgue, I was going to lose it. "Okay," I said.

"You're a dear." She squeezed my arm. "Thank you!" She went off to take care of something else and I headed downstairs. I really, really hoped I wouldn't bump into a dead body.

I went down the stairs and found the storage room easily enough. I gathered up a couple of bags of candy, some pretzel sticks and potato chips, and was about to head back upstairs when I heard voices coming. Urgent, quiet voices, from somewhere out in the hall.

"I can't believe this. It was you all along. You let me think, for forty years, that Henry had done this. And pretended to be my concerned friend this whole time. How could you?"

It was Lilah Gilmore. I would recognize that voice anywhere. My eyes widened. Who was she talking to? Was Sal here? I took a quiet step forward, catching sight of a partially closed door down the hall. Light spilled out of the room.

"Lilah. Please." Donald's voice. Frantic, pleading. "I didn't even mean to do it. It was an accident. We were just supposed to threaten him, get the money back. He'd been stealing from both of us!"

"You killed a man!" Lilah's voice rose to a shriek. "Did you kill the psychic too? Did you sneak back and do that before you drove me home that night, like the good friend you've pretended to be all these years? You never cared about me. Just your business!"

I froze. Donald? Donald had killed Archie Lang? Meek, quiet, funeral director Donald? Lilah had to be mistaken.

"Lilah, please." Donald sounded like he was about to cry. What was going on in there?

I took another step forward but lost my grip on one of the bags of candy. It fell to the ground with a smacking noise that I didn't think was that loud, but suddenly the voices went silent.

I rushed to the door and shoved it open, stepping back with a gasp. Lilah had Donald backed into a corner and was holding him there with a large knife. His eyes were as wide as saucers as he held up his hands in front of him.

"Lilah! What are you doing?" I cried. "Put the knife down. You don't want to do that."

"Go away, Maddie," Lilah said without turning around. "It doesn't matter now. The story is coming out. Everyone will know anyway. And my Henry isn't going down for what *you* did," she spat at Donald.

I slid my hand into my pocket where my phone was. Before I could pull it out, my arm was jerked back roughly. The snacks fell to the ground and I felt something cold against my neck. And a voice in my ear said, "Sorry, girlie, but you're not making any calls."

Chapter 50

Sal. I'd know that voice anywhere.

And he had a gun on me.

A gun. Sal had a gun? It seemed completely surreal, but I guess once a gangster, always a gangster.

"I'm not doing anything," I said, trying to pull my arm away, but he held on. His grip was like a vise.

"I'll tell you what you *are* gonna do. You're gonna tell that friend of yours she's not running a story in the newspaper."

I shook my head slowly. "I can't do that. It's not up to me—"

"Well, then this isn't gonna go so well," he said. "Lilah. Put the knife down and back off."

Lilah had frozen too, not sure what to do now that there was a gun in the mix. I thought almost hysterically about that old adage—don't bring a knife to a gun fight. Donald looked relieved to see his friend, but he kept his eyes trained on Lilah and her knife.

"I said, put it down!" Sal's voice rose.

Lilah's eyes met mine. I nodded. She let it fall to the floor.

Donald stepped past her, looking relieved, and started for the stairs. "We have to get out of here," he told Sal.

I imagined those were the same words they'd exchanged that night forty years ago, after Archie Lang had gone down the elevator shaft for the final time. And for some reason, they infuriated me and I couldn't keep my mouth shut. "You think you can get away now?" I asked, incredulous. "Everyone knows. The story's already done and ready to go. Someone heard you that night. You guys are screwed."

I felt the gun dig into my neck even harder. "You know, I respect your grandfather even though he always cramped my style," Sal said. "I'd hate to have to kill his precious granddaughter."

"You killed Balfour," I said. "It wasn't Donald. You caught him coming outside and, what? Followed him to the cliff? Coerced him? Someone saw you with him."

Sal sneered. "I followed him. He made it too easy. Backed himself into a corner. I had nothing against the kid. Just wanted him to mind his own business. I couldn't let him expose that . . . indiscretion from all those years ago. It had been way too long. I mean, no one had any clue. What was I supposed to do, let him blow up everything I spent my life trying to create?"

"You didn't want him to come here at all. You were worried he would be able to figure it out," I said.

"Of course I was! Not like *that* knucklehead," he said, nodding at Donald, who was still kind of frozen. "He didn't believe in it at all, but then he started to realize the kid knew stuff somehow. I don't know how he knew it, but he knew it. It was never worth the risk to me."

"Why did you kill Archie?" Lilah asked Donald, her voice almost pleading now. "You didn't have to kill him! I know he wasn't a good man, but he didn't deserve to die. You were still going to get your money. I could have given you more!"

"I didn't mean to kill him. You wouldn't believe he'd done anything wrong when I came to you with my suspicions, and then we couldn't find the money! He was stealing from *you*, Lilah," Donald said desperately. "It was an accident. Sal. We can tell them it was an accident!"

"Too bad the psychic wasn't an accident," Sal said. "And since I did it to cover for you, you better shut your mouth right now."

"Well, killing me and Lilah isn't going to help your case," I said, swallowing the fear that was building in my throat. Sal sounded like a desperate man, and I knew all too well what desperate men did.

He shrugged. "I got no choice. And I got connections that'll help me get out. I just gotta get off the island."

"Your mob friends won't be able to help you all the way out here. And you think you're going to get off the island with no one noticing? You're delusional. Everyone knows you." I caught a movement out of the corner of my eye, just a flash of something down the hall. I wondered if there might be another way in and out of here and felt a ray of hope. If Mick had eyes on Sal, maybe they'd followed him here. I made a conscious effort not to focus on whatever it was so Sal wouldn't get suspicious. "Just let us go. There are tons of people upstairs and they're going to be looking for me any minute."

"She's right," Donald said to Sal. "We can't stay down here like this."

"Well, we can't let them leave either," Sal pointed out. "So we need to get out of here before anyone finds them. Where can we put them?"

"We can't . . . kill them," Donald said, looking horrified.

"I'm not going to kill them unless they try anything," Sal said. "We're gonna tie them up and leave them. And we have to go now. I already called my contact. There'll be someone waiting for us when we get off the island."

"In the morgue, then," Donald said. "This way."

He grabbed Lilah and pulled her down the hall after him. Sal removed the gun from my neck and motioned for me to follow. As I turned to do so, plotting how I was going to get away from him without getting Lilah killed, a figure darted out of the shadows and launched at Sal from behind. Alice was smaller, but she was younger and more determined. And, she caught the big man off guard, causing him to lose his footing and pitch forward, dislodging the gun in the process.

I shut my eyes and threw myself to the ground as it went off.

Chapter 51

Daybreak Island Gazette

October 24

Local Men Arrested for Murder of Psychic in Bizarre Twist Connected to Cold Case

The murder of Archibald Lang in 1983 had investigators stumped for the past forty years. But yesterday, police arrested Donald H. Tunnicliffe, owner of Tunnicliffe Funeral Home, in connection with the cold case. Another local businessman, Salvatore Bonnadonna, was arrested for the murder of Balfour Dempsey, the psychic medium who hailed from Daybreak Island and had returned to headline the Daybreak Island Haunted Halloween Festival.

Dempsey was killed Thursday when, police allege, Bonnadonna followed him to the cliff behind the Inn at Daybreak Harbor and shoved him over the edge.

Bonnadonna was allegedly trying to protect

Tunnicliffe, who allegedly murdered Archibald "Archie" Lang forty years ago by pushing him down an elevator shaft at the Inn at Daybreak Harbor. The men were reportedly concerned that Dempsey had uncovered details of the murder and was about to come forward.

In another shocking twist, Dempsey's mother herself came forward with details about the crime and revealed that she was the subject of yet another forty-year-old cold case. Alice Dempsey told police that her real name is Theresa St. Clair—the maid who went missing from the Inn at Daybreak Harbor a few weeks after Lang's death.

Ms. Dempsey told police she'd been hiding under a trapdoor in an adjoining room when Tunnicliffe and Bonnadonna approached Lang in his room and accused him of stealing funds from an investment firm. The funds were earmarked for the Tunnicliffe Funeral Home. When a fight ensued, Tunnicliffe shoved Lang into the exposed elevator shaft, and the two men fled.

Lang was pronounced dead at the scene.

St. Clair vanished a few weeks later.

"I'm thrilled that we were able to solve these cases and give some closure to Mr. Lang's family," said Daybreak Harbor Police Chief McAuliffe. "It shows the hard work and dedication of our detectives and, hopefully, brings some peace to the citizens of Daybreak Island."

Chapter 52

"Violet wants to stay another few days," Sam said to me. "Is that okay?"

It was a few days after all the excitement and we, along with Grandpa, Val, Ethan, Violet, and Sydney were headed into the local community playhouse for the early performance of *Macbeth* and my mother's debut as a Weird Sister. Normally I would've balked at the question, wanting a little privacy and for things to go back to normal, especially after everything that had happened, but I surprised both of us when I said yes without hesitation. "Sure. She's fun to have around," I said. And I meant it. I was also getting some lessons on crystals and had accepted Violet's gift of a large amethyst to put in my bedroom. She'd promised it would help me sleep better after all the recent stress, and she'd been right.

"Yay!" Sam clapped her hands. "I'll go tell her." She hurried ahead to catch up with Violet and Sydney.

"I'll be right back," I told Lucas, pausing on the theater steps when I saw Becky and Damian getting out of Damian's car. I hurried over to them. "Hey, you two."

"Maddie!" Becky gave me a huge hug. I hadn't actually seen her since everything had gone down on

Sunday, mere steps away from where a ton of kids were carving Halloween pumpkins. "How are you doing?"

"I'm good," I said. And I was. Just still a little traumatized. After Sal's gun had gone off, thankfully missing hitting anyone by some miracle, everything had just seemed like a blur. Mick, who had been alerted by his patrol guys to Sal's whereabouts, had just arrived on the scene with backup when he heard the gunshot from outside. Thankfully, the crowd upstairs was so boisterous no one had really noticed it—and those who had assumed it was a car backfiring.

But Mick and his guys moved fast and had Sal and Donald in custody within moments—so fast that even Donald's wife hadn't realized what was happening. The poor woman was still upstairs waiting for me to bring a snack refill to her table when her husband was hauled out in handcuffs.

"Quite a week," Damian said. "I finally convinced Becky to take a night off." Becky had been working nonstop since Sunday. Between Alice's story coming out and this news, her tongue-in-cheek dream of solving two forty-year-old cases had become a reality—with a current murder thrown in for good measure.

"Well, it's been a little hard to take time off. Especially with the national media down our throats—" Becky broke off as we both started to laugh. "I still can't believe Alice took Sal down," she said finally.

"I know. It was wild." I shook my head. "But you know what they say about mothers protecting their kids. She knew he'd killed Balfour. I think she could've ripped him apart with her bare hands if Mick would've given her a chance. Is she still going to work at the paper?"

Becky nodded. "I might be giving her a new role. A column. She wants to look at unsolved crimes. I might even have her work with me on the podcast."

"Carrying on Balfour's dream," I said. It must be so bittersweet for her.

She nodded. "What about his crew?"

I wasn't sure what would happen to them, honestly, especially the twins. "They've all left the island. They probably need to go figure their lives out. I'm sure they'll land on their feet, though. Especially Maeve. She adopted one of our cats. Cindy." The kitty she'd fallen in love with, whom Balfour had tuned in to. I wondered if that was one of the reasons she'd come back for her. As a way to stay close to him.

"No kidding," Becky said.

I nodded. "I was on the fence at first, but I think she really needed the friend."

"And how's Lilah doing?"

"I don't know. My mother's talked to her, but she won't talk to anyone else right now."

"Is she in any trouble?" Damian asked.

I shook my head. "She didn't know what Donald did until this past weekend. But they definitely questioned her and Henry extensively. Lilah was the driving force behind Green Farm, after all. Henry just glommed on to her. But Sal and Donald thought Archie Lang's affair with Lilah would keep Henry from funding the funeral home, and apparently Donald was in bad shape and about to lose the business.

"I'm not sure how the two of them are holding up, but I'm sure they'll figure it out. It wouldn't look good to get divorced now." I was being a little facetious, but it was true. People like Lilah Gilmore didn't get divorced, especially at almost eighty. If the issues that came up were too much for their relationship, they'd probably just ignore each other and coexist.

"I can't believe two big-time locals were involved

in all that," Damian said. "Just goes to show you never really know anyone, do you?"

We were all quiet for a moment, then I said, "Let's talk about something happy. What about you two? Looks like things are going well." I looked at them expectantly.

Damian grinned and slipped an arm around Becky's shoulders. "I think it's going very well. What do you think?" he asked her.

"Still gathering the facts," she said, but I could see the twinkle in her eye. "Come on, we better go in. We don't want to miss anything."

I followed them into the playhouse. Lucas waved at me and I veered off to meet him just as the house music started to play while we waited for curtain. As I reached him and he took my hand to lead me to my seat, Ella Fitzgerald's sweet and plaintive voice came over the speakers singing "I Can't Get Started."